TO PROTECT
AND SERVE

What Reviewers Say About Bold Strokes Authors

KIM BALDWIN
"*Force of Nature* is filled with nonstop, fast paced action. Tornadoes, raging fire blazes, heroic and daring rescues…Baldwin does a fine job of describing the fast-paced scenes and inspiring the reader to keep on turning the pages." – *L-word.com Literature*

ROSE BEECHAM
"…her characters seem fully capable of walking away from the particulars of whodunit and engaging the reader in other aspects of their lives." – *Lambda Book Report*

GEORGIA BEERS
"Beers weaves a tale of yearning, love, lust, and conflict resolution. She has constructed a believable plot, with strong characters in a charming setting." – *JustAboutWrite*

RONICA BLACK
"*Wild Abandon* tells how these two women come to realize that 'life was too precious to be ruled by…fears, by…demons.' While these two women struggle with their issues, there is some very, very hot sex. If you enjoy complex characters and passionate sex scenes, you'll love *Wild Abandon.*" – *MegaScene*

GUN BROOKE
"*Course of Action* is a romance…populated with a host of captivating and amiable characters. The glimpses into the lifestyles of the rich and beautiful people are rather like guilty pleasures…a most satisfying and entertaining reading experience." – *Midwest Book Review*

CATE CULPEPPER
"…an exceptional storyteller who has taken on a very difficult subject …and turned it into a spellbinding novel. As an author, she understands well that fiction can teach us our own history." – *JustAboutWrite*

JANE FLETCHER
"*The Exile and the Sorcerer* is a mesmerizing read, a tour-de-force packed with adventure, ordeals, complex twists and turns, and the internal introspection of appealing characters." – *Midwest Book Review*

JD Glass

"*Punk Like Me*…is different. It is engaging. It is life-affirming. Frankly, it is genius. This is a rare book in that it has a soul; one that is laid bare for all to see." – *JustAboutWrite*

Grace Lennox

"*Chance* is refreshing…Every nuance is powerful and succinct. *Chance* is not a novel about the music industry; it is about a woman discovering herself as she muddles through all the trappings of fame." – *Midwest Book Review*

Lee Lynch

"Lynch, with a dozen novels to her credit dating back to the early days of Naiad Press, has earned her stripes as a writerly elder. She was contributing stories to the lesbian magazine *The Ladder* four decades ago. But this latest is sublimely in tune with the times." – *Q-Syndicate*

JLee Meyer

"*Forever Found*…neatly combines hot sex scenes, humor, engaging characters, and an exciting story." – *MegaScene*

Radclyffe

"…well-plotted…lovely romance…I couldn't turn the pages fast enough!" – Ann Bannon, author of *The Beebo Brinker Chronicles*

Susan Smith

"This disparate duo's lush rush of a romance - which incorporates reincarnation, a grounded transman and his peppy daughter, and the dark moods of a troubled witch - pays wonderful homage to Leslie Feinberg's classic gender-bending novel, *Stone Butch Blues*." – *Q-Syndicate*

Ali Vali

"Rich in character portrayal, *The Devil Inside* by Ali Vali is an unusual, unpredictable, and thought-provoking love story that will have the reader questioning the definition of right and wrong long after she finishes the book." – *JustAboutWrite*

By the Author

To Protect and Serve

Visit us at www.boldstrokesbooks.com

TO PROTECT
AND SERVE

by

VK Powell

2008

TO PROTECT AND SERVE

ISBN 10: 1-60282-007-4
ISBN 13: 978-1-60282-007-4

THIS TRADE PAPERBACK ORIGINAL IS PUBLISHED BY
BOLD STROKES BOOKS, INC.
NEW YORK, USA

FIRST EDITION: MARCH 2008

CREDITS
EDITORS: JENNIFER KNIGHT AND STACIA SEAMAN
PRODUCTION DESIGN: STACIA SEAMAN
COVER DESIGN BY SHERI (GRAPHICARTIST2020@HOTMAIL.COM)

Acknowledgments

My first book would not have been possible without the following wonderful women: "Red," Mate, Vern, Doc, Pat, and Nancy. Your love, friendship, support, and guidance sustained me during this project and continue to fill my heart.

To Len Barot and Bold Strokes Books, my heartfelt appreciation for taking a chance on an unknown author and helping to make my dream come true. Your vision for the future of Bold Strokes Books and your dedication to the development of its writers make me proud to be a part of this wonderful family of professionals.

Senior consulting editor, Jennifer Knight, you are brilliant! I am forever grateful for your keen instincts, knowledge, and guidance. You're a gifted teacher with a wonderful sense of humor. You make me sound like the writer I hope to be. To Stacia Seaman, your meticulous attention to detail is awe inspiring and greatly appreciated. To Sheri, BSB graphic artist, my thanks for wrapping my baby in such gorgeous clothes for her debut. Because of your amazing work, Bold Strokes Books readers know they can judge a book by its cover.

No writer could survive without the valuable assistance of competent beta readers and proofreaders. For your untiring hours of careful scrutiny and input, I give special thanks to beta readers JM, Ev, and Linda. You kept me on track. To the dedicated BSB proofreaders, my gratitude for your efforts on my behalf.

And to all the readers who support and encourage my writing, thank you for buying this book, visiting my Web site, sending e-mails, and showing up at signings. You make writing fun!

Alex gave herself a moment to take in the simple beauty before
Perfectly shaped lips parted to reveal teeth so white against the
complexion, they seemed to glow. An oval face was highlighted
es that brimmed with curiosity and something else, a hint of barely
ined passion that beckoned to Alex.

She wouldn't normally explain herself to a subordinate, but Keri
an was flustered and Alex decided to cut her some slack. "I've
in Vice/Narcotics for a while."

She extended her hand, half expecting it to be ignored. Keri had
ed away from the simple courtesy the last time they'd encountered
other. When a cool palm finally slid briefly against hers, Alex's
es sparked with a jolt of excitement she hadn't experienced in far
ong. "You look well," she said.

"Thank you." Keri folded her arms across the file, which she held
r chest as if suddenly self-conscious of her questionable attire.

Her guilty demeanor made Alex curious, and she paid closer
tion to the color-coded folder. "I assume you're authorized to
'eyes-only' documents pertaining to a known drug lord." The
mation originated in the Vice/Narcotics office and had to be
sed by someone at the rank of captain or above.

"My captain told me to review it." Keri's tone was polite, but it
obvious that she yearned to tell Alex to go intimidate someone

Alex found it hard to believe three years had passed since
excessive force interview in her downtown office. The officers
lved, one of them Keri, were not her direct reports, and under
nal circumstances she would not have been involved in the
stigation. But the incident had occurred in an affluent area of town
the evaluation had to be above reproach. The chief had requested
handle the distasteful task personally.

Keri had been angry about the violation of her usual chain of
mand and the investigation itself, proclaiming the innocence of her
ner. Their interview had rapidly degenerated into scathing looks
heated comments, until she accused Alex of conducting a witch
and stormed out of the room. The same heat sparked from her eyes
y. Evidently three years had done little to temper her resentment.

Shortly after the investigation, Alex was transferred to the Vice/
cotics Division satellite station. Keri had remained on the graveyard

Dedication

For TLS—finally.

Chapter One

Lieutenant Alex Troy wondered what could be
for the chief to pull her from high-priority
cop's intuition smelled trouble. As she mentally flippe
scenarios, she punched the elevator call button agair
else in this central North Carolina municipal buildin
at the pace of the bureaucracy housed within the beig

When she pushed the button again, a woman
down, sorting a file of papers as she rushed. She colli
Alex. Numerous pages burst from her file and flutter
landing around Alex's feet.

"Damn, I should watch where I'm going." Th
even bother to look at Alex directly. She dropped
swept the scattered pages together with her hands, off
she was not expecting.

A silky red tank top hung loosely on her bral
nothing to the imagination. A pair of unencumbered br
most perfectly shaped olive mounds she'd ever see
by erect dark-chocolate nipples that beckoned invitin
quickened. She still couldn't see the woman's face
chestnut hair brushed her bare shoulders and fell loos
if finger-combed by a lover. As the woman cramme
back into the file, she offered an apology that was at
stood.

"You." Shocked cobalt blue eyes lifted to
immediately a hint of challenge entered her gaze. "Lie
expecting to see you."

Dedication

For TLS—finally.

Chapter One

Lieutenant Alex Troy wondered what could be important enough for the chief to pull her from high-priority surveillance. Her cop's intuition smelled trouble. As she mentally flipped through possible scenarios, she punched the elevator call button again. Like everything else in this central North Carolina municipal building, the lifts moved at the pace of the bureaucracy housed within the beige walls.

When she pushed the button again, a woman approached, head down, sorting a file of papers as she rushed. She collided headlong into Alex. Numerous pages burst from her file and fluttered through the air, landing around Alex's feet.

"Damn, I should watch where I'm going." The woman did not even bother to look at Alex directly. She dropped to her knees and swept the scattered pages together with her hands, offering Alex a view she was not expecting.

A silky red tank top hung loosely on her braless body, leaving nothing to the imagination. A pair of unencumbered breasts, the firmest, most perfectly shaped olive mounds she'd ever seen, were centered by erect dark-chocolate nipples that beckoned invitingly. Alex's pulse quickened. She still couldn't see the woman's face. Soft waves of chestnut hair brushed her bare shoulders and fell loosely into place as if finger-combed by a lover. As the woman crammed her documents back into the file, she offered an apology that was at best routine, then stood.

"You." Shocked cobalt blue eyes lifted to Alex's. Almost immediately a hint of challenge entered her gaze. "Lieutenant, I wasn't expecting to see you."

Alex gave herself a moment to take in the simple beauty before her. Perfectly shaped lips parted to reveal teeth so white against the olive complexion, they seemed to glow. An oval face was highlighted by eyes that brimmed with curiosity and something else, a hint of barely restrained passion that beckoned to Alex.

She wouldn't normally explain herself to a subordinate, but Keri Morgan was flustered and Alex decided to cut her some slack. "I've been in Vice/Narcotics for a while."

She extended her hand, half expecting it to be ignored. Keri had walked away from the simple courtesy the last time they'd encountered each other. When a cool palm finally slid briefly against hers, Alex's nerves sparked with a jolt of excitement she hadn't experienced in far too long. "You look well," she said.

"Thank you." Keri folded her arms across the file, which she held to her chest as if suddenly self-conscious of her questionable attire.

Her guilty demeanor made Alex curious, and she paid closer attention to the color-coded folder. "I assume you're authorized to have 'eyes-only' documents pertaining to a known drug lord." The information originated in the Vice/Narcotics office and had to be released by someone at the rank of captain or above.

"My captain told me to review it." Keri's tone was polite, but it was obvious that she yearned to tell Alex to go intimidate someone else.

Alex found it hard to believe three years had passed since the excessive force interview in her downtown office. The officers involved, one of them Keri, were not her direct reports, and under normal circumstances she would not have been involved in the investigation. But the incident had occurred in an affluent area of town and the evaluation had to be above reproach. The chief had requested she handle the distasteful task personally.

Keri had been angry about the violation of her usual chain of command and the investigation itself, proclaiming the innocence of her partner. Their interview had rapidly degenerated into scathing looks and heated comments, until she accused Alex of conducting a witch hunt and stormed out of the room. The same heat sparked from her eyes today. Evidently three years had done little to temper her resentment.

Shortly after the investigation, Alex was transferred to the Vice/Narcotics Division satellite station. Keri had remained on the graveyard shift housed in the central municipal building and their paths had not crossed since. Time had been kind to Alex, allowing her to forget the tug of attraction she'd once felt to the younger woman, or that's what she'd believed. Seeing Keri now, an uncomfortable feeling settled in her chest.

"The elevators in this building are always so damn slow." Keri's gaze was fixed straight ahead at the unyielding steel doors.

"Yes, they are." As Alex mashed the lift button a third time, she made another covert visual evaluation. Nice, very nice indeed.

The past three years had only improved Keri. Her body was sleek and well-muscled, and her honey-colored skin shone with healthy radiance. She appeared a little thinner, and signs of premature graying showed in a few strands of the wavy brown hair that fell recklessly across her forehead. But now as then, her expressive eyes pulled Alex into their depths. Though the fire still burned in them, she seemed to be able to contain her emotions and remain civil. Alex smiled to herself. Perhaps the young officer was maturing.

She was surprised when Keri asked bluntly, "Lieutenant, do you like Vice/Narcotics?"

"Yes, it's actually my favorite assignment so far. Why?"

As soon as she'd spoken, Alex regretted inviting more discussion. She was well aware that the guys on her squad warned everyone about the ambitious female lieutenant. They described a superhuman cyborg able to regurgitate procedures verbatim, arrest fleeing felons, and defend the rights of the downtrodden, all while spooning out bitter doses of discipline to the deserving. If Keri needed any more reason to dislike her, she would find it the first time she sat down for a beer with anyone in the division.

"I've always had an interest in narcotics work and do a lot of street-level enforcement. I'd like to take it to the next level someday." The cool blue of Keri's eyes turned dark. The intensity of her words hinted at something deeper than a simple career move. She seemed to ponder her next statement. "I was wondering, if you don't mind my asking, is it important to insulate yourself from people on the job in order to *do* the job at your rank?"

"I beg your pardon?"

"I'm sorry. Is that too personal?" Keri paused, enjoying the flicker of discomfort on Alex Troy's face. She recognized the look: suspicious, untrusting, and perhaps…lonely. Curious to know if anything besides blue lights and sirens got this woman's pulse racing, she asked, "I just wonder if it's difficult and how much of a toll it takes."

A trace of conflict in Alex's eyes told her she wasn't going to get an answer. Aware that she was treading on Alex's toes, Keri said quickly, "Lieutenant, with all due respect, I was only trying to…never mind."

Alex regarded her evenly. "Do you always say what's on your mind? That can get you in trouble around here."

"I'll remember that." Keri held her gaze, eyes steady.

God only knew what lay behind those cool pools of innocence. Trouble, Alex decided. Mentally adding "still sensitive and emotional" to her growing list of adjectives to describe Keri Morgan, she said, "Morgan, it was just a suggestion. You don't have to take it personally."

The minute she said the words, she wanted them back. She'd said something very similar in that room with Keri three years ago and the response had been swift and emotional. She held her breath.

"I take everything personally. Otherwise what's the point?" Keri tried for a flippant tone, but the criticism stung.

She caught a mental flash of the two of them staring across a table at each other during that unforgettable interview. Thankfully, she could hide her feelings better now and had learned to think before she opened her mouth. She wished she'd made a better impression, but the formidable lieutenant would not be easily impressed. Keri glanced down at her skimpy top. It was just her luck that she was dressed for a night on the town. She and her best friend had partied until early morning and she hadn't had time to go home before work. She was going to change the subject but she realized they were still standing in the middle of the hallway in front of the elevators, oblivious to the people maneuvering around them. The steel doors were finally open. Alex was moving with the crowd.

"It was nice to see you again, Morgan," she said as she followed a man into the confined space. "Keep up the narcotics work."

"I will." Keri stepped aside as the doors swished closed. She had no plans to ride the elevator jammed up next to Alex Troy.

Irritated, she hurried toward the stairway exit. It was almost time for lineup and she wanted to review the confidential file before her shift. She knew she shouldn't have allowed Alex's stoic attitude and criticism to get under her skin. She wondered why she cared what that woman thought. Hadn't she lost all respect for Alex Troy a long time ago?

❖

Alex stared straight ahead as the elevator ascended a few floors. She felt unsettled by the surprise encounter with Keri Morgan, and irrationally annoyed that Keri had avoided taking the lift at the last minute. Obviously she'd interpreted Alex's comment as another criticism. Alex reminded herself that she didn't have time to baby-sit an angry officer with a chip on her very lovely shoulder. Officer Morgan's tender feelings were not her responsibility. Her intentions hadn't been malicious, and if Keri could get over herself perhaps she would have seen that. All the same, Alex was reluctant to end their brief conversation on a sour note. Three years had passed. It was time for both of them to move on.

As she exited the elevator and entered the chief's office, she made a concerted effort to clear Keri from her thoughts. Glancing around the reception area, she marveled that instead of memorabilia of the chief's career, the walls were lined with photographs of officers who had been recognized for their accomplishments. The collection continued into the chief's private office.

Chief of Police Rudy Lancaster rose from behind his vertically enhanced desk, towering over Alex as he greeted her. Framed by the light pouring in through a bank of windows opposite the door, he seemed even larger than his six-foot-four. Alex liked this amiable African American man and had come to respect him as a boss since he took up the position a year ago.

"It's good to see you, Alex." He shook her hand and motioned her to a chair. "How are you holding up?"

Alex's jaws clenched. "It's still hard to believe they're both gone, but I'm doing okay, sir. Thanks for asking."

"If you need anything, let me know."

His sincerity touched her. Blinking back tears, she said, "Thank you, Chief. How're Carol and the kids? Do they like it here?"

"They love it. I wasn't sold on the move, as you know, but Carol's family is here. It's convenient for vacations, too. Four hours from the coast and four hours from the mountains."

Granville, North Carolina, was a midsized town with a small-town mentality. Alex had lived here since college and it felt like home. She'd attended UNC and had decided to stay on because of the know-your-neighbor feeling. And there was enough nightlife to keep an experimenting lesbian in playmates. The thought made her frown. She could hardly remember when she'd last enjoyed either. The occasional one-night stand made little impact. Her parents' deaths a year earlier, coupled with the end of a painful relationship, had led to months of self-imposed solitude. To return to work without falling apart, she had exercised all the emotional self-restraint she was capable of. She still wasn't back to full steam, and frequently skipped meals and restless sleep hadn't helped her health or state of mind. But she'd accepted the personal price as a necessity.

The chief slid the family photos on his desk to one side and pulled a piece of paper toward him. "I don't get to see much of you, but your name crosses my desk often. You and Wayne are doing good work."

"We try, sir."

Alex thought about her supervisor and mentor, Wayne Thomas. He and Alex's father had been best friends, and when her parents died, Wayne had become like a surrogate father and kept her from falling apart, personally and professionally. She owed him so much and wanted to make him proud. But she was surprised he wasn't here. It was unusual for him to miss a meeting with the chief unless something more important came up.

Chief Lancaster got to the point. Handing her a single sheet of Granville Police Department memo paper, he said, "Alex, I've got a special assignment for you. Wayne and I discussed it earlier and agreed on the basics."

Alex scanned the memo and her pulse quickened. This was the opportunity she'd been waiting for ever since making lieutenant five years ago. When she looked up, the chief was smiling.

"I take it you have no objections to heading up a multijurisdictional task force to target our most notorious and elusive drug dealer?"

The multijurisdictional aspect sent a shiver up Alex's spine and she took a deep breath. "I have no problem whatsoever, Chief. I'd love to make life hell for Sonny Davis."

"I know I don't have to tell you this, Alex, but the series of deaths recently from drug overdoses on college campuses has the community in an uproar. We've got five institutions of higher learning in this town. You and Wayne have been to enough of the meetings to know what the citizens are saying about—" Lancaster paused as the phone at his elbow rang. "Excuse me a second."

Alex watched his brow furrow with what could only be bad news. He was silent for a few seconds before asking, "Any ID on the victim yet?" He covered the mouthpiece with his hand and murmured to her, "Another overdose."

They needed to get this creep off the streets, Alex thought. Sonny Davis had been on their radar since he ran a gang of drug dealers in high school, but he'd never been convicted of anything. He dealt every drug that came down the pipeline and often used brutality to keep his people in line. They'd sent several of his cronies to prison but Davis's hands were always clean.

"Thank you for calling," the chief said. "I'm going to send Alex Troy down there right now. She'll be running the Sonny Davis task force, and I want her to take a look at what you have. Keep me posted."

He hung up and turned back to Alex. "The MO's not quite the same as the others. This one is off campus, but I'd like you to take a look anyway." He scribbled the address on a piece of notepaper and handed it to her. "Come back by when you finish, if it's not too late, and we'll wrap up the task force details."

"Will do, sir."

Alex was halfway to the door when the chief added, "Whoever is bringing this poison into our town is turning it into a death trap for our young people. I want it stopped, Alex. Whatever it takes, make it happen."

❖

The drive to the crime scene in the low-income housing area of town took only five minutes. Captain Ted Joyner, the evening watch commander, met her in the parking lot of the complex, handed her a pair of latex gloves, and led her into a modestly furnished apartment.

"She's back here in the bedroom. We still don't know who she is, didn't have an ID on her. We're canvassing the other members of the group."

"What group?"

"This girl was trying to help organize a community watch group in the neighborhood. Guests from half the complex were in the house and the backyard for a cookout."

Alex worked her hands into the gloves on her way to the back bedroom. Dodging officers pretending to be busy, she stepped into the small space. The young woman's body lay face down on the bed. Alex moved in for a closer examination. The body was in full rigor and the skin had an ash-gray tone that made it appear death had occurred days ago instead of hours. "Looks like she had some sort of seizure," Joyner said.

"Help me roll her over," Alex directed one of the paramedics standing by the bed. She took one arm and turned the body toward her.

As the victim's face came into view, Alex froze. Time collapsed around her as she looked into the thinly clouded eyes of Stacey Chambers. Those haunting orbs of once-living human substance begged for help. The young woman's mouth gaped open. Emesis had dried around her lips and nose. Alex wondered what words had died on Stacey's lips as her last breath passed over them. A knot rose in her throat and bile churned in her stomach, threatening to escape.

"Oh my God," she whispered.

"Alex, do you know this girl?" Joyner asked.

"Yes. Stacey Chambers. She worked for me as an intern in Vice/Narcotics last summer." Alex backed up to the door and grabbed the frame for support. "She just graduated from college."

"You don't mean Councilman Chambers's daughter, do you?"

"Yes." Alex couldn't take her eyes off the lifeless form that once hosted the lovely and vibrant spirit she knew. Her breath came in staccato bursts. She'd seen more than her share of dead bodies, but never someone she knew, not even her parents. "She didn't do drugs, Ted. This has to be investigated as a suspicious death. We can't afford to leave any questions on this one."

He nodded. "You don't need to be here. Would you brief the chief? He'll want to tell the councilman himself."

"Of course."

As Alex exited the room and hurried from the apartment, images of Stacey's contorted features flashed through her mind over and over like a hiccup in an old reel-to-reel movie. Once in the confines of her vehicle, she allowed the hot tears pooling in her eyes to escape. The drive back to police headquarters seemed to take twice as long as the earlier trip.

Chief Lancaster was pacing in his reception area when Alex walked in. He motioned her back into his office and closed the door. "From the look on your face, I'd say you don't have good news for me."

"This one hit close to home, Chief. It'll be in the papers before morning. The dead girl is Stacey Chambers, the city councilman's daughter. She interned in Vice/Narcotics last summer."

"Jesus."

"She collapsed at—of all things—a community watch meeting in one of our low-income neighborhoods. It was called in as an overdose, but she had no drug history. It's just not possible. I knew her. I worked with her. I'd stake my reputation on it."

Alex had liked Stacey Chambers immediately and they'd formed a sort of mentoring bond. Stacey wanted to become a drug abuse counselor. Now all that potential was snuffed out. Gone. There was no way on earth Stacey would have been using drugs. Something was badly wrong and Alex planned to get to the bottom of it.

Lancaster wiped a bead of sweat from his brow and shook his head in disbelief. "I'll have to break the news to Councilman Chambers personally. I can't imagine losing a child, especially like this."

"There was no trauma to the body," Alex said. "But Captain Joyner is handling it as a suspicious death for now. We'll have to wait for the coroner's report before we know anything definite." She flinched at the thought of the state ME impassively probing Stacey's body in search of clues. "It has all the signs of a drug overdose, but we'll need to see a copy of the tox report before that can be confirmed."

"The councilman and the mayor are going to want answers on this one in a hurry."

"So far, we know the tainted ecstasy in our area is coming from a single source," Alex replied. "And all our street informants finger Davis as the distributor. If we can link Stacey's death with the others through the toxicology results, we might be able to follow the trail to Davis and build a case for negligent homicide."

Chief Lancaster wiped his broad hand over his face again. "I don't need to tell you how it looks for us when we have a bunch of kids ending up dead because we can't nail this guy." He paused. "Get this tied up in a neat little package and we'll discuss a promotion for you."

Alex didn't point out that bringing down Sonny Davis wasn't all about kudos and a pay raise. "None of those dead kids deserved an end like this. I'm going to find out who's behind Stacey's death and weave a chain of evidence so tight that Sonny Davis will never draw another free breath. *And* some of the asset forfeiture money from his holdings would go a long way in a small department like ours."

Lancaster nodded. In a pensive tone, he said, "Quite honestly, Alex, I need a perspective like yours on my command staff, a vision beyond the ordinary, if you get my drift. A woman's perspective."

Alex's enthusiasm rose. She couldn't deny the part of her that was competitive. She wanted to be among the very best at her job, and a promotion would be her ticket to make some long-overdue changes in the department. Her anger boiled just beneath the surface as she remembered her less-than-ceremonious promotion to lieutenant. The good ol' boys' club worked hard to keep people like her and Lancaster "in their places." The chief had struggled to diversify the force from the bottom up without much support. Many of the white male supervisors in the five-hundred-member department viewed him with distrust. It would really chap their asses if she made captain. Meantime, finding Stacey's killer and putting Sonny Davis away came first. She would have plenty of time to think about getting the railroad tracks on her collar later.

Chief Lancaster continued. "Now, about the task force team. DEA will kick in a techie to help with surveillance and hardware. Caldwell PD is contributing one detective and Layton PD will send a black male-and-female team. You'll be choosing a sergeant and two detectives from our department."

Anxiety shot through Alex's system like splinters. Layton's involvement could be problematic, given her history with an ex who worked there, but she could handle Helen Callahan if their paths crossed. Adrenaline surged as she began to map her plan of attack. "What are the limits on my choices internally?"

"Actually, there's only one." Lancaster studied her closely for a moment before explaining, "I know you have a history with Keri Morgan, but one of my commanders submitted her name to serve on the team. He thinks very highly of her and I have to admit, her narcotics work in the field is quite impressive."

Something about the chief's hesitation stirred anxiety in the pit of Alex's stomach and she gently chewed the inside of her cheek. Her first instinct was to raise an objection, but she counted slowly to ten. The investigation into Keri's partner was old news. She didn't want her boss to think she would allow emotional baggage to affect her decision making.

"I'm certain you've moved on and I'd like to give her a chance to do the same," he said, making her glad she'd kept silent. "One of the things I admire most about you, Alex, is that you never let your feelings get in the way of the job. You have connections to both Stacey Chambers and Keri Morgan, but I'm confident you'll put the job first."

Alex forced a smile and hoped the same could be said when this assignment was over. Her mind flashed to Keri Morgan, stooping to pick up the papers, her clinging red top leaving little to the imagination. "I'll do my best, Chief. So I'll be choosing a detective and a sergeant?"

Lancaster nodded and stood, signaling the end of their meeting. "I'll send out the order this afternoon. Start recruiting immediately. You'll work out of the office next door to Vice/Narcotics. The mutual aid agreements have already been signed. If you hit any roadblocks with the other agencies or their reps, let Wayne run interference for you. I want you totally focused on this. Any questions?"

"No, sir…and thank you again. I won't let you down."

Alex left the chief's office torn between exhilaration and apprehension. The earlier conversation with Keri replayed in her mind. The last thing Alex or this assignment needed was a team member with a grudge. If Keri was serious about moving into Vice/Narcotics, this would be the ideal opportunity. If she wanted to prove herself, she would have to toughen up.

Alex headed for the afternoon lineup with a sense of anticipation she hadn't felt in a long while. Her feelings had nothing to do with Keri Morgan, she reasoned, but her heart continued to beat faster than it should. Alex found that very unusual.

Chapter Two

In the musty police locker room, Keri switched mechanically from street clothes into her uniform, her mind on the frustrating woman she'd left at the elevators twenty minutes earlier. Alex Troy still had the power to intrigue her and anger her after three years. No one ever had that effect. Keri could not understand why her reactions to the arrogant lieutenant seemed to be frozen in time. She would never forget the browbeating she'd received over the complaint of excessive force against her partner. Alex had practically accused her of being complicit in the battering of a suspect and of lying during the investigation. Her emotionless questioning and nitpicky badgering were typical of administrative pencil pushers who hadn't worked the street in years. What level of detachment allowed her to turn on her fellow officers? Was her motivation strictly political, her aim merely to hurdle another rung in the departmental hierarchy?

Keri thought back to the encounter at the elevator and flushed again. She'd rehearsed her next meeting with Alex Troy a hundred times since the day of that interview, planning on a calm discussion. She wanted to provide a levelheaded account of events that would clear her partner's name and restore her own reputation. In her imaginary encounter, Alex would realize she'd been wrong and she and Keri would become...what, friends? Amiable coworkers?

It infuriated Keri that when she saw Alex today, she was too disconcerted to think calmly. The gorgeous, auburn-haired woman with the roguish grin seemed at odds with the coldhearted, ambitious lieutenant locked in Keri's memory. The lightly etched lines of her face were carved by a greater depth of caring than Keri recalled. And the gaze from her cinnamon-brown eyes had the precision of a laser and was equally impossible to hold.

Keri pushed Alex Troy from her mind. The last thing she needed before going on shift was to be distracted by a three-year-old nightmare and a woman she probably wouldn't see again for three more years. She snapped the keepers securing her ten-pound gun belt to the smaller pants belt, grabbed the brown paper bag her mother had filled for the squad, and headed to lineup.

"That's my girl," Brian Saunders, her zone partner, yelled when she entered the small assembly area just outside the lineup room. "More snacks from Mama Marie?"

The other six officers redirected their attention from gun cleaning and inched closer as she placed the bag on the rickety metal-legged table. "Yeah, she thought you guys might not get a dinner break. Dig in. There are enough ham biscuits to go around. But only once."

One of the other officers piped up. "You know, I'd ask your mom to marry me if she wasn't already attached."

"Right, I know your wife would appreciate that," Keri replied. "By the way, how are she and the baby doing?"

"Good. She said thanks for coming by the hospital and for the gift you sent."

"Sure, no problem." Keri grabbed her hat and fell in line for inspection as Sergeant Larry Barnes entered the gray-walled lineup area. The distinctively pungent odors of solvent and gun oil permeated the air as officers holstered freshly cleaned weapons and moved to the side of the room.

"Lieutenant Troy from Vice/Narcotics is with us today," Barnes announced. "She'll address you after inspection."

Alex marched into the cramped room and stood opposite Sergeant Barnes in formation. Keri wondered why she was here. Perhaps to skewer another unfortunate officer in return for a second bar on her collar.

Keri conducted a thorough appraisal of the lieutenant, which embarrassment and haste had prevented earlier. A beige linen jacket accentuated her neatly cropped auburn hair. Threads of silver at each temple gave her an air of distinction. She wore tailored jeans and a white cotton blouse that clung to her muscular body. Except for the beginnings of crow's feet, Alex's years of experience weren't physically evident. She exuded the energy of a rookie with the confidence of a seasoned officer. The combination was almost breathtaking.

Keri stole a glance at her eyes, wondering if she'd imagined the sorrow she glimpsed there earlier. Something in Alex's expression told a story of too closely guarded emotion. How did a woman so attractive and accomplished arrive at such a desolate place? Maybe stepping on the little people was taking a toll.

After calling the squad to attention, Sergeant Barnes waddled toward the end of the line and began his methodical inspection. He sidestepped in front of each officer, scrutinizing hair length, shine of hat and breast badges, press of uniform, placement of tie tack, and finally gloss of leather gear and shoes. When he stopped in front of her, Keri prayed he wouldn't linger as he often did, staring needlessly at her breast badge or trouser cut. His overattention made her the butt of jokes from guys on the squad. To her relief, he passed quickly with only a cursory glance at her uniform, leaving the stench of stale cigarettes in his wake.

Her relief was momentary as he executed a military-style turn and continued the inspection behind the officers. "Morgan, button that pocket." He poked her left buttock with his pudgy finger.

Keri caught her bottom lip between her teeth and continued to look straight ahead. She thought she saw Alex's jaw tense as she snapped a return salute to Barnes and stepped forward to speak.

After ordering the squad to stand easy, she said, "I've been advised by Chief Lancaster that I'll be heading up a task force to target Sonny Davis and his expanding drug and prostitution business. As some of you may know, Councilman Chambers's daughter was found dead of an apparent drug overdose earlier today." Her throaty, enticing voice seemed to fracture slightly and Keri had the impression she was containing a strong emotion. "Sonny Davis may be connected to this young woman's death. He probably sold the drugs responsible."

Keri found herself fascinated by the way Alex stood and the confidence she exuded. Her slender fingers sliced the air in controlled gestures, their perfectly manicured nail tips healthy with a shine free of polish. She made direct eye contact with each officer, her intense gaze a quiet plea and a challenging invitation to action. No wonder her subordinates followed so readily.

"I'm sure most of you are familiar with this guy's history," Alex continued. "But for the new and uninformed, Davis is the kingpin of narcotics and prostitution in the city. He drives an old-model Cadillac, pale yellow in color, with personalized tag 'SD.'"

One of the officers cautiously interrupted. "If he's so bad, why haven't we nailed him before now?"

"Davis has the highest paid lawyers and the best Teflon coating I've seen in years. We haven't been able to get anyone inside his operation. Hopefully this task force will change that."

"We're going to infiltrate Davis's organization?" The voice was skeptical.

Alex shook her head. "Infiltration is probably not going to be a possibility, but we're considering all options. Our best chance may be a hand-to-hand buy directly from him through a trusted source. This isn't going to be a glamour job. There'll be a lot of grunt work. Information and intelligence gathering, surveillance, and informant buys before we even think about trying to nail this guy. I'll be assembling my team over the next few days. If any of you are interested, please let me know. Also, if you encounter Davis or his associates, use extreme caution. They're usually armed. Forward all intelligence up the chain to my office so we can keep building our case against him."

Alex exchanged a glance with Keri and a spark flashed between them. Keri had never seen such intensity or singularity of purpose before, but there was something else, something she couldn't name. Keri weighed her chances of being chosen for the task force, considering her history with the lieutenant. Her next thought caused even more consternation: *Why would I want to be on a team supervised by someone I can't trust?* Her heart sank. The opportunity was everything she could have hoped for, but her dream of becoming a narcotics officer evaporated. Alex could pick and choose. Why would she pick someone who had insulted her?

Barnes dismissed the troops and followed Alex into the cubicle adjacent to the lineup room. Behind them, Keri veered into a musty supply room and sensed immediately she shouldn't be there. Alex's calm but forceful voice penetrated the wall.

"What's your problem, Barnes? You're a twenty-year veteran with eight years' supervisory experience. What were you thinking...or do I want to know?"

"I beg your pardon, ma'am?" Barnes stammered. "What do you mean?"

"I mean don't ever let me see or even hear a rumor that you placed your hands on a female officer's butt or any other part of her anatomy again. In private such behavior is forbidden, in front of her peers it's even more degrading and inappropriate. Do I make myself perfectly clear?"

"Oh, you mean the button thing?" Barnes must have smiled.

"Precisely. And wipe that stupid grin off your face or I'll have your ass up on charges so fast you'll wonder why you didn't have time to resign. Do we understand each other?"

"Yes, Lieutenant, you're right. It was uncalled for and I apologize."

"I'm not the one who deserves an apology, Sergeant."

"Right, ma'am, I'll see to it immediately."

Keri grabbed her reports and dashed toward the lineup area, unable to keep the smile off her face. For the first time in her career, somebody had called one of the boys on his sexist behavior. Alex had sliced Barnes like a zero-degree wind chill. She would've probably done the same for any other officer, but Keri was glad it had been for her.

Barnes stuck his head in the door as he passed the squad room. He shot her a blistering stare and mumbled, "Morgan, sorry about earlier, you know, the button." His squinty face was splotchy and contorted with anger.

Keri felt vindicated, but before she could reply, Barnes vanished. Knowing there'd be hell to pay for that apology, she gathered her equipment bag and walked the frayed carpet path from the squad room to the parking exit. A suffocating blanket of heat and exhaust fumes enveloped her when she kicked open the metal door to the parking deck. Not far from her, Alex was rearranging something in the trunk of an unmarked Crown Victoria.

Keri dropped her bag beside her patrol vehicle, took a deep breath, and approached. "Excuse me, Lieutenant."

Alex closed the trunk and turned, her piercing eyes momentarily devoid of their customary defenses. Keri noted the up-and-down evaluation of her body. The intensity of it unnerved her and she shifted uncomfortably. She inhaled the light musk fragrance already embedded in her olfactory memory, the subtly commanding fragrance she recalled from earlier. It defined this woman.

"Yes, Officer Morgan?"

The openness of her gaze caught Keri off guard. Reluctant to break the connection, she said, "I just wanted to say thank you. I mean, I wasn't eavesdropping. I appreciate what you did for me with Sergeant Barnes."

With a blink, the contact was broken and her customary guarded façade was in place. "You shouldn't have heard that, Morgan. Women have a hard enough time in this job. I just think we should try to keep the playing field as even as possible."

Keri couldn't believe it. The woman sounded almost sincere. "Well, I appreciate it, but I don't want any trouble."

Alex regarded Keri with a mixture of what appeared to be curiosity and confusion. "I'm afraid I don't understand."

"I don't want to file a complaint against my sergeant."

"That won't be necessary. I observed the violation myself, so if any charges were going to be brought, I would do it. You needn't worry."

"Good, just so we're clear." Keri hesitated, trying to decide if and how to broach her next subject. No guts, no glory, she finally concluded. "So, I guess the fact that a councilman's daughter is our latest victim elevates the case to APE status."

Blood drained from Alex's face. Her brown eyes turned to deep pools of pure sadness and welled with tears. One of her hands flattened against the side of her vehicle as though she needed support.

Keri knew without a doubt that she'd said something terribly wrong. "I meant an acute political emergency. You know, bad case, bad press."

Alex's lips moved but no sound emerged. A quick flick of her hand dispatched a single tear.

Keri wanted to hug her and erase the anguish so painfully etched into her delicate features. She stepped closer, the sorrow drawing her in. "My God, you knew her, didn't you? I'm so sorry. I had no idea."

The ever-present icy exterior had vanished before her eyes and Keri saw a woman deeply affected by the death of a friend. She watched in disbelief as Alex straightened, nodded in affirmation, and regained control of her crumbling façade.

Alex nervously combed the sides of her auburn hair with her

fingers. "She interned for me last summer. Stacey is—was a wonderful young woman." Her voice cracked at the end and she turned to open her car door.

"I'm really sorry, Lieutenant. We'll catch this guy. Don't worry."

"Thank you for that, Morgan." Alex closed the door of her Crown Victoria and started the engine.

"Have a nice day, ma'am."

Keri waited for her to drive off before strolling back to the patrol car. She couldn't believe the glimpse of uncharacteristic emotion she'd seen from Alex. Was it possible she'd misjudged the lieutenant? She had to admit she was now more intrigued than ever about her, yet despite that unguarded moment and the fact that Alex had taken up for her with Sergeant Barnes, a nagging feeling remained. Keri didn't trust Alex's motives, and she doubted that would change anytime soon.

❖

Alex pushed open the oak front door of her ranch-style house with her sneaker-clad foot and dropped her briefcase. As she did most evenings, she took in the collection of inherited antiques mingled with junk that served as furnishings and vowed to have a tag sale. It was time to upgrade her home and her life. Both had been prisoners of the past for too long.

Her body ached with physical fatigue, and a deep sadness clung to her like a wet woolen pea coat. She couldn't shake the image of Stacey Chambers's body, lifeless and frozen in an epileptic twist of disfigurement. It was hard to comprehend how that once lively young woman had been taken away. Alex was convinced Stacey's death was not from a self-administered overdose. Whatever had happened, someone else was responsible, either deliberately or accidentally. She needed to know who was with Stacey immediately before she died, and exactly what was going on at that community watch meeting.

Alex slumped into her father's worn leather recliner and rested her head in her hands. She and Stacey hadn't been close personal friends but they'd formed a bond of mutual respect and appreciation. They shared an understanding of dedication to purpose and service for the greater good. This was a young woman who would've made a difference in the world. Alex lost track of time as the tears started without invitation and refused to stop. Memories of Stacey's laughter, her plans for the future, and her compassion for others faded with the sobs Alex had held in all day.

The world sucks, she thought as she slammed her fists against the chair arms and rose to pace her cluttered living room. Whoever did this to Stacey would not go unpunished. She owed it to her and the other young people who had died before realizing their potential. She wanted this killer of dreams and purveyor of poison to rot in prison for the rest of his natural life. Better yet, she wanted him to do something stupid and invite a bullet.

For the first time in her career, Alex considered the risks she was willing to take in order to make this case. The very idea of anything illegal, immoral, or unethical grated at her nature, but she wondered if her strict adherence to the rules all these years had allowed others like Sonny Davis to go unpunished. Other officers occasionally skirted procedures or bent the rules, and didn't the end justify the means, especially if the end result was justice? The thought sent a shiver up her spine.

Her mind flashed unwanted pictures of Keri Morgan's unencumbered breasts under that tank top. She wondered if the skimpy attire had been the result of a wardrobe oversight or an intentional effort to attract attention as she came into work. Alex tried to dodge her wayward thoughts as she walked to the bathroom. The old reel-to-reel answering machine on the phone stand in the hallway blinked that she had a message waiting. She ignored it. All she wanted was a hot shower to soothe her aching muscles followed by a vodka tonic to erase Keri Morgan from her mind.

She turned on the hot water and undressed. How could she possibly work with Keri on the task force when Keri gave her killer looks like today? Not to mention the fact that Alex had physically craved her breasts not six hours earlier. What a mess. Questionable professional ethics were bad enough, but add to that Keri's... Alex struggled for the right word. She was just too damn...vibrant.

You're making no sense at all, Alex chastised herself. One of the reasons she was drawn to Keri was that she bristled with life. Alex hadn't felt that energy in herself or anyone else for a long while. She showered and dressed without wasting time, then wandered out to the hallway and mashed the rewind button on her blinking machine. The tape backed up with a slow whirring growl, then began its delivery.

"Hello, gorgeous, it's Helen."

Alex jabbed the rewind button and stared at the phone. She suddenly hated the antiquated technology that prohibited immediate erasure of that deadly sweet voice. But she'd been unable to part with her father's only concession to the high-tech age in their home.

Alex rattled off a list of reasons Helen Callahan might call her. Maybe she'd already heard about the task force and wanted to horn in on the political action. Or perhaps she was just horny and thought Alex was weak enough to entertain the idea of having sex with her again. The most likely reason was that she was drunk and lonely again. Alex dropped into a turquoise vinyl chair at her kitchen table and stared at the Formica and chrome top, feeling as dated as the hand-me-down dinette set. Different emotions warred in her mind. She knew what was coming every time she allowed herself to remember Helen: seductively promising words followed by the skillfully manipulative hands and mouth, ending with the inevitable knife to the heart.

Helen had strolled into the Granville detective division five years ago, a newly promoted Layton PD lieutenant, with an in-your-face confidence. She was supervising an organized crime task force involving the two agencies. Methodically working the room, she shook hands with everyone, saving Alex for last. Helen's five-foot-five frame was perfectly accentuated in a navy suit. Her beauty was topped off with blond hair and blue-gray eyes that pierced Alex's soul. When their hands touched, Alex was captivated by Helen's warmth and seductive charm. They quickly became inseparable, making excuses for unnecessary meetings just to see each other.

Two weeks later they made love for the first time in the lift of Helen's building, and Alex was undeniably lost. Even now, she couldn't escape the vivid memory. She didn't even bother to fight it; she simply gave in, letting herself drift back in time. Helen had punched the Stop button. The tiny wood-lined cubicle jolted to a halt and Alex's breath caught in her throat as Helen pressed her against the wall. She ripped Alex's blouse from her jeans and quickly unfastened the buttons. Her lips were hot and hard against Alex's breasts, sucking and biting them into erection. Alex's knees trembled and her clit ached with pulsing beats. She tried to regain her composure and calm the fire that threatened to blind her to all sense of decorum. Her protests were pointless.

Helen said, "I have to fuck you right now. I can't wait."

Alex had melted into her arms, moisture gathering between her legs. No one had ever been so desperate for her.

Helen unzipped Alex's jeans and slid her hand into the slippery warmth. "See? You want me."

"But we're almost to your apartment." Alex struggled to move away but Helen lowered her to the floor and pinned her. She was vulnerable. It turned her on and Helen knew it.

"You're so wet. I know you want it as badly as I do."

"But the alarm…people will come." The fear of interruption only served to heighten Alex's arousal.

"It's broken. Fuck them anyway. I only care about you."

Helen's mouth covered hers with bruising kisses as her hand claimed Alex's center. She rode Alex's thigh as her fingers plunged deeper and deeper inside. Her expert hands stroked Alex with such intensity that the sensations fluctuated between pleasure and pain. Alex could feel Helen's need to have her, to possess her. She wanted to please Helen, but something held her back.

"You're safe with me, Alex. Let go for once in your life."

And God help her, she did. Alex had wanted to trust someone to love her and take care of her. She'd grown weary of always being on guard, never feeling safe. Need that intense must have been love. She gave in to the feeling. Desire overtook her and physical pleasure became her only goal.

Helen felt her response and drove her fingers deep inside, making Alex's body burst into a wave of light. Tears, sweat, and come spotted the elevator floor as Helen continued to devour her. Alex had never imagined such passionate physical gratification.

As their bodies trembled, Helen whispered, "You're mine now."

If Alex had only known the literal intent of those words. She had trusted Helen totally and felt safe. She'd surrendered to the emotional involvement and craved the sexual excitement. Helen had filled a void, and Alex had allowed her to control their life together. The four-year exchange aroused passion and volatility beyond Alex's wildest imagination and nightmares. Ultimately it almost destroyed her. Helen was a violent alcoholic, who came from a long line of similar relatives.

Her obsessive jealousy had isolated Alex from friends and family. Alex's attempts to extricate herself from their relationship always ended in a scream-fest followed by threats of further violence.

How could she have been so stupid? And why did she still feel drawn to Helen?

Maybe it was because everyone she loved had left her all at once. Helen had dumped her for another woman a week after Alex's parents were killed in the crash of their private company plane. She felt orphaned and abandoned, and she knew that made her vulnerable. She didn't trust herself right now and she certainly couldn't trust other people. Self-pleasuring and anonymous sexual liaisons satisfied her physical needs. Intimacy was an indulgence she couldn't allow.

Alex picked up the phone and ordered a pizza. As she waited for the delivery, she agonized again over the same old questions. How could she have trusted Helen so completely? When did her judgment go so off track? Her heart ached with the loneliness of too much control and too little hope. Maybe it *could* be different. *I may be bruised, but I'm not broken*. Perhaps it was time to find out. She allowed the thought to sit with her for a moment before common sense reasserted itself. No, the only true safety was in maintaining distance and not getting involved.

Chapter Three

Alex was about to check off when she heard the hostage situation call. She'd attended two afternoon lineups and three night-shift assemblies and had been running calls for the past three hours. She wanted to find the other candidate for the task force ASAP, and seeing officers in action was a good start. She fought the urge to respond directly to the scene. The field was not her command, and male egos were fragile.

"Dispatch, this is Lieutenant Troy. I'm in the vicinity. I'll be at the staging area."

She pulled into the Quick Stop parking lot at Cypress and Fourth, threw her jacket in the backseat, and took a ballistic vest from the trunk. She pulled it over her shirt as she approached officers already at the staging area.

Great, Keri thought, *that's all I need, Lieutenant Hard-Ass looking over my shoulder again. As if one hostage taker isn't enough.* She crouched at the corner of the residence behind a row of dense pampas grass, her pulse pounding as she awaited further instructions. She could hear the television next door, a barking dog, and even crickets in the grass with pinpoint clarity. Worst-case scenarios flashed through her mind and she played each out to its logical conclusion. Her skin tingled with sensitivity as the seconds crawled.

"All units on the scene…" The dispatcher's voice had gone up an octave. "We just received a call from a relative of the reported victim that the male subject at this address is holding a female hostage and threatening to kill her if anyone interferes. They say he's hooked on meth and sounded high. For information only, our original call came from the victim. She advised he has a gun."

Sergeant Barnes arrived at the command post as Alex was reviewing a sketch of the street with the zone officer. "Lieutenant, I didn't realize you'd be here." His clipped tone made it clear her presence was neither necessary nor welcome.

"You didn't realize we'd have a hostage situation, either."

Barnes hitched up his utility belt. "I checked on the way over and the Special Response Team is out on another situation. It could take two hours to get back. We need viable intel ASAP, and Morgan's in a perfect position to serve as forward point."

A tinge of something unfamiliar sneaked into Alex's usually flawless, operational mind. "Do I detect some reservation about sending her in?" She wasn't sure if she was asking herself or Barnes.

Barnes's lips tightened as he offered the explanation. "Morgan always volunteers for these types of assignments. She can get emotional. I don't think she'll act unless she has to, though."

Alex questioned his motives. Would he make that comment about a male officer? "What kind of assignments?" Prickling hairs on the back of her neck indicated she knew the answer.

"Anything dangerous. If you ask me, she's got something to prove."

"It's your call, Sergeant." It galled Alex to give him control of the situation. "I'd suggest you make sure she understands not to engage the subject unless directed to do so. If he's on meth he'll be extremely volatile. Also, get some officers on the other corners of the house and a backup for her. If this guy bolts we need to be on his tail."

Keri listened to Barnes's instructions while she scoped out a position nearer the house. Just because she couldn't go in didn't mean she couldn't get as close as possible. She needed to know what was going on inside. She skirted across the patchy lawn, flattened herself against the concrete foundation of the building, and called in her location. The partially opened window she squatted beneath offered an excellent vantage point. She was close to danger; it permeated the air.

"Car 260, can you tell us anything?" Barnes asked Keri by radio.

"There's a car in the driveway, older Buick with no tags. It looks like it's been here a while and— Stand by. I hear something."

Alex felt beads of perspiration forming under her vest in spite of the cool night air. Screams from inside the house could be heard in the background of Keri's transmission.

"Sarge..." Keri's voice was barely audible. "It sounds like he's assaulting her right now. Permission to go in."

Through the open window, Keri heard the pleading voice of a woman. "I just wanted you to get some help. These drugs are going to kill you."

The unmistakable slap of fist against flesh brought renewed cries from the house. The sounds elevated Keri's adrenaline levels and made her feel invincible.

"Can you see anything, Morgan?" Barnes wanted to know.

"No, sir, but it's getting worse. I need to go in. Is my assist close? It sounds like he's killing her." Keri was already on her way to the door, her heart threatening to beat out of her chest.

When it came down to it, Barnes passed the responsibility and looked to Alex for confirmation. She quickly assessed the new information. The only justification for sending an officer into this type of situation unassisted was imminent danger of death or serious injury. Her tactical experience dictated the necessary course of action, but for the first time in her career she felt unaccountably reluctant. That troubled her, but she didn't have time to consider the reason or its possible implications.

She nodded to Barnes and he relayed the command. Sirens sounded immediately down the street as the officers complied. "All other units, maintain your perimeter posts."

As Keri approached the door of the residence, the sickly sweet smell of fresh blood assaulted her senses. One side of the entryway was covered with bloody drag marks leading back into the house. She slammed her foot against the wooden door, sending a jolt up her leg. At the same time she announced, "Police!"

The flimsy lock gave way and the door frame splintered to the floor. Everything slowed to half-time as Keri entered the residence. She cleared the living room with a quick scan and followed the moaning toward the back of the house, checking each room as she passed. She found the bloody victim in a south-facing bedroom sprawled across a queen-sized bed.

At that moment Keri heard footsteps pounding through the house. The victim pointed and Keri gave chase. Her legs seemed to move effortlessly as she approached the back door.

"Car 260, send the paramedics in, now. The victim's been cut. The suspect's running out the back on the east side toward the tree line. He's armed with a gun and possibly a knife. I'm in pursuit. Have the other units move in."

Alex visualized the scene as Keri described it. Her heart pounded as the situation escalated. She struggled with an urge to race to the residence but protocol demanded that she remain at the command center until the scene was stabilized. Sirens wailed as the seconds dragged by.

Keri crouched at the back door to get a feel for the area before continuing pursuit. She heard the unmistakable crack of weapon fire against concrete blocks as she dove for cover.

A round whizzed past her head. She belly-crawled behind a stack of firewood. Peering through the logs, she keyed in on the suspect and pointed her weapon at him. Her voice choked in her throat when he stood his ground and took aim.

"Freeze!" she challenged him. "Don't make me have to shoot you."

At that moment two other officers flanked the suspect from behind the trees, yelling, "Drop the weapon! Do it now! Drop it!"

The suspect seemed to notice the odds were against him. He dropped the gun at his feet and raised his hands. "Okay, don't shoot. The bitch ain't worth all this."

As the officers handcuffed him, Keri rose shakily to her feet, holstered her weapon, and sent up a silent prayer. The adrenaline oozed from her. She trembled and began to feel weak as she recalled what could've happened. It was the same reaction every time she faced a potentially deadly situation. She stood by the woodpile, surveying the scene and giving her pulse and breathing a chance to return to normal. When her hands finally stopped shaking, she walked slowly toward the front of the house.

Red lights from the ambulance flashed eerie shadows across the lawn and Alex seemed to move toward her in a rapid series of still photos. Even in freeze-frame, Alex was the epitome of military bearing and personal grace. Keri thought for a second Alex was going to touch her as she stopped inches away, well within Keri's personal body space, a violation no cop ever committed on duty. Instead, Alex gazed at her with a look that caused more apprehension than being shot at. Her eyes momentarily burned with something stronger than fear, then softened.

"Are you all right?"

"Yes, ma'am, I think so. At least I'm not hit."

"Do you always get into this much trouble?" Alex's lips curved slightly at the corners.

"I don't go after trouble. It just seems to find me. But I really had no choice. Did I do something wrong, Lieutenant?"

"You saved the victim from further injury, got the bad guy, and no cops got hurt. I'd say that's a pretty good day. We can talk about the rest another time."

Keri's confidence rose at Alex's compliment, then immediately vanished as she thought about the accusatory interview years before. "What do you mean the rest? What else is there?"

Alex hesitated. Keri's complexion had paled and Alex longed to see its characteristic color return and hear a snappy comeback from the young officer. She didn't want to hurt Keri's feelings again, but she did want to understand. Her interest was mission specific, Alex assured herself. It had been an extremely tense situation. Motioning Keri to the side, she asked, "Why do you always volunteer for positions like forward point on these dangerous calls?"

"Who told you that? Barnes, right?"

"That's not really the issue, Morgan. It's an officer safety thing."

"I think this officer is pretty safe, ma'am." Keri knew she'd been right not to trust Alex, and she hoped her attempt at levity would mask her growing irritation. The last thing she wanted was Alex Troy poking around in her inadequacies and insecurities.

"You can't always hide behind humor. What are you trying to prove?" Alex's internal edit alarm sounded. But the words were out. She knew they were beyond the true scope of operational evaluation and into the personal arena. Why she'd asked she wasn't exactly sure.

"I'm a police officer. It's my job to keep other people from getting hurt. The guys on my squad have families, and that woman needed help fast. I couldn't wait. If you're going to write me up for something, go ahead. I won't fight it."

She cares more than she wants to admit and is willing to risk her life to prove it. An unfamiliar feeling crept into Alex's chest. "This isn't about writing you up. I'm just trying to…" *Understand you.* The thought was sobering and Alex shook her head to dismiss it.

"Trying to what?"

"Never mind. It's not important." Alex added as Sergeant Barnes approached them, "Just make sure your relief asks this guy about his connection. We need to know where he gets his drugs."

Barnes avoided Alex's stare, directing his comments to Keri. "Morgan, it's time for you to go off shift. Debrief with Ventura, hand the investigation over, and head in."

After Barnes finished, Keri turned to complete her conversation with Alex, but she was gone. Driving toward the station, Keri felt proud of her performance on the call, but dismayed that Alex Troy had suddenly started haunting her again.

❖

"Hey, Morgan, over here." Patricia Walters, Keri's best friend, waved from the parking lot across from the police station as Keri crossed the street toward her Jeep. Flashing lights from patrol cars sprayed a jittery luminescence through the night as officers checked their equipment.

Keri smiled as Pat covered her ears against the short yelps of siren tests and motioned her over. "My God, you cops sure are a flashy, noisy bunch," Pat said, giving her a quick hug. "I thought I'd drop by on my way to the hospital and see how it's going. Haven't heard from you since our near all-nighter. I hope you didn't get into trouble for showing up to work in your trolling attire." She studied Keri closely. "So, what's up?"

Keri thought about her exchange with Alex Troy not an hour before and felt her spirits sag once again.

"So what's going on?" Pat settled her five-foot-five frame against the side of Keri's vehicle and raked pudgy fingers through her jet-black spiked hair.

"Just the usual police department administrative bullshit."

Pat gave her a concerned look. "Wanna go to the bar and check out the scenery? I'm sure I can find somebody to cover for me tonight. We've both been on the high-and-dry list for a while."

"Don't you ever think about anything but sex?" Having known the feisty ER nurse for five years, Keri already knew the answer was a resounding no.

"Why would I? Our jobs are all about life and death. Why waste time waiting for one when you can be enjoying the other?" Pat eyed Keri mischievously and smiled.

They'd met in the ER after a vehicle chase ended in an accident. Pat was the trauma nurse who'd flashed a tiny penlight in Keri's eyes, asking, "Can you see me now?" They'd based their subsequent friendship on laughter and complete honesty. Keri knew Pat would understand her feelings about Alex and give her the second opinion she needed. Maybe she was just paranoid where Lieutenant Troy was concerned.

"Mind if we skip the bar tonight? I'd like to run something by you." Keri unlocked the Jeep and motioned for Pat to get in.

"This must be good if you're passing up liquor, laughter, *and* lesbians. Unless of course this involves another lesbian." Pat directed a sharp stare at her. "Oh, my God, tell me already. The suspense is killing me."

"Can you get your mind out of your pants for a second? It's not about a *woman*, it's about a frigging lieutenant who's trying to make my life total and complete hell."

"Just tell me who the bastard is. I'll have my cousin Frankie and his buddies stump-break his ass."

"It's not a guy."

"Aha, so this *is* about a woman."

Keri groaned. "Pat, remember Lieutenant Troy, the one who conducted the use-of-force investigation I was involved in a few years back?"

The laugh lines around Pat's eyes vanished. "Tough on you—and unfair?"

"You could say that." Keri swallowed a knot of anger that threatened to choke her. "She just came on one of my calls tonight and lit into me again. This time it was about officer safety."

"I thought you told me she was assigned to Vice/Narcotics now. What's she doing answering calls in the field?"

"Recruiting for a Narcotics task force," Keri answered offhandedly. "It was a hostage call. I thought I did pretty damn good, securing the victim and catching the suspect. She seemed okay with me, then the criticism started." Keri paused, reevaluating something in her mind. She could have sworn she saw genuine concern in Alex's eyes for a few seconds, but no way was she giving her the benefit of the doubt.

"Did you get a chance to talk about it at all?"

"Oh, no. She issues decrees from her high perch and rides off into the sunset unconcerned about their effects on her minions."

Sliding her hand over Keri's on the console, Pat ventured into the hot zone. "Is it at all possible that your past with this woman is casting everything in a bad light? You obviously still have very strong feelings about that. I'd hate to see that stuff interfere with your career forever." She gave Keri's hand a squeeze. "And how anyone could accuse you of dishonesty, I have no idea, sweetie."

Knowing Pat would see through anything but the truth, Keri acknowledged, "I'm not sure what I think, or why, anymore. But I know one thing for sure. I could *never* work for her, no matter how much I want to be on that task force. I don't trust her."

"I'm really sorry, Ker. I wish there was something I could do. Just keep the faith. It'll work out." Glancing at her watch, Pat opened the Jeep door. "Wish I could stay and talk because I know you're too wired to sleep, but duty calls. We're meeting in the morning for our run, right?" When Keri nodded, Pat added, "Get out and give me a hug."

Keri exited the vehicle and joined Pat in a full-body hug. "I love you, girl. And thanks for listening."

Pat hugged Keri tightly. "I love you, too. And remember another very important thing…never say never."

At that moment Lieutenant Troy walked through the lot toward a red Corvette parked on the street. She paused, surveyed Keri and Pat with a lingering visual examination worthy of a couple of nudists. Without a word, she continued to the curb and joined a woman Keri recognized as Sergeant Beth Price.

As the two officers headed back into the station, Keri cringed. She could just imagine what Alex was thinking. Probably *Slut.* Or worse, *Unprofessional.*

❖

"So, did you see any good prospects for the task force tonight?" Beth asked.

Alex bit back the reply that burned on her lips. Did Keri get off making out in public? Her embrace with the dark-haired woman was just another example of her immaturity. At least she wasn't in uniform. Alex decided her response to Keri's behavior was concern for the department's image. Had Keri been a male officer groping his girlfriend, she'd have had exactly the same reaction.

"That Morgan girl we just saw in the parking lot was impressive on a hostage call, although that display just now wasn't exactly what I'd call appropriate behavior outside the police station."

"From what I hear, she's a damn good officer." Beth hesitated.

Alex knew her friend well enough to know there was more to the story. "But?"

"Nothing about the job. She has a few family issues, like we all do. But you would, too, if your old man throttled you every time you tried to take a liberated breath."

Alex's body stiffened as though she'd been fisted in the gut. How could a parent strike their own child? For that matter, how could anyone hit a person he or she supposedly loved? Her mind flashed to Helen and she forced the memories away immediately, resenting their power to surface.

"How do you know about her father?"

"I overheard one of the guys on her squad talking about it. Keri speaks her mind, and that didn't set well with her father. Her twin brother was apparently the chosen one, always pampered and protected. He didn't have Keri's adventurous streak."

Alex tried to make sense of this latest news in the context of what she thought she knew about Keri Morgan. "But doesn't she still live with her parents?"

"Yeah, she moved back to help out when her mother developed Alzheimer's. Her dad's supposedly mellowed a lot with age, and stopped drinking. He's in poor health now, too. Heart, I believe."

"I can see why she's always joking around. I had no idea. But how can you live with someone abusive?"

Beth cleared her throat. They both knew the answer to that question and didn't need to revisit it now. "I think she'd be worth a look for the task force if you can get past your first run-in with her. Besides, that turned out all right in the end."

"I don't think she'd agree with you. She still seems pretty angry." Alex chose not to tell Beth that Keri Morgan was virtually on the project already. She needed more information about the young officer before finally adding her name to the short list. Maybe with just the right piece of intel she could talk the chief out of a personnel assignment that could only prove disruptive and unproductive for the entire team.

"Give her some slack," Beth said. "She doesn't know all the facts about that incident three years ago and you do."

"I don't have time to baby-sit on this one. Councilman Chambers is already climbing the chief's ass about Stacey's death. She was a great kid, but her father can be a pain in the butt. I don't blame him, though. I'd be doing the same thing if she was my daughter."

Beth stopped halfway up the building steps. "Is this really just about Morgan sulking over past history? Or is there something else?" Her sideways smile told Alex she liked the young officer's potential and looks.

"I'm afraid she's a time bomb waiting to go off, and I don't need to be dealing with anybody's issues in addition to..." Alex felt her insides tighten.

"In addition to what?" Beth eyed her with concern.

Alex hesitated, knowing her friend's reaction would be immediate and strong. "Layton PD is in on this."

"Oh, hell no. Who do I have to talk to? Ain't no fucking way this is happening. You know Callahan will try to make you look bad and take over the case. And you can bet your sweet ass that she'll try to get you in bed again—that's a given."

"It's a done deal, Beth. I've just got to work with it. I want this guy bad, and if he had anything to do with Stacey's death, I'll find out and bury him. Besides, there's a promotion waiting for me." Just the thought of it quickened her pulse.

"One more promotion won't change anything in this shithole of male ego and favoritism, and I don't think it's worth the fresh hell of dealing with Callahan again. Besides, it's not like you do it for the money."

"No, I don't. So will you come by tomorrow and look over some names with me?"

"Sure." Beth checked her wristwatch. "Want to work out now? It's still early."

"No, let's skip it tonight," Alex said. "I've got to get some rest so I can get this task force rolling in the next few days."

"That's right, go to your *old* home with your *old* things and think about this *old* problem that's getting ready to be brand new. Take it from me, nix this thing quick, Lieutenant. You don't need Helen Callahan in your life again." Beth's tone was teasing, but Alex knew she was very serious.

She was also dead right. The last thing Alex needed was another round in the ring with the only woman who had ever made her wonder if life was worth living.

Chapter Four

The next morning during their warm-up at the running trail, Pat's inquisition began. "Who *was* that gorgeous auburn-haired vixen last night in the parking lot? The way that gym suit clung to her body made me want to run interference. Do you know her? Is she single? Can I meet her?"

Keri bit down on her lower lip. She could tell Pat was nowhere near finished with this topic.

"Did you get a load of how she was looking at us?" Pat sighed. "It was like she was trying to decide between calling the fire department to hose us down, the vice squad to arrest us for indecent conduct, or just joining us. It made me horny, watching her watching us."

Keri's heart raced uncharacteristically. Thinking of Alex Troy as anything other than her nemesis was unsettling. A tingle of physical uneasiness rippled through her body. Alex had given them a scathing look, but Keri interpreted it as her usual disapproval.

Pat finally noticed Keri's silence. "What? Are you going to hook me up? That's what friends are for."

"That was Alex Troy."

"*The* Lieutenant Troy? Damn, she's hot."

"She was hot, all right, but not in a good way. If looks could kill, I'd have been dead when she crossed that lot last night."

"Okay, so I'm letting my hormones get the best of me—again." Pat focused unnecessary attention on her shoelaces.

Keri thought again about the look Alex gave her and Pat last night and wondered why it felt so personal. Maybe she *was* too focused on the past. She just needed to do her job and let her performance speak for itself.

"It probably wasn't personal," Pat mused. "The senior staff is the same at the hospital. Always worrying about the department's reputation. What are the chances you're going to have to deal with Troy, anyway? You're not even in the same division."

"Are we running today or talking?" Keri took off at a sprint.

"Hey, wait up. I didn't mean to piss you off." Pat huffed, trying to catch up.

Keri slowed her pace. "You just hit a sore spot." Another of many where this woman was concerned. "She's going to be handling the Narcotics task force I told you about last night."

Pat stopped and caught her breath. "You've always wanted to be in Narcotics."

"Exactly. And now it looks like my chances are shot to hell. Whoever gets on this team is pretty much assured a permanent slot in Narcotics."

"Is there anybody who can help you?"

Keri understood what she was getting at. Politics would be pretty much the same in a hospital or a police department. Nothing was ever beyond favoritism, bribery, or blackmail. "Even if I could pull some strings, I'm not working with this woman. I just can't, Pat. After the way she's treated me, I could never expect a fair shake. End of story. Let's change the subject."

Pat easily converted to her default topic of choice: sex. "Great. So when are we going trolling again? There's nothing so wrong that can't be fixed by a hot, anonymous fuck."

Keri smiled at the ease with which her friend talked about, and through the years, engaged in sex. Pat's philosophy about relationships was simple—do your best until one of you gets over it, then move on. Keri had begun to wonder if there was something wrong with her physically. She enjoyed sex but had never experienced the all-consuming passion people raved about. Perhaps it would be different if she were in love with someone.

"I guess I could handle a little stranger sex," she said. "It couldn't hurt my frustration level."

Pat threw up her hands. "Sex isn't to be 'handled.' You need to jump in with both feet and go wild. How many times have I told you that you don't have to love everybody you sleep with, despite what you read in the lesbian handbook."

Keri smiled. "Don't get me wrong. I enjoy sex, at least the physical part. It's the lack of emotional connection I have a hard time with."

She slowed her pace, then stopped, taking in the glassy stillness of the lake. Pat stood behind her and wrapped her arms around Keri. Her warmth and compassion filled Keri with a deeper longing. She craved such intimacy with a lover. Why did it seem so hard to find?

"This is what I'm talking about." She leaned back into Pat. "I've never felt this level of intimacy with anyone I've slept with. When someone holds me, it's usually for sex. But I want a friend *and* a lover. Maybe I'm asking too much."

"You just haven't met the right woman," Pat said. "Believe me, when you do, all the loose ends will connect just fine. Meantime, don't sell yourself short for anyone. You deserve to have exactly what you want."

Keri nudged Pat and nodded toward the track. "Thanks. Let's go."

Making the turn at their halfway mark, Keri was ready for a change of focus. "So what about you, my wise friend?"

"What do you mean?"

"Come on, don't play dumb with me. How's your love life?"

Pat jogged several minutes before responding. "Same old, same old for me. I'm basically the opposite of you. I fall for anything in a skirt, love them as long as it lasts, and move on. They never seem to love me back anyway, so it's just as well."

Keri was touched by the sincerity in Pat's voice. "What did you just tell me? You haven't met the right woman yet, either. And when you do, she'll see the same great person I do and she'll love you back."

"We're so good for each other's egos. Why haven't we ever slept together?"

Racing her friend to the end of the trail, Keri called back, "Because it's just sex to you, and I want to fall in love. What a perfect way to end a good friendship."

❖

Being summoned to the chief's office before start of business was never a good sign. The long hallway leading from the back stairway to the executive suites lacked the usual din of the workday, but Alex heard urgent voices echoing as she approached the partially opened door. She tapped lightly and immediately understood the chief's tense expression when he waved her in.

"You know Councilman Byron Chambers," Lancaster said. "We're just discussing the investigation."

"Councilman Chambers, I'm so very sorry for your loss. Stacey was a wonderful young woman. She'll be missed."

The man in front of the chief's desk shook hands with her, tears pooling in his eyes. Even with the obvious differences, Alex could have picked him out of a lineup as Stacey's father. His reed-thin frame was more angular where hers had been curvy and soft, but they both had the same intense blue eyes. Stacey's had always shone with laughter and promise. His mirrored the anguish so apparent in his defeated posture and pale features. He cleared his throat and said, "So, Chief Lancaster tells me you'll be leading the investigation."

The chief motioned for them to be seated. "Alex is heading the drug task force aspect of the case. The homicide squad is handling the death investigation, but Alex has been read into the specifics. You have my word—"

Councilman Chambers raised his hand to stop the chief. "No disrespect, Rudy, but I want someone on my daughter's case who knew her. I don't want this handled like any other case. I want them to *care* what happened to her. And she always spoke so highly of Lieutenant Troy."

Alex started to speak, but Lancaster replied, "Byron, I can assure you that none of our death cases are considered routine."

"I'm sure, but you'd want the same thing if she were your daughter."

The comment stopped Rudy Lancaster. Alex knew it touched his heart as a father. After a beat, he said, "I'll make sure everyone knows Alex has the lead."

Seeming satisfied with the chief's answer, Chambers returned his attention to Alex, asking, "What can you tell me?"

"At this point, the team is still being assembled that will look into the drug-related aspect of the case. It would be helpful if you could give me a list of the people Stacey associated with, professionally and personally. I know she went into counseling after graduation but we hadn't had a chance to talk about it much."

The knowledge that they never would saddened Alex to her core. Why hadn't she kept in closer touch?

"I'll give you anything you need. But please keep me in the loop." Byron Chambers took a notepad the chief offered and wrote furiously for several minutes. "This is everyone I can think of. I'll check with her mother and see if she can add anything."

Chief Lancaster stood and moved around his desk toward the door. "We should probably be going, Councilman. The press conference starts in five minutes. Hopefully someone will come forward after we've made the appeal. Alex will keep us both informed every step of the way."

Alex knew the chief's last statement was not just a reassuring comment for Byron Chambers's benefit but an indirect order to her. After shaking hands with both men, she headed back to her office and poured a fresh cup of coffee. As she sipped she went over the names on the councilman's list. Stacey Chambers was obviously a very popular and well-connected woman. Her register of contacts resembled a who's who of Granville politics and society. It would take an entire team of officers weeks to interview everyone. She decided to let the homicide glory boys handle the legwork and her guys would take any really promising leads.

Unfortunately, no one on the list stood out. Her next hope was that someone Stacey worked with or counseled at the Granville Drug Rehab Clinic would have some worthwhile information. Once she had the names from every other statement, she could cross-reference them with known associates of the other victims. Maybe there would be a connection. And just maybe, if they were really lucky, someone would respond to the councilman's appeal for information.

❖

Alex's desk phone buzzed and Shirley's sharp tone reverberated against the predominately bare walls in her makeshift office. "Lieuten-ant?" She pulled the word out like hot taffy. "Sergeant Price is here. You remember her, don't you?"

"I'm not sure. Refresh my memory." Her secretary knew she and Beth had attended recruit school together and remained best friends.

Beth opened Alex's door and shot her the bird. "Does this refresh your memory?"

"I'll take it from here, Shirley," Alex said into the speaker. "And hold my calls for a while. We've got a lot of work to do."

Beth closed the office door and dragged a worn fabric armchair next to Alex's. "I'd know that tone of voice anywhere. You've already gotten a call from the soul-sucking bitch. Right?"

"She left a message on my machine last night, but I didn't listen to it."

"I told you, Alex. It's not going to work. Helen's not a team player. She'll either try to take over or she'll blow the whole case with her petty power plays. Just remember what she put you through on that other task force, and there wasn't nearly as much at stake." Beth shook her head. "She's just aching to ride you down that dark road again."

"Thanks. I promise to keep her at arm's length." A Helen-induced uneasiness crept into Alex's mind. Distracting herself, she slid a handful of M&Ms from the mason jar turned candy dispenser on her bookshelf. "Want a hit?"

"No, thanks. Do you have some names for me to look at?"

"I've narrowed it down to a dozen, but that's as far as I can get." Alex pushed the files in front of Beth. "You've been in Vice/Narcotics for a while now and you've been a field sergeant. You know how things work."

"Guilty on all charges."

"So tell me what you think."

For the next few hours they discussed the pros and cons of each officer, reviewed their previous work assignments, evaluations, Internal Affairs jackets, and field performance. They narrowed the list to four names, two male and two female.

"All right, boss, I'm tired of looking at paper and I'm hungry as hell," Beth said. "Can we continue this over lunch? And you're buying."

"Sounds good to me." Alex welcomed the break to erase Keri Morgan from her mind. She kept resurfacing as the number one choice, even if the chief hadn't made his choice clear. But Alex's defenses still warned against it as they walked across the street to the deli.

She and Beth settled into the last church-pew booth. The early lunchers at the Main Street Deli had already claimed most of the wall-hugging booths and were busy swigging sweet tea and eating the barbecue lunch special. The blue-haired waitress smiled when they came in and shouted their usual order to the cook.

Beth studied the pained look that crossed Alex's face. "I'm sorry about Stacey. I know you liked her a lot."

"Yeah, she was a great kid. That's just one more reason I've got to make sure we do this by the book."

When Alex's chef salad and Beth's cheeseburger platter arrived, Beth took a mouthful and returned to business. "In that case, I don't think you should eliminate her just because you like her."

"Who?" Alex tried for her most innocent look, but her clenching jaw and the heat in her cheeks gave her away.

"You know exactly who—Keri Morgan. We've been over these files a dozen times and you have yet to say one thing about her, pro or con. That tells me you like her. And if you like her, you don't want to work with her because, because, because…pick a reason. You've got a lot of them."

"It's not that I like or dislike her. She's already on the team, chief's orders, unless there's a very good reason not to have her."

"Then why are you working my ass off going through all these files?"

"Because I need to know how she stacks up on her own merits, not because of a political favor the chief owes one of his commanders. You'd do the same thing if you were in my place."

Beth searched her face. "Yeah, I would. But you do like her. I know how you operate. You stay closed off by avoiding anything that resembles feelings."

"Okay, so she's attractive and, do I need to remind you, a subordinate. *And* if that's not enough, she seems impulsive and emotional. Would you trust her on a case this big?"

"You bet I would. Your other candidate's been on the force a long time. She's got more experience but she's also got a better chance of being known by Davis or one of his associates. Keri can be impulsive, but that often works in her favor. She's got keen instincts and she's got a hard-on for dopers that started about a year ago."

"What brought that on?" Last time Alex had an in-depth

conversation with Keri, the only thing she seemed serious about was covering her bent partner's ass.

"I'm not sure if something happened or she just developed her skills in drug investigations," Beth said. "Give her a chance. I'll keep you both out of trouble." She gave Alex a plastic grin and batted her eyes.

"That brings me to the last reason I asked you to help. I'd like you to be my team sergeant."

Beth's forkful of French fries hovered in midair. "You really do want to throw me in the fire, don't you?"

"You've got experience, and I trust you with my life."

"When you put it like that, how can I refuse? But there's something you need to know."

"Yeah?"

"I've arrested Davis before, and he'll probably remember. I broke his damn smart-assed jaw when he resisted. So I won't be much use to you undercover or even on close surveillance."

"That's fine. I need you for planning, direction, and supervision, but thanks for telling me."

"Absolutely. So, who's the final pick?"

"Steve Alston from Vice/Narcotics. He's the best, and I think they'll get along."

"That's a great idea. It sounds like you've got your team. When do we meet the others?"

"I'll call you as soon as I can pull it together. Thanks for your help."

"You bet. And stay away from psycho bitch. You want me to tell Keri about the job?"

"No. I'll do an interview first, just to be on the safe side. I don't want her, or anyone else, thinking she was an automatic choice."

"You got it, boss. This'll be the first time we've worked together. It could get interesting."

Alex's mind flipped through the things that could go wrong with the case: the team, the supervisors, the politics, and her mixed feelings about Keri Morgan. Right now she felt like she could handle anything, even the latter. Whether the same would prove true for Keri was another matter.

Chapter Five

K eri lurched into groggy consciousness. The afternoon silence of her parents' house was shattered by the ringing of her bedside phone. Any possibility of a nap before her shift disappeared. She grabbed the offending device and held it to her ear.

"Yeah…"

"Officer Morgan?"

"Yeah?"

"This is Lieutenant Troy. I'm not disturbing you, am I?"

Immediately awake, Keri bolted upright in bed coming to seated attention. "No, it's fine, what can I do for you?"

"If you recall in lineup last week I referenced a Narcotics task force. I was wondering if you had any interest in being a part of that assignment."

Keri shook her head to clear away the haziness of sleep, unsure that she'd heard correctly. "I'm not sure I understand."

A slight edge of irritation hardened the voice on the other end of the line. "I asked if you'd consider the task force assignment."

The pulse in Keri's temples throbbed and she felt almost light-headed. A woman she detested was offering her the position of her dreams, and she had never been more confused. "I'm not sure how to answer that, Lieutenant."

"If you have a few minutes before your shift today, I'd like to talk with you about it."

"I'll come in early." Keri's heart pounded with a combination of excitement and trepidation. She wasn't sure what Alex Troy had up her sleeve. Was it possible that she was trying to make up for past wrongs?

"My temporary office is beside Vice/Narcotics Division in the annex on First Street," Alex said. "Park in the gravel lot across the street and walk over. And please don't wear your uniform."

"Yes, ma'am. I'll see you shortly."

Keri jumped out of bed in her T-shirt and gym shorts the minute the phone hit the cradle. She dashed into the kitchen, grabbed a Diet Coke from the refrigerator, popped the top, and took a hefty swig. As she guzzled it, she looked at the brown plaid den furniture her parents had purchased on their thirtieth wedding anniversary. A series of mixed memories ensued: her parents sitting on the sofa holding hands watching television, her sick mother lying in the recliner dazed and confused. Herself, knocked to the floor in front of the coffee table. She emptied the soda can and discarded it, along with her sadness, just as her father walked into the kitchen.

Bobby Morgan moved around the table between them and approached the refrigerator from the opposite side. He always gave her a wide berth when they shared space, her unspoken rule. "Thought you were gonna take a nap before your shift."

"Got called in." Keri took her usual defensive sideways stance, glancing at her father periodically but never really making eye contact.

Bobby opened a Coke and leaned against the sink. His brown work boots were covered with dirt from the garden and his face was flushed from the heat. "You want something to eat? I could make you a sandwich right quick. I'm fixing one for your mom."

Keri could see he was trying, but sometimes the memories were just too strong. "No thanks, Dad. I've got to go."

"Will you be back for dinner? Kevin and Jean are coming over. I'm making your favorite, fried chicken and mashed potatoes." His attempt at a smile vanished and Keri felt guilty.

"I don't think so." She thought of her twin brother and his overbearing wife and was glad duty called. Kevin as a pussy-whipped husband wasn't a pretty sight. They both knew she had all the guts in the family.

❖

When in doubt, Keri reverted to the top three rules her mother taught her: Listen before you speak, Be honest, and Be yourself. Waiting outside Alex Troy's office, she tried to control her breathing. She paced the small, sparsely furnished reception area, fingering the police-badge key ring her mother gave her on her last birthday. It already showed signs of the constant rubbing Keri applied for luck. She needed more than luck today with the Ice Princess.

Keri wondered what kind of woman Alex Troy really was underneath the ever-present smile and cool confidence. The hints of emotion she kept seeing made her uneasy. It was harder to detest and mistrust Alex when she came across as a sensitive human being. "Morgan, come on in."

As their hands pressed together in greeting, Keri noted an unmistakable current pass between them. She withdrew and hoped Alex hadn't noticed.

Alex motioned to a plastic, straight-backed chair at a small conference table, then dragged another one up beside Keri. She sat, leaned casually back, and studied Keri in silence. Keri returned her gaze but knew instinctively that she shouldn't speak. The lieutenant had used this ploy during her interrogation three years ago. Keri wasn't about to fall for it. She surveyed the green metal desk, circa 1970, and a short bookcase with a jar of M&Ms on top. With the exception of a single picture on the old desk, the room was unadorned.

When Keri looked up again, Alex was studying her with what appeared to be a mixture of confidence and curiosity.

"I like that," Alex concluded.

"I beg your pardon." The quiet scrutiny and approving statement sent tingles of excitement through Keri's body, which she attributed to nerves and rising irritation. She was pleased that she'd passed Alex's unspoken test but annoyed to be subjected to it.

"Most young officers are so nervous and eager to impress that they can't bear the sound of a silent inspection. They start talking to fill the void. But you just waited until I was ready to begin. That tells me a lot about you."

"How's that?" Keri asked reluctantly. At this point she just wanted Alex to speak her piece and let her go.

"It says that you're confident, reflective, and don't open

your mouth until you actually have something to say. Is that a fair assessment?"

Keri controlled her surprised satisfaction. "Some would probably disagree, but I like to think so…most of the time."

Alex tapped her pencil eraser on the table and actually looked slightly uncomfortable. Her brown eyes locked with Keri's for an instant before returning to some notes in a file folder.

"Your work record speaks for itself, Morgan. You've done well in your tenure and your evaluations are good. Supervisors and peers speak highly of you, but this is a different kind of operation than you're used to."

There had to be a legitimate reason to exclude her from the task force, Alex rationalized. Her gut instincts said Keri was perfect for the job, but her defenses still argued against it. Keri's work performance was good. What about her motives?

"Morgan, why do you want to catch drug dealers?"

The look that clouded Keri's face told Alex she'd found the weak spot she was looking for.

Keri's lashes fluttered several times as her blue eyes rimmed with tears. "Have you ever lost someone you love, Lieutenant?"

The question was so direct and unexpected that Alex struggled to remain unaffected. She swallowed to dislodge the knot that choked speech. Keri's pain was palpable and absent any malicious intent, but still Alex couldn't answer. How could such a matter-of-fact question hurt so deeply?

Keri caught the imperceptible shift in Alex's facial expression. The corners of her laughing eyes drooped, her full lips quivered slightly, and she seemed to have trouble swallowing. The professional demeanor slipped momentarily into personal mode and quickly back to guarded control. Keri regretted being the cause of such conflict. She fought off a strange urge to console Alex.

"I'm sorry, Lieutenant. It's obvious that you have. I just don't think anybody should lose someone they love to something as senseless as drugs. We can fight it, and we owe it to ourselves and society."

Keri's pulse quickened as she considered what Alex could be thinking. She'd sounded like a public service announcement. When would she ever learn to keep her mouth shut?

"The fact is," Alex regained her voice, "I do know how it feels and

I agree completely." She immediately regretted the admission. Morgan was a subordinate, not a confidante. "I'm assuming you've lost someone as a result of a drug-related incident of some sort. Is that correct?"

"Yes. One of my best friends, Josh, died of an overdose at a party about a year ago. He didn't even do drugs. Somebody slipped something into his drink." Keri's hands were clenched into fists.

"Do you think this loss could interfere with your ability to remain focused and objective if you're chosen for this assignment?"

"Absolutely not. I want justice, not revenge."

"That's good. Revenge can be a powerful motivator but it can also lead to poor judgment." Alex paused. "Stacey Chambers worked for me as an intern. I've never met a young person as dedicated to her work or as unlikely to do drugs. So I understand how you feel. The truth is that we *may* be dealing with the killer of both our friends, but we can't make that assumption without proof. So my next question is very simple. Are you interested in working on this task force and getting the proof we need to put Sonny Davis where he belongs?"

The fact was, Keri Morgan had earned the task force position and so far she'd said nothing that offered a valid reason to sideline her. The only hope Alex had was that Keri would decline. Her insides fluttered with a mixture of excitement and old-fashioned fear. Her gaze slipped from the file in front of her to the white button-down shirt that clung to Keri's breasts. The fabric rose and fell unevenly, keeping time with her breathing. Alex feared her own erratic breaths would betray the desire spreading through her system.

Keri was silent. She had expected a little more preamble before having to answer the question directly. More information, that's what she needed. The decision was too important.

"I think you already know that I like drug work, but I'm a little vague on the specifics of this assignment. I need more information. Like who'll be supervising the team, and how we're supposed to get evidence on Davis. What are we going to do that hasn't already been done?"

Alex studied Keri's gorgeous face, impressed that she wasn't rushing into a decision, pro or con, at least she was willing to listen. "Fair enough. This will be a case based predominately on documentation, following the money trail, surveillance, and controlled buys with a reliable informant. There is always the potential for violence of some sort where Davis is concerned. He's very unpredictable and surrounds himself with a whole posse of unstable individuals."

"And the team leader?" Keri prompted.

"Sergeant Beth Price. She has previous narcotics experience and knows the legal and departmental protocols for this kind of operation. We can hit the ground running with her."

"How do you envision your own role in this investigation, Lieutenant?" Keri knew the question was a little cheeky, but she had a right to know. Lead officers ran their teams differently. Some were hands-on. Others kept more distance. She met Alex's eyes and saw a slight twitch at their corners followed by a foreboding darkening.

Alex's insides clenched as she surveyed the woman beside her. There it was, the issue that loomed between them like an elephant in a wading pool. Keri might as well have said she didn't want Alex anywhere near her own officers as they worked. The discomfort between them was obvious but Keri was proceeding with calm and confidence.

Rattled, Alex replied, "The chief wants all my attention focused on this case. In that capacity I will be reviewing every piece of intelligence gathered and every report submitted, and approving every operational plan proposed for execution. It's my job to compile a solid, leakproof case against Sonny Davis. Is that specific enough?"

Keri's heart sank. She already knew the answer to her next inquiry, but had to ask, "And what about the day-to-day operations?"

"My presence will be much more evident in this case than any other, since it is my only focus. And to be perfectly honest, operational involvement isn't out of the question. However, my intent is to let Sergeant Price handle that as much as possible."

"I see." Keri only hesitated for a few seconds. "I'm not sure I'm the right person for this job, Lieutenant."

The rebuff caught Alex off guard and she fought to keep the simultaneous flashes of relief and disappointment from registering on her face. She had seriously doubted that Keri might turn down the assignment. If she did, Alex would be in the clear with the chief. She should be thrilled.

Before she could stop herself Alex said, "You might want to give some serious thought to your future, Morgan. This case can make or break a career."

There it is, Keri thought, her motivation. *She's definitely bucking for another promotion.* And that had to spell trouble for anyone in her path. "I'll have to think about it—in light of everything we've discussed. Can you give me some time?"

"Time is short." Alex's voice was suddenly terse and unfriendly. She was obviously annoyed, probably not used to being turned down. "I'll need an answer by the end of business tomorrow, at the latest."

Keri's legs shook as she stood and followed her to the door. She didn't care what Alex thought; she wasn't about to jump into this hotbed of political land mines without careful consideration of all the facts. "Thank you for your time, Lieutenant, and for considering me. I know it couldn't have been easy for you."

Alex noticed the almost imperceptible tightening at the corners of Keri's mouth and the focused stare of her cobalt blue eyes. The anger was still there, carefully contained, but present nonetheless. Maybe it was best if Keri declined the offer. Without giving her time to respond, Keri turned and exited the office, leaving Alex speechless in the doorway.

As Keri walked away, she replayed the conversation and weighed her decision carefully.

Over the past few days, she'd glimpsed a softer, more personal side of the woman behind the badge, even hints of actual compassion. But she'd also seen the sharp edges of her ambition rise to the surface again, and Keri had a feeling if she got too close to that edge she'd be ripped apart, just as she was three years ago. Her first instinct was to take the assignment. But she wasn't the same impulsive person she'd been a few years ago, and she would never allow Alex Troy to compromise her again. If she joined the task force, she would make sure to watch her back.

❖

Keri ended her shift with a sense of anticlimax. She'd made her decision but when she tried to find Alex to tell her, the lieutenant had already left. Looking forward to releasing some tension, she strode into the women's locker room and was instantly assaulted by the odor of wet towels and perspiration. The beige concrete walls displayed a collection of dirty handprints and scuff marks from neoprene police shoes. As she sat on the narrow bench that ran the length of the tall metal lockers, her waning enthusiasm was mimicked by a flickering fluorescent tube that threatened to go out permanently.

She changed from jeans to a pair of white running shorts she kept in her locker for such occasions. She didn't have another T-shirt, so the white, rain-splotched one she had on under her vest would have to do. The sudden torrent of rain had soaked her through on her last call and her body shook. Raking her fingers through her curly wet hair, she opened the gym door and froze.

"Jesus, Alex, I'm dying here. Can you slow down a little?" Beth panted from the center of the room. She and Alex were on a worn, gray floor mat doing synchronized push-ups to a rapid count. Alex's well-muscled body glistened with perspiration and moved gracefully beside Beth's more compact version.

"You never could keep up with me."

"Maybe not in the gym, but I kept you sweating…" Hearing the gym door slam, the two collapsed on the mat, faces frozen, as if caught in an inappropriate moment.

Alex looked stunning in body-hugging bike shorts, tank top, and a headband just below the hairline. Keri never imagined just how exquisite the body was that hid beneath Alex's tailored clothes. Beth wore a black police-issue sweatsuit. Both women stared at Keri so hard she almost turned around and walked back out. She was suddenly self-conscious about her almost transparent white shorts and wet T-shirt, nipples cold and erect underneath.

Beth broke the uncomfortable silence. "Damn, what happened? You look a little shell-shocked."

"Nothing, really. Got caught in the rain coming in, that's all." Alex's eyes still appraising her body, Keri felt her face grow warm. She watched a deep shade of scarlet spread across Alex's cheeks. Their eyes locked and held until Alex finally diverted her gaze and reached for a towel thrown across the weight bench.

"I'm going to take off. We're almost done here anyway."

"No, please. Don't go," Keri said, surprised by the urgency of her tone. She stared down at her shoes, puzzled that she could feel such intense anger toward Alex one minute and strong attraction the next. "I didn't mean to interrupt your workout. Please finish. I just needed to have a run."

"Are you sure you should be running?" Beth moved to her side and placed a hand lightly on her shoulder. "You look a bit shaky."

"Thanks, Sergeant Price, but I'm really fine."

"Whatever you say." Beth shrugged her shoulders and returned to Alex. "Okay, Alex, name your pain." Under her breath, she whispered, "Has she decided about the assignment yet?"

Alex shook her head and waved Beth off. "I'll work my way through the machines and meet you at the bench press in about half an hour." She avoided looking at Keri again. For some reason the easy way she and Beth had just connected bothered her. She envied Beth's ease with physical intimacy and wished she could have reached out to Keri herself. She looked so disheveled and anxious. Alex wondered if the task force decision was the only cause. Every time she'd thought about Keri lately, her mind and libido had been at war, and for the first time, she could see signs of the same internal conflict in Keri. She hadn't imagined the sexual tension between them just moments ago, and she knew Keri was equally aware of it.

Alex cursed beneath her breath as she headed for the lat machine. As if the situation wasn't complicated enough, would she now be working with a subordinate she had the hots for?

The next thirty minutes dragged. Keri punched the treadmill speed up to six and easily kept pace. Every time she looked at Alex her mind reeled from the possibilities of what could happen between them if she accepted the task force assignment. Maybe Alex would give her a second chance. Or perhaps she'd just prejudge her again. Or maybe they'd become friends bonded by professional necessity. And it was even possible that they could become involved with each other. Keri's legs weakened at the visual her mind played and she momentarily lost her rhythm. Alex was certainly attractive and Keri's body responded to her readily. But Alex was her superior and nothing could ever change that. Their relationship was and always would be professional.

Keri adjusted the treadmill speed, stumbling to remain vertical. A strange tension mingled with the rising heat in the room. With only an occasional grunt or moan of exertion, the other two women worked silently through the exercise machines that lined the gray gym walls. Beth offered occasional thumbs-up of encouragement in Keri's direction and some not-too-subtle glances at her small bouncing breasts.

Alex hadn't looked at her since she started her run. An infrequent word of motivation or a brief consultation about weight or technique was the only conversation that passed between Alex and Beth, unlike the friendly banter she'd witnessed upon entering the gym. She felt as if she'd interrupted something private then.

Keri mashed the treadmill Stop button and stepped off, wet clothes clinging to her body. She pulled a towel from the storage rack and wiped her face and neck. Beads of perspiration trickled down between her breasts. She raised her shirt and captured the moisture in the ribbed cotton material. Eyes closed, enjoying the rough-textured fabric on her skin, she wiped the flat surface of her stomach to the top of her shorts just below the navel. With an exhausted sigh, she opened her eyes and noticed Alex look quickly away.

"Are you ready to spot me?" Alex asked Beth.

"I've got a few more leg presses first."

"I'd be glad to help out," Keri said.

"No, I wouldn't want to impose." Alex was unwilling to encourage a closer proximity of their bodies. "I can wait for Beth to finish."

"Oh, let her spot you, Alex. I'll be on this a few more minutes."

Reluctantly, Alex agreed. "If you're sure it's no bother."

Keri admired Alex's fluid movements as she positioned herself on the bench, long legs up, feet resting on the edge of the seat. Placing her gloved hands equal distance from the weights on either side, she wrapped her slender fingers around the bar, stared straight up at the ceiling, and began the exercise.

Veins bulged in her neck and hands as she pumped the weight up and down. Perspiration dotted her forehead and rolled away from the headband. Keri observed the rhythmic rise and fall of Alex's toned chest muscles, the dip of her stomach, and marveled at the beauty of a well-formed female body, clearly visible under the clingy outfit.

"Set," Alex said, placing the weights back on the rack. As she let go of the bar and withdrew her hands, a wet strand of hair fell across her face. Without a thought, Keri reached to push it aside.

Alex saw Keri's hand moving in slow motion toward her face. She wanted that touch more than she realized but simultaneously feared it. She turned her head to avert the connection and rose from the bench. "Please, don't."

Keri thought Alex's voice sounded deliberately polite but strangely cool. "Sorry. I didn't mean anything." The warning in Alex's eyes had been clear. "Write me up for an invasion of PBS." She tried to laugh off the encounter.

Beth was instantly at Alex's side. "How about violating my personal body space? I could use a good massage."

Alex grabbed her towel off the bench. "I'm going to head out. Thanks for the workout, Beth…and the spot, Morgan."

Keri stood motionless, watching Alex's retreating back. When the locker room door closed behind her, she turned to Beth. "What was that?"

"That's just Alex. She's a private person and that's how she likes to keep things."

"Fine with me." Keri flipped the thin gym towel over her shoulder. "Good night, Sergeant, and thanks for your concern." She headed for the locker room fully expecting Alex Troy to be long gone. But when she opened the door, Alex stood in front of her opened locker as if waiting.

Keri spoke without invitation. She had to strike before her courage waned. "Lieutenant, I'm sorry—"

"Morgan, I didn't mean—"

"No, please, let me." Keri stepped within touching distance of Alex and felt the heat radiating from her body. A misty sheen of perspiration glistened over muscles straining with tension. Keri's breath caught in her throat as she struggled to speak. "I'm sorry if I overstepped. It was just a reflex." *And what about this urge you have to touch her right now? Is that a reflex?* Keri wondered.

Alex's gaze hadn't left Keri's mouth since she entered the room. It was as if she watched the words form on her lips but never heard the sounds. Wiping a bead of sweat from her forehead, she responded, "Don't worry about it. I'm just not very good with being touched."

Keri watched the pulse along Alex's neck quicken and her body posture tighten as she spoke. "I don't know who did that to you, but I'm so sorry."

Alex's eyes grew wide with disbelief. "I didn't say anyone—"

"It's okay. I've been on the receiving end of an out-of-control loved one and I know the look." Keri moved carefully toward Alex and in slow motion raised her hand to Alex's face. "Touch is meant to be loving and healing. Don't accept any that isn't."

She cupped Alex's cheek in her palm and felt Alex lean into her. The simultaneous warmth of her face and the lean hardness of her body fired jolts of desire through Keri's system. Maybe she was oxygen deprived after the vigorous run. She'd never felt this excited, and there had to be a logical reason. Arousal spiraled from her core. Her muscles trembled with an unfamiliar need. Moisture flooded the suddenly aching folds of her sex. *What is happening to me?*

Alex lightly touched Keri's arms and slid her hands tentatively upward. She raked her fingers through the damp curls at Keri's temples and teasingly dragged her index finger across Keri's bottom lip. The pink tip of her tongue appeared between her lips and left a moistened trail. Keri felt herself moving closer to those inviting lips, unsure if the advance was hers or Alex's. Brown eyes, hazy and hooded with desire, bored into her soul. Hot breath caressed her face. She closed her eyes and lightly parted her lips in surrender.

Suddenly the room around Keri turned cold.

"I can't do this." Alex backed away from her as if she were poison. "I apologize. This is wrong on so many levels." She grabbed her gym bag, slammed her locker, and raced toward the exit without a backward glance.

"But what about the task force? I've made a decision." Keri couldn't believe what she'd said. It wasn't until she touched Alex that she realized why she'd made the decision that felt so uneasy earlier that day. The last thing she wanted to talk about was the damn job, but she thought that might stop Alex's hasty retreat. The slamming of the locker room door was her only answer.

Miserable and depressed, Keri changed clothes and thought about what just happened. Had she really almost kissed the woman who'd tried to destroy her credibility? She had strong feelings about Alex but they weren't sexual. Or were they? She and Alex had almost kissed, of that she was certain. But why did Alex stop? Was she really so concerned about professional propriety? Her eyes said she wanted that kiss. Her body definitely wanted that kiss. So what could possibly elicit such an obvious withdrawal from simple human touch?

❖

Alex clutched the rough steering wheel cover of her old Mercedes, marveling at the contrast to Keri's soft skin only minutes before. Her body reacted immediately to the tactile sensation, as it had then, with a strong bolt of sexual energy. Her nerve endings vibrated with a need bordering on addiction. How had her feelings gotten so out of control so quickly?

It all started with that damn skimpy outfit. The water-spotted T-shirt had the same effect on Alex that it would've on the hormonally challenged male of the species at a wrestling match. She'd never wanted to simultaneously strip and completely swaddle someone's body before. She'd managed to avoid Keri's first attempt at contact, but her gut registered a desire for that touch much deeper than Alex could've imagined.

It had been a long time since anyone aroused her interest, emotionally or sexually, so it was only natural that she responded to the deadly combination of beauty and honesty. The latter was something Alex had always craved in her relationships and seemed unable to find. Keri Morgan seemed to spout the truth like an innocent child, unaware of its impact or implications and unsure why others should care.

Her compassion and empathy in the locker room affected Alex deeply. And the courage it must've taken for Keri to physically reach out to her again tugged at something well buried. How had they gotten so close, close enough for her to effortlessly stroke Keri's arms and caress her full, hot lips? Sensory memory sent a shard of uncontrolled passion down Alex's body and she mashed her foot against the accelerator to stop it.

As the car shot forward, Alex thought, she too was charging toward a collision with this train of thought. Had she actually confessed her fear of being touched to a subordinate while in a lust-induced haze? Then she'd leaned against Keri and almost kissed her. *Almost kissed her, for God's sake.* Miraculously, Keri hadn't pulled away. Her eyes closed and those gorgeous lips opened in an invitation Alex wanted desperately to accept. Keri had wanted that kiss as much as she did. Longing coursed through her anew as she relived the softness of Keri's skin under her fingers and the heat of her breath.

When she was near Keri Morgan, the well-defined and never-violated boundaries between work and personal life blurred unrecognizably. But it was her job to maintain those boundaries at all costs. Anything else was out of the question. An attraction to someone as vibrant, open, and candid as Keri was easy to imagine. But they were like antipodal points of a sphere, exact opposites. And just like the softly curving sides of a sphere, people had the capability of changing and melding into one another.

Stop it, Alex cautioned herself. Sexual chemistry was understandable and could be enjoyed at a safe distance through fantasy, but that's where it had to end. Keri Morgan was the job and the job was Keri Morgan. *Repeat it until you believe it.*

Alex tried to remember what Keri had said to her as she exited the gym. Something about a decision regarding the task force, but the demanding pulses between her legs had made rational thought impossible. She only knew she had to get away from Keri quickly. What if she'd agreed to work with the team? As Alex pushed the garage door opener and pulled inside, she wondered if she'd be able to keep her double-crossing emotions in check and remain focused on the assignment. Stacey Chambers deserved her best, and a fleeting lapse into previously contained passion wasn't going to interfere with her determination to find justice for the young woman. Her professional integrity demanded nothing less.

But what about her integrity where Keri Morgan was concerned? She'd already violated her number one rule: Don't even *think* about getting involved with a subordinate. That coupled with their unresolved history spelled disaster. Not to mention the other deception Alex was perpetrating. She had led Keri to believe she had to compete for the task force assignment just like everyone else. If Keri found out that the chief had all but ordered her inclusion, she would probably consider the interview another betrayal by Alex. Maybe she should tell her. After all, Alex had put her through the process because she genuinely intended to see how she stood up on her own merits. But would Keri understand that or see another reason to distrust her?

Distrust seemed to be a theme with Keri, an unsettled past, secrets about the assignment, and Alex's own annoying attraction to the woman. Needless to say, there was more than one conflict of interest. But Alex had risen in her career predominately by handling conflicts. She thought about the last task force she'd worked on and the myriad of problems with Helen. Her ambition had made Alex's look like a childhood dream. She'd commanded the organized crime team and

Alex with unquestionable authority. To Helen, bending the rules a little was acceptable to achieve the desired results, and those results had everything to do with making her look good and receive the glory.

Alex didn't plan to let Helen jeopardize this investigation with her questionable tactics or her overt attempts to bed her. Thoughts of her time with Helen still stirred an array of emotions Alex could not control; fortunately, the bad times outweighed the good and made it easier to stay focused on the main priority—this assignment. And Keri was a big part of this task force, assuming she'd decided to accept the opportunity. How would she figure into the mix: in a new position, working for someone she despised, chasing a drug dealer who could very possibly be a killer, watching acrimonious lovers at each other's throats, and dodging a supervisor with a crush on her?

Alex sighed. Why did combining attractive women and police work always involve drama?

Chapter Six

Any chance of restful sleep vanished into visions of Alex's full, moist lips coming closer to hers again and again through the night. The fluttering in her stomach woke Keri long before the alarm sounded. She listened to her father make coffee in the kitchen as he did most days since her mother's health began to decline. Coffee had been her job, but now he prepared it the very same way, even though he never drank it.

Her body craved caffeine and the complete muscular meltdown she knew would follow her morning run with Pat. She dressed quickly and started down the hall, pausing to tiptoe into her mother's bedroom.

Marie Morgan opened her eyes when Keri dropped a light kiss on her forehead, and gazed at her with the blank look that was becoming more and more frequent. She attempted a weak smile before she drifted back into the dark void that was consuming her life.

"Coffee?" Bobby Morgan motioned toward the steaming pot when Keri shuffled into the large country kitchen. His coveralls showed wear on the outsides of the pockets where he rubbed his weathered hands as he looked over the garden from their kitchen window every morning.

"Thanks. Been up long, Dad?" Keri grabbed her usual coffee mug with the Granville PD logo from the dish tray and poured it full of the steaming brew.

"A while." He didn't look at her much when she spoke, and she understood why. Her resemblance to her mother was uncanny, and some days she sensed he just couldn't bear it. It must be one of those days. He swept back his thinning gray hair, not bothering to comb it anymore.

"I've been checking on the garden. The peas and new potatoes are coming in."

Keri's chest tightened. Her mother loved sweet peas and new potatoes. They picked the first batch together every year and ate them for supper the same night. Her father would be thinking about that, too.

She gave a phony cough and changed the subject. "I had my interview for that drug task force assignment yesterday." She glanced sideways at Bobby Morgan, always afraid he'd slip back into his angry default response.

"Are you going to do it?"

Keri thought about her decision anew. It would be her first major assignment, and all the other officers on the team wanted to make a name for themselves with this case. There was Alex to contend with every day. She was like a splinter in the back of Keri's mind, always just beneath the surface, waiting to be teased out and finally exposed.

"Yes, I want this chance," she said.

He turned away from the window to face her. "You're sure?" His voice cracked. "I just don't want you to get hurt."

"Yeah, I have to do it." Keri knew she couldn't explain to her father that he, as much as her mother and Josh, was part of her decision.

"You gotta do what you think is best. I understand that." He shoved his hands inside his faded bib pockets. "Keri, I want to talk to you about something."

Keri's muscles tensed and her hands fisted automatically. "We don't have to talk about it."

"We do…someday, maybe not today, but soon."

"It'll keep. We've got vegetables to pick."

Keri took another sip of the rich, dark coffee, washed her cup, and placed it back on the drain board. "I've got to go. Pat's waiting for me. I've got just enough time to get Mom dressed. I'll help with the garden when I come home."

Bobby Morgan reached out to pat her on the shoulder, and then pulled back. He took a deep breath as if his next thought was painful, changed his mind, and settled on, "Just be careful."

❖

Alex glared at the phone coiled like a predator on the edge of her ancient desk. So far the calls to DEA and the Caldwell Police Department had gone smoothly. Their officers would be reporting for duty in the morning. The last call, the one she'd avoided all afternoon, was to the Layton Police Department. Alex leaned an elbow on her desk and propped her forehead in her hand. Her droopy eyelids grated. She felt like she hadn't slept in days. Her mind refused to let go of last night's near kiss in the gym. Every time she thought about Keri, feelings flooded through her in waves. Emotions she'd tucked carefully away poked at her and demanded attention, and her body throbbed with a wanting she hadn't experienced in years. The need for an intimate human connection gnawed at her insides.

Frustrated with her lack of focus, she picked up the phone. She had an appointment to get to later this afternoon and she needed to get this conversation out of the way. It would help if she could concentrate enough to form coherent sentences. Alex steeled herself as she dialed.

"Captain Callahan, Tactical Division, can I help you?"

The voice cut through Alex with precision. It plunged into her heart and stuck there, slicing deeper with each ragged breath. "This is Lieutenant Troy with the Granville Police Department."

After the slightest pause from the other end, Helen Callahan's voice changed to liquid sex. "Well, aren't we formal today, darling? To what do I owe this definite pleasure?"

"You know why I'm calling, Helen. It's about the Sonny Davis task force. I understand officers Siler and Fields are under your command. I need to arrange—"

"Slow down. Don't I even get a hello and how're you doing? It's been almost a year."

"This is business. Let's keep it that way. Can your officers report for assignment in the morning at ten hundred?" Alex knew Helen's tactics and waited for the inevitable barrage of personal comments and sexual innuendo.

"I think we should get together and talk about it first. I left a message at your home, but you didn't return my call. Can we meet for drinks after work? Please, honey, I've missed you."

Helen's sultry voice was the definition of phone sex. In spite of her best attempts at control, Alex felt herself responding. She closed her eyes and was back in the elevator in Helen's apartment building five years ago, Helen's hands cupping her breasts, teasing her nipples into pinpoints of erection and that exquisite mouth and tongue working feverishly between her legs, licking and sucking the life out of her one pleasurable morsel at a time.

"Alex...are you still there?"

Alex's nails dug into the flesh of her palms. Summoning darker memories of her drunken ex, she regained her composure. "No, Helen, I won't meet you for drinks. Just have your people at the meeting on time."

Before Helen had a chance to snare her in further with her verbal foreplay, Alex dropped the receiver noisily in its cradle and scooted her chair back. Plopping her feet on the corner of the desk, she took a deep, relieved breath. Afternoon sun spilled into her office through the antiquated metal crank windows around the room. Its warmth induced another wave of sleepiness and Alex let her thoughts retreat from the bitterness of Helen to take sanctuary in Keri.

An authoritative knock on the door disrupted her musings and she dropped her feet to the floor, calling, "Come in."

The face she couldn't dislodge from her mind appeared around the corner of the door. "Your secretary wasn't in. Am I disturbing you?"

Disturbing was certainly an interesting way to describe the jolt of excitement that ran through Alex at the sight of Keri Morgan. Her pulse escalated and heat rose to the surface of her skin. She remembered the caress of Keri's breath on her face as they'd almost kissed and involuntarily licked her lips.

"No." Alex motioned for Keri to take one of the chairs in front of the desk. She was thankful for the physical barrier between them. "What can I do for you, Officer Morgan?"

Keri hesitated. It had been too long since those amazingly deep brown eyes gazed into hers. The last time, Keri knew what she'd seen in them and knew Alex had seen the same yearning in her. Now she was mesmerized by the slight upward curve at the corners of Alex's mouth. She couldn't explain the simultaneous feelings of disbelief and exhilaration for the woman she'd once considered her archenemy. She didn't understand when she'd begun to see Alex Troy differently, when her feelings started to change. And more importantly, she wasn't sure what, if anything, it meant.

"I tried to tell you last night." She flushed with the memory of Alex's lips so close to hers. "I've made a decision about the task force assignment."

Alex held her breath as her pulse pounded deafeningly in her ears. She started to send up a silent prayer for the answer she wanted but realized she was no longer sure what that was.

"I'd like to be on the task force, if it's not too late." Even as she said the words, Keri questioned her own motives. She wanted the chance to prove herself in Narcotics, but now, perhaps just as much, she wanted to figure out this enigma that was Lieutenant Alex Troy. Walking away was no longer an option, professionally or personally.

Alex released a long breath, unsure if she felt defeat at having to accept Keri on the team or relief that she would now have a legitimate excuse to spend more time with her. The quiver of arousal in her core hinted at an answer she wasn't ready to acknowledge. "The last time we spoke, you had serious reservations." Amazed that her voice sounded even, she asked, "Have you resolved your concerns?"

"I'm not sure anything has been resolved." Keri sat back in the chair and crossed her jeans-clad legs, muscles bulging along their length in a seductive dance of invitation. "All I know is that I very much want a chance to work on the team."

"And what about our history—the investigation—can you let that go? This case is too important to let personal feelings get in the way." Alex felt hypocritical as the annoying ache between her legs persisted just being in close proximity to the young woman.

Keri wanted to be honest and reassure Alex, but words failed under the searching look Alex was giving her across the desk. Something in her expression tugged at Keri's heart and in that moment, she ached to give Alex whatever she seemed to be asking for, if only she could be sure what it was. Alex cleared her throat, obviously awaiting an answer. Of course, Lieutenant Troy was all about business. Anything else Keri wanted to read into her stare was all about her own tangled-up fantasies and sexually deprived libido.

Alex continued, "I want us to have a very clear understanding about this. If you're willing to put the past behind us, I'm willing to move forward, to start fresh."

"All I really want is to be treated fairly," Keri said. "If you can promise that, I promise I'll put everything else behind me." Keri wondered if she would ever be able to leave the memory of Alex's touch behind. The thought of it heated her flesh still.

Alex studied Keri's expression and body language for signs of deception. Seeing none, she said, "Good, it sounds like we agree."

"Great. When do we start?" Keri's eyes sparkled with enthusiasm.

In spite of her best efforts to stay focused on work, Alex wished she was the reason for that glimmer of excitement. But now that the deal was done, she had no choice but to put thoughts like those out of her head and do what she did best—run a professional, focused investigation.

"The first meeting is here in the morning at ten hundred hours. At that time we'll make the assignments and develop a game plan." The usual ease with which Alex shifted into supervisory mode was disrupted by a nagging thought. She was now the one who would decide how deeply involved Keri became in the case, who would place her in harm's way. Only she would be ultimately responsible if anything happened to her. A shiver ran up Alex's spine as the realization fully registered. "To protect and serve" suddenly took on a whole new meaning—a personal one with the highest stakes of her career.

"Keri, this case could prove dangerous. We've already tied the deaths of several coeds to the same batch of street drugs, and there's the possibility that Stacey Chambers's death may also be connected. If we can prove the bad ecstasy is coming from Sonny Davis, we'll have a good chance of indicting him on more than just drug charges. But in order to do that, we need much more evidence."

"It sounds like you're trying to talk me out of this before we even get started." Keri cocked her head to one side and gave Alex a mischievous grin. "I'm not afraid of hard work, and you've already seen that I don't scare easily. Not administratively and not on the street."

Keri's point was clear. She hadn't backed down in the past, or during the hostage call. Alex could respect that determination; in fact, she intended to use it. Keri could turn out to be quite an asset in an investigation like this. Already Alex's mind raced at the possibilities. She'd ruled out infiltration so far, but having a beautiful young woman on the team could change that equation.

"I just want to make sure you know what you're getting into," Alex said.

"I do, Lieutenant, and I'm in all the way. I've developed some pretty good informants. We might be able to use one of them."

"We'll have to evaluate that possibility as we go along. But I'll keep it in mind."

"Okay then, guess I'll see you in the morning."

Keri rose and extended her hand. Alex smiled at the irony. This was the first time Keri Morgan had offered to shake her hand first. She clasped the younger woman's hand in hers. The sensation of their flesh pressed together dispatched surging pulses of heat into her body. Time seemed to crawl as each nerve registered Keri's presence. Then like lightning the moment was gone and their hands slid reluctantly apart.

As Keri turned to leave, Alex watched the rise and fall of her perfectly shaped ass, already wishing for tomorrow.

❖

Hours later Alex still couldn't evict Keri from her thoughts or her body. The restless stirring of her senses made her shift uncomfortably in the leather chair opposite Norman Smith, her family's lawyer. She glanced around at the diplomas and certificates that cluttered the paneled walls, then tried again to focus on the gray-haired man seated across from her. Norman Smith had been a fixture in her family as long as she could remember. The least she owed him was her complete attention.

"I know this is difficult, but unfortunately, the world doesn't slow down when terrible things happen," he said. "It's been almost a year and some matters need your attention. As the only child, you're sole beneficiary to your parents' estate."

"Yes, that's fine." Alex interrupted. She'd already had enough to deal with today. Having her parents' lives reduced to a stack of legal mumbo-jumbo gave her cold chills.

She supposed emotional trauma over finalizing her parents' affairs was inevitable, and Norman was right: she'd delayed the process long enough. But every box of papers she opened contained more memories and pain she was not ready to face. Her parents' tidy preparations for the future made Alex all too aware of her failure to enjoy the present. Grief began to choke her and tears stung her eyes.

"What about the company?" Norman asked. "Have you given any thought to what you want? There's the parent company here in the

States and several foreign subsidiaries. I can help with a sale if you wish. I've already had inquiries."

"I can't decide that right now." Alex took a deep breath. "Whoever's been running it for the last year seems to be doing fine. Let them do it a while longer."

For most of her childhood Alex had believed her parents ran a simple computer store. They'd tried to convince her to come into the business with financial incentives and properties before she joined the police department, but Alex wanted to make her own way. Their privately owned corporation, the Trojan Horse, handled all facets of high-tech surveillance, from basic night-vision equipment to advanced satellite components. The clientele spanned the globe. Then as now, Alex had been unable to imagine herself doing anything but the job she loved. But selling the business her parents spent their lives building didn't seem like an option at this point, either. It was too soon and too final.

"Don't wait too long," Norman said. "Your parents were dear friends of mine and I just want to make sure their daughter is taken care of." He paused as if waiting for his comments to register. "I assume you're keeping the house. The title and insurance have been transferred into your name. What about the cars? Do you want to keep them?"

A lump formed in Alex's throat. She'd never considered returning to her parents' home, but now it belonged to her. Her infrequent visits the past year had barely been enough to keep cobwebs from forming in the corners. It felt like her parents' lives were being disassembled piece by piece and she was being asked to dispose of them. Her knowledge of the business was insufficient to make such important decisions at this point. But her childhood home and all its memories would also have to wait. "I'm not ready for all this."

Norman shuffled through the stack of papers in front of him, pulled one out, and continued, "There are also the other properties to consider, in addition to the business. The two vacation homes, various real estate investments locally, and a sizeable stock portfolio."

"But hasn't everything been going along fine for the past year? The company seems to be doing well from the quarterly statements I receive. The vacation homes are being properly maintained as they were before, and the other real estate properties are currently occupied by long-standing tenants. So what is the urgency today, Norm?"

"The stock investments are due for rollover soon, and with all the recent market fluctuations it's time for a portfolio review. You could leave it in place or reinvest it in something else. Whatever you decide, we're on a two-day deadline and I'll need your signature to make it happen."

"Fine, just let it ride, if there's no penalty involved. I don't need any huge influxes of cash anytime soon." She signed the proffered form and pushed her chair back from the desk.

"There is one final thing," Norman added. "The board of directors meeting is next month. I think you need to be there. The CEO and board have been doing a great job running the show, but they need to know the company is still important to the principal shareholder, and that's you."

"I'll give it some thought. Everything else can wait." Alex rose stiffly from the chair, shook hands with the lawyer, and took the probate documents from him. "I'll read all this and make some decisions. Just give me a few days, okay? And thank you for everything you've done for my family, Norm."

Norman walked her out to the elevators. He seemed a little more relaxed than when she arrived. Some of the tightness around his mouth had disappeared, but Alex knew the heavy creases in his forehead were only one sign of the gravity he attached to his responsibilities to her family. Alex thanked him again for being patient and for the care he'd taken with her parents' affairs. As she rode down, she realized she had finally moved from disbelief to a form of acceptance. Her parents were gone. The finality she'd refused to accept until now washed through her.

She sat in her old Mercedes coupe outside the lawyer's office for a while. Her throat felt raw as a sickening feeling clawed its way up. Her eyes watered and stung, blurring her vision. She pounded her fists on the steering wheel as tears streamed down her face. It was the first time since the funeral she'd allowed herself to cry, and the timing couldn't have been worse.

There were too many responsibilities, too many things demanding her time and energy. Entirely too many to waste time crying. But the feelings continued to bubble up and spill over. She'd stuffed them down, avoided them, ignored and denied them for too long.

"But why now?" Alex asked aloud, wiping her eyes on her shirt sleeve. "I don't have time for a nervous breakdown." Something her father said years ago came to mind: "You have to grieve your loss to embrace the future." The tears began anew and she let them fall.

She thought about her mother's perfectionist expectations and her father's tenderness, constant encouragement, and acceptance of all things Alex. They'd only asked one thing of her, and that was to be happy. And it was the one thing Alex couldn't give them.

It should be easy. Find your passion and the person who makes it all worthwhile and live. Right? Law enforcement was definitely her niche, but the personal component proved more elusive. The thought of disappointing her parents brought another round of soul-tearing sobs.

"I miss you so much." She slammed her palms against the roof of the car. "I don't know what to do about all this."

She didn't know if it was the business, loneliness, feeling like an orphan, or the feelings suddenly surfacing around Keri that upset her most. Alex buried her face in her hands and rubbed the tears from her eyes. She shook her head and hammered the lid shut on her emotions once again. *Life needs my attention. I can't fall apart.*

She drove home mechanically and pulled into her driveway, scanning the street out of habit. With her keys already in hand, she walked to the house, unlocked the door, and went inside. Her living room was more welcoming now that she had decorated with some memorabilia of her parents' lives. A picture of her parents occupied the focal point on the entryway table. Every day now she looked at them, celebrated their lives, and vowed to live hers more fully. She felt comfortable among their things and appreciative for the physical connection to her parents.

She knew Norman was right. It was time for her to take the responsibilities her parents had entrusted to her and make the decisions they would have expected. But the investigation was heating up and she needed to stay focused for a few more days. After that, she'd deal with the estate and everything else that seemed so splintered in her life at the moment.

Alex dropped into her father's old leather recliner and picked up the rotary phone. She dialed the number and waited for the familiar, soothing voice.

"Hello?"

"Wayne, it's Alex."

"Alex, it's good to hear your voice. We haven't talked, other than at work, for months."

Alex mentally kicked herself. "I know. I've been a terrible friend."

"I didn't mean it like that. I just meant I've missed you. I know you have a lot going on right now. And I also know when you're hurting, you work that much harder."

"You know me too well." Secretly, she was glad. Wayne Thomas reminded her of her father in so many ways. They were both strong and supportive but gentle and intuitive, especially when it came to her. Wayne supervised her in Narcotics and mentored her toward a more politically advantageous position in the department. His advice in matters of the ol' boys' club politics had proven invaluable. But it was his support when her parents died that changed their working relationship to friendship.

"So, how's the assignment coming along?"

They spent the next thirty minutes discussing progress and possible directions the investigation might take. He offered encouragement and advice. She listened to the kindness and acceptance in his voice as he reviewed tactics that, thanks to him, were already second nature to her.

Talking to her friend and mentor helped. She felt more reassured and comfortable about the case. "Thanks for listening and letting me bounce some things off you."

"No problem. You'll get this guy. I have faith in you."

"You're good for my ego. Don't stop." Alex hesitated.

Wayne's voice softened. "You're really missing them tonight, aren't you?"

Alex exhaled a long breath. "Yeah, I am. Sometimes I just feel like I failed them." She wanted her parents to be proud.

"You know your parents just wanted you to be happy. Remember, your father used to say that real living wasn't based on the size of a bank account or a successful career. It was based on love and commitment."

"I remember." Alex thought of Keri and her pulse quickened.

"So, Alex Troy, whoever's got you thinking about your parents, disappointment, life, and the future, go after her. Don't let her get away."

Alex was stunned by Wayne's insight. "But I didn't say—"

"You never do. Life's too short, Alex." A slight hitch sounded at the end of Wayne's statement. "Now, I've got to go. There's a gorgeous woman in my bed and it sounds like you've got a big day tomorrow."

Alex had no idea she could be so transparent, but she knew he only had her best interest at heart. She hung up the phone with Wayne's encouraging comments like a warm blanket around her. Perhaps life was too short to rationalize her feelings away or pretend they didn't exist. The more she thought about Keri, the more the younger officer entrenched herself in Alex's mind and soul. But it seemed everything in her life was suddenly happening at warp speed. Everything demanded her attention and everything was critical. How was she going to juggle it all at once to honor her parents' lives, vindicate a friend's death, catch a killer, and fall in love?

Something would have to wait, and with sadness and regret she hadn't imagined possible, Alex knew what it would be. As she prepared for the first task force meeting the next day, Alex relegated her interest in Keri Morgan to the pending file. She only hoped her feelings could be so easily contained.

CHAPTER SEVEN

When Keri entered the cramped conference room, Alex felt the temperature rise by degrees. She was dressed in tight jeans with a baggy denim shirt and a pink camisole peeking out at the neckline. Her mahogany brown hair waterfalled across her shoulders, hanging in naturally curly ringlets around her face. An infectious smile radiated enthusiasm and way too much happiness.

She waved a paper bag in the air and the smell of warm bread permeated the room. "I brought bagels for everybody. I hope there's coffee." When Alex didn't respond, she teased, "Come on, Lieutenant. I know you want it," and shook the bag in her direction, apparently determined to get some kind of response.

Alex allowed herself only a momentary glance at her. That disarming smile and those piercing blue eyes could prove hazardous, or at the very least, distracting. And distraction was something Alex couldn't afford. "Thanks for the bagels, Morgan. Help yourself to some coffee and grab a seat. The others should be here shortly."

The room was lined with worn, black fabric chairs pushed against the walls and gathered around the scarred table. It smelled of stale cigarettes and cold coffee. On one side of the space, a scratched green chalkboard hung and on the other, a corkboard overflowing with wanted posters. In a corner just inside the door, a child's desk functioned as a serving table for the industrial-sized coffeepot, sugar, and fake cream packets. As officers arrived, they gathered around the makeshift coffee bar to collect their morning shot of stimulation.

Alex snuck M&Ms from her pocket one at a time. She carefully cracked the hard outer shell between her tongue and the roof of her mouth, felt the creamy chocolate melt, and waited for the inevitable sugar high. She watched Keri joke with the other officers as though she knew them personally. Everybody took to her immediately. But Alex's impatience grew as she shuffled papers and tried to look busy. By ten o'clock everyone but the Layton officers had arrived. *Damn you, Helen Callahan.*

Refusing to be manipulated into a late start, Alex sat down at the table next to Beth, her back to the door. She faced the chalkboard. "Okay, everybody take your seats."

Once the team was settled and the shuffling had ceased, a few heads turned and Alex heard footsteps at the end of the hall. When the door opened, Beth's body morphed into attack mode. She pushed back from the table and slowly rose to her feet, eyes narrow and focused. As Alex stood, the woman behind her spoke.

"Good morning all, sorry we're late. We were detained by an accident on the interstate. I'm Captain Helen Callahan from Layton PD and these are my officers, Renee Siler and Mike Fields."

Muscles knotted throughout Alex's body. She set her expression and prepared to face the woman she'd avoided for over a year. Never again would she permit Helen Callahan to make the rules. From now on their dealings would be on her terms alone.

Keri's nerves prickled. Except for the incident in the gym the other night, she had never seen Alex's eyes so dark. Her face was void of emotion, cold and determined as she turned to greet the late arrivals.

Captain Callahan stood well inside Alex's personal body space and seemed oblivious to the others in the room. She was dangerously beautiful in a black business suit, gray satin shell, and blond hair that flowed past her shoulders. Her blue-gray gaze swept over Alex like a caress and lingered on her lips. She offered her hand. From the look on Alex's face, Keri thought she'd rather shake the business end of a rattlesnake.

Alex took in Helen's beauty with a cynical smile. Gorgeous but deadly. *She should really travel with a caution sign and flares.* She clutched Helen's hand in a two-fisted grip, and using her superior strength, forcefully backed Helen out of her body space and toward the row of chairs against the wall.

Helen's eyes never left her face, but Alex saw a flicker of surprise.

"It's a pleasure to see you again, Lieutenant. It's been entirely too long."

Keri disliked Captain Callahan immediately. The possessive way she looked at Alex and assumed a position close to her made Keri uncomfortable. *Maybe Alex and this woman...* Keri couldn't finish the thought. Something hot and foreign rose in her throat. Helen Callahan was gorgeous, elegant, refined, and certainly sexy. All the things Keri knew she'd never be. But there was something off with her.

Beth cleared her throat. Eyes burning with contempt, she said, "We didn't realize you'd be joining us this morning, Captain." Her tone was cold and unwelcoming. "Let me find you a seat."

"That won't be necessary, Sergeant."

Keri thought Callahan's emphasis on "sergeant" relayed a definite dislike for Beth. It was obviously mutual, and if Sergeant Price didn't like her, that was good enough for Keri.

Helen grabbed an empty chair and indicated that Keri should make room for her. "You don't mind, do you, sweetie?" Without waiting for an answer, she rolled the chair close to Alex and sat down.

Keri took several deep breaths to slow her pulse. She wasn't sure what was causing more anxiety, waiting for her assignment or watching Callahan's doe eyes fawn all over Alex as she introduced the team members. She knew the look of lust, and Callahan wore it like a badge of honor. Keri was thankful that Alex seemed completely unimpressed. The thought made her cross and uncross her legs beneath the table. She would have been jealous, she realized, if Alex had returned the alluring captain's interest.

Alex refused to be shaken by Helen's proximity. As she looked around the room at the officers gathered to do battle under her command, confidence flooded her and she pushed away from the table enough to avoid Helen's body grazing hers "accidentally."

"Our target is probably the biggest and most dangerous drug dealer in the tristate area," she said. "And it's entirely possible that his dope is responsible for the deaths of some of our college students recently. This isn't simply a drug case anymore. There's a homicide investigation as well, and the chief has agreed to let us handle all of it. That's a huge honor and an enormous responsibility for each of us. Detective Spagnola of the homicide squad will bring us up to speed on their investigation after our briefing."

The image of Stacey Chambers's contorted features and lifeless body flashed through Alex's mind. Her stomach churned and she fisted her hands into tight balls in her lap to regain focus. "This is criminal investigation one-oh-one. I want it played by the numbers. Background checks, criminal histories, DMV runs, water and sewer listings, wanted persons checks, IRS histories, the works." Alex looked directly at Helen when she added, "There'll be no shortcuts on this one, folks. I want surveillance, night and day. I want to know where this guy goes, who he sees, for how long and why. I want to know how many wives, girlfriends, boyfriends, children, and relatives he has. I want to know where he eats and how often he takes a crap." A laugh from the officers broke the gathering intensity in the room.

"In other words, I want us so far up this guy's ass that when he burps, we know what he ate for lunch." Alex concluded, "Sergeant Beth Price will be your immediate supervisor. She's going to make the assignments based on our evaluation of your abilities and the operation profile. Sergeant Price, if you would."

Beth moved to the chalkboard. "Here's what it looks like. Agent Paige Hunter with DEA has generously agreed to provide the technical equipment and expertise we need for all surveillance. Detectives Mike Fields and Renee Siler from Layton PD will provide long and roving surveillance when needed."

Helen scooted her chair over, placed her hand on Alex's forearm, and leaned in. The swell of her breasts against Alex's upper arm and the hot breath on her ear sent electricity shooting down her spine. She rolled her chair away, breaking contact. "If you have a concern, Captain, share it with everyone. We're a team."

Helen gave her another sweltering gaze before standing. With a long, seductive stroke, she smoothed an invisible crease in the front of her thigh-revealing skirt. "I assumed Mike and Renee would be lead detectives since they have the most undercover experience."

"That's not possible, Captain. I'm sorry to disappoint you." Beth almost sneered.

"I think you should take advantage of their longevity. They know drugs better than anyone here and can work under pressure," Helen fired back.

Alex felt her ire rise at Helen's veiled insults. "Captain Callahan, what Sergeant Price says is correct." She stood, towering over Helen. "We thought about your officers for the lead position, but our target is a racist white male. He doesn't mind selling to African Americans, but he won't let them into his inner circle. We needed someone who can get close to him fast."

Helen locked stares with Alex and her look changed from defiance to acquiescence. "Very well. As you wish, Alex. So who takes the lead?"

"If you'll allow Sergeant Price to continue, she'll finish the assignments." Alex motioned for Beth to resume. Helen Callahan would not come onto her turf and insult her officers, past lover or not.

Keri suppressed a childish urge to stick out her tongue at Helen, give her a "so there," and slap a high five with Alex. She'd watched the exchange between Helen and Alex with increasing annoyance. Everything about Helen Callahan screamed sex. Alex was obviously trying to remain focused, but Helen had a different agenda.

"Our primary team is officers Steve Alston and Keri Morgan," Beth continued. "We'll try to insinuate Morgan into an undercover role with an informant."

Keri felt a shock charge her body. She hadn't expected to be a lead officer on the case, just being assigned was enough. But everything had just changed. The stakes were much higher now.

Helen shook her head, a disapproving frown crinkling the space between her perfectly plucked brows. In a steely calm voice, she said, "You've got to be kidding. Look at her." And everyone did. "She's obviously as shocked by this assignment as I am."

Keri's initial surprise and excitement turned quickly to anger as Helen unapologetically expressed her dissatisfaction in front of everyone.

Helen continued with the verbal assault. "Have you ever worked undercover? Have you even made a single drug arrest, ever?"

Before Keri could assemble a reply, Alex said matter-of-factly, "Officer Morgan has extensive drug experience and *will* serve as one of our lead investigators."

Keri could see the anger on Alex's face, but this was her fight. "Lieutenant, if I may?" She knew how to deal with bullies. Helen was playing her game now.

Secretly pleased, Alex nodded her approval.

Helen caught the exchange and her eyebrows arched.

Keri drew a deep breath and began. "Captain...Callahan, is it? You're right on two counts. I am a little shocked. And I've never worked undercover."

The corners of Helen's mouth curled into a self-satisfied grin.

Keri kept her breathing steady and continued. "But you're wrong about my drug experience. I've made over two hundred drug arrests in the past two years and I've got an informant who can probably get us into Davis's inner circle."

Gasps sounded as the other officers calculated the amount of time and focused attention that accomplishment required. Even Alex looked surprised and gave Beth a questioning glance.

"Now, if you still don't think I'm capable of running point on this operation, I'll defer to the better officer, whoever that may be." Keri's knees shook under the table but she forced herself to remain steady and confident.

Helen seemed taken aback. "I still think your lack of undercover experience will be a detriment, sweetie." Helen's condescending tone and lingering appraisal only slightly diminished Keri's feeling of victory as she leaned back in her chair.

"It looks like we've already got a foot in the door since Keri has an informant who may be useful," Beth said. "I'd like to break for a long lunch so you folks can get to know each other better. We'll meet back here at fourteen hundred hours."

The officers gathered their paperwork and immediately hovered around Keri, escorting her out like a team of bodyguards. She was elated that her colleagues had taken to her so readily, but she couldn't help glancing back over her shoulder. What was going to happen when they left Alex alone with that woman? Beth must've been thinking the same thing because she hung back, taking far too long to get her notes together and tidy up the room. Alex watched as Keri was swept down the hallway.

"Lieutenant, you'll be joining us for lunch, won't you?" Beth asked. "The troops need to get a sense of both of us."

Helen spoke before Alex could respond. "Actually, we probably need to talk privately." She smiled up at Alex and licked her lips slowly.

"Don't you think, darling? I still have questions about the operation and this new kid."

"Well, if you have questions about Keri, you need to talk to me." Beth glared at Helen. "I'm her immediate supervisor and know more about her than anyone."

"I'm sure that won't last long," Helen continued, eyeing Alex suspiciously.

"Just what the hell does that mean?"

"I knew it…you've already got the hots for her. Have you fucked her yet?"

Alex felt Beth bristle beside her. She knew her friend wanted to throttle Helen, but she shook her head, murmuring, "Let it go, Beth." She nodded toward the hallway. "I've got this. Close the door on your way out."

Helen gave a patronizing smirk and fired another slam. "It's gratifying to see such devotion from the women who want to fuck you. We're certainly a loyal though small group of thwarted rejects. I hope Little Miss Innocent can stand the heartbreak when it's over."

Alex cautioned Beth with another sharp look and waited for her to leave, then Helen purred, "Thank God, alone at last." She scooted up on the conference table, spread her legs, and reached for Alex.

"Don't even think about it." Alex's words sounded much more confident than she felt as she tried to step back from Helen's grasp.

But Helen caught her around the waist in one swift motion and guided her between her parted thighs. She wrapped her legs around Alex and locked her in place. With her right index finger she traced the outline of Alex's lips. "I'm way beyond thinking about it, darling."

Alex squirmed backward, trying unsuccessfully to free herself from Helen's clutches. "We're in a police facility, for God's sake, Helen. Anyone could walk in."

"And I know how you love that fear of getting caught." The fingers of Helen's left hand slid up the inside of her leg and disappeared under her short skirt. "I'm already wet…feel."

"No, damn you, I won't. Let go of me." But in spite of her words, Alex's physical responses had already begun. Her neck and face grew warm. Moisture gathered between her legs and her mouth dried. It happened every time Helen unleashed her ultimate weapon. Something about the way she just took charge, with no doubts and no hesitation, like no one could possibly refuse her. And Alex never had.

"You want it as much as I do," Helen whispered into her ear. "I can feel you getting hot. I can smell it."

Sparks shot through Alex's body as Helen's tongue rimmed her ear and stroked down the side of her neck. Her mind was screaming, "Snap out of it, get control of yourself," but the sensation felt so good, she heard an audible moan and feared her body had betrayed her out loud. Helen's soft chuckle provided confirmation.

"Come here, baby. I know what you need."

Alex froze. *How dare this bitch claim to know what I need?* "Oh, hell no, you don't. Let go of me, now." All the energy that had fueled her passion morphed into anger. Alex raised her arms with such force when she broke free that Helen slid backward onto the table.

The conference room door flew open and slammed against the wall as Keri barged into the room. "I forgot my car keys…" Her face paled. "What the hell?"

Keri fought a wave of sheer fury as she took in the sight of Helen Callahan's body splayed across the conference room table with her skirt above her thighs. The woman was pure sex and she was obviously working her witchery on Alex. *How dare she come into a police facility and act like a slut?* In the next instant Keri knew her contempt was less about the violation of sacred police space and more about the violation of Alex's body.

Helen rose up on her elbows and laughed at her. "What's the matter, sweetie, jealous? Why don't you run along? We've got some unfinished business here. Or haven't you had the pleasure yet of seeing what Alex looks like when she's aroused?"

Alex reacted immediately, leaning toward Helen with cold menace. "Get out of my building. Now."

Helen took her time sliding off the table and straightening her clothing. As she walked toward the door, she blew Alex a kiss and said, "See you later, lover." Her laughter echoed down the hallway as she exited.

Alex turned toward Keri Morgan. The shock and disillusion in her eyes was unmistakable. Now this young officer would think she was not only a spiteful ladder-climbing opportunist but also a sex-craved woman who couldn't control her appetites on the job. "It's not what it looks like." The explanation sounded lame, and Keri's face said she wasn't buying it.

Without a word, she grabbed her keys and slammed out of the room.

Seconds later, Beth Price walked back in. "What was that about? I just saw Keri running out of here like her ass was on fire."

"She walked in on one of Helen's finer moments—draped across the table half naked."

"Don't tell me you let that skanky bitch touch you again."

"She tried, and I got caught up in the attraction for a second. She's like an Altoid, curiously strong." Alex shook her head as the reality of what almost happened sank in.

"Haven't you learned anything?"

Alex threw up her hands. "So I'm a little horny. Shoot me."

Beth stared at her for a split second before breaking into laughter. "You're sick, Troy."

"She has that effect."

"If you're that hard up to get laid, I know several women who'd love to have a go at you and they wouldn't cause any trouble. Hell, I'll even give you, a pity fuck if that's what you need." Beth paused as if considering her last statement. "Strike that. Tammy would kill my ass."

"And mine," Alex said dryly.

Beth lifted Alex's briefcase from the chair and motioned toward the door. "Lunch?"

They didn't speak again until they drove out of the lot and were on their way to the designated lunch spot. Alex wished Beth would just drop the subject, but her friend loathed Helen and she also had responsibility for the team. In her position, Alex would want to know if personal dynamics would compromise the investigation.

Before she could offer some reassurance that Helen was dealt with, Beth demanded, "I really need to know what's going on. You said you were done with Helen and now you're playing grab ass with her in the conference room. What gives?"

"I let it go too far. Her persistence was flattering again for about half a second, but you can bet your sweet ass that I'm not getting mixed up with Helen Callahan again, ever. Now, can I get a little slack?"

Beth tapped the steering wheel absently. In a troubled tone, she asked, "Are you still in love with her?"

"God, no! Haven't you ever been with somebody who just makes you crazy every time they touch you?"

"Yeah, but it's a good kind of crazy and I'm living with her. Helen is a head case and you know it."

"You're right, and I plan to stay far away from her." Alex meant it, and for the first time since the relationship had ended, she knew she was strong enough to deal with Helen.

"I told you she'd use the task force as an excuse to reel you back into her smarmy clutches."

"That's not going to happen."

Beth gave Alex a sideways grin. "If it's just about the sex, we need to get you laid, fast, and I've got the perfect candidate." She pulled into a parking space in front of the pizza house and pointed to Keri Morgan entering the restaurant.

"Talk about jumping out of the frying pan into the fire. No, thanks." Alex got out of the car. "I can't afford a distraction on this case. Not with Helen or Keri."

"I know, but didn't you love the way she stood up to Helen?"

Alex thought about Keri standing her ground and defending herself. "That was definitely a thing of beauty. That girl's got potential. I just might take her under my wing and teach her a thing or two…about police work."

Beth grinned. "Yeah, right. Let's go eat."

"If you don't mind, I'm going back to the office. I need to clear my head and finish the op plan so I can get it to the chief. You can get a ride back, can't you?"

"Sure, boss, whatever you need."

But it wasn't her head or the op plan Alex needed to work on, it was the tumultuous waves of feeling that racked her body and mind. After four years on an emotional roller coaster with Helen and a year of simply being afraid to express herself at all, it was almost joyful to feel something positive and to have a sense that she could trust herself again. But the timing of her newly realized feelings was way off. The job had to come first. Still, Alex realized that she was running. Right now, she couldn't face the intensity of Keri Morgan's blue eyes, searching, questioning, and maybe discovering things Alex could not disguise.

Chapter Eight

Yeah, I can give you Sonny Davis, but it's gonna cost you."
The self-serving voice at the other end of the phone line belonged to Chad Williams.

Keri had put the conversation on speakerphone so her partner, Steve Alston, could listen in and help evaluate the call. The cramped conference room, which was being used as work space for the entire team, remained surprisingly quiet as the recording continued.

"I've already told you that I'll make it worth your time, Chad." Keri tried to conceal her growing impatience with the petty thief turned informant. "So what's the deal?"

It had taken a few days to track Chad down. Then Keri had gone through the process of proving him reliable with documented drug buys from two of Davis's street dealers. Now it was finally time to set up the meet between Davis and Keri. If Chad backed out, she'd look like the new kid with a good game but no substance. This was her opportunity to impress the team and Alex all at once.

Once again, the image of Helen Callahan sprawled across the conference room table made prickly-sick heat gather in the pit of her stomach. Keri wished she could stop thinking about it, but the strong current between Alex and Helen had been palpable and that bothered her. She wondered about the nature of their connection. Obviously they weren't just professional colleagues. She'd hardly seen Alex since that day and had a feeling the lieutenant was avoiding her. That bothered her as well, and it made her nervous. Alex wouldn't want the entire division to hear about that indiscretion. What would she be willing to do to keep it quiet?

Keri had thought about saying something but decided the best idea was to keep her head down. It would soon be clear that she knew how to keep her mouth shut, since there would be no gossip. Holding back a sigh, she returned her attention to Chad's monotone.

"Sonny is having a party at his place soon. You know, a little blow, some broads. He told me to drop by and check out the action to see if I'm interested in hooking up with his crew."

How could anyone trust this man, with his schoolboy good looks and morals of a snake? Sad to think her whole career could depend on a scumbag like Chad Williams. But most drug dealers weren't arrested hanging out with society's elite. She had to get down and dirty for the big payoff.

"Soon doesn't cut it, Chad. I want specifics. That's the only way you get paid. We need to get this ball rolling."

Steve gave her a quick nod of encouragement. He already knew her well enough to know this call wasn't just important to the case but also to her. She didn't bother to pretend that she had nothing to prove. She liked Steve and felt safe with him.

"Chad, I need to make contact now. There's got to be a way. Where does he hang out?" Keri prodded Chad's drug-fried brain to come up with other options.

"You might have something there. He goes to a bar called Shelly's over on Murray Street. I heard he'll be there tonight. We could accidentally bump into him. How's that?"

"Keep it in your pants. Go by and see if he's there. If he is, page me and I'll come over." Keri got the thumbs-up from Steve.

"Okay, that'll work, but don't bring no skin-headed, cop-looking dude with you. Bring another chick or something."

"You just take care of your end and I'll do the rest." Keri hung up and looked at Steve. "What'd you think?"

He stroked his scraggly brindle beard pensively between his thumb and forefinger, a mannerism that went along with the long-haired biker look he'd adopted for his cover. "I think we need to find you a female partner for the night."

They both glanced toward Paige, the quiet, honey blond techie, and Renee, the talkative African American, and couldn't see either of them partnering with her for this job.

Steve shook his head. "If we decide to wire you, Paige'll be monitoring. Renee can't go and Sergeant Price popped him that time. I think he'll remember her."

"The lieutenant can do it." Beth's voice came from the other side of the room.

Keri hadn't noticed her come in. Without thinking, she said, "What?"

"She's been in Vice/Narcotics four years and fills in all the time," Beth said. "Right, Steve?"

"You're right, Sarge. Why didn't I think of it? She'd be perfect."

"Then it's settled." Beth flashed that sideways it'll-make-you-a-better-person grin Keri had come to know during their few days together.

Her pulse kicked up at the thought of spending time alone with Alex. "Will I be wired?"

"No, this is just an introduction," Beth said. "You'll have to wear something a little sexier, and you won't be armed. This is the honey to lure the little pervert into our trap."

"Shelly's?" Keri had heard the name but wasn't sure of the clientele or how upscale it was. If she was going to blend in, she needed the right look. "What kind of place is it?"

Steve burst out laughing with the rest of the team. "Shelly's is sort of like a wi-fi coffee shop. You can hook up with anyone there, gays, straights, trans, whatever your little heart desires."

The surprise must've been obvious on Keri's face because the guys continued to laugh.

"What's the matter? Never played for the pink team before?" Rick Jones teased. The Caldwell PD detective was in his thirties with Andy Griffith looks. His affable personality had already made him a favorite on the team.

"Yeah," Renee joined in, "I hear it's kinda like going black. Once you been there, you never go back."

Mike Fields, the African American officer from Layton PD, looked confused. "What does that mean?"

Renee elbowed him. "I'll explain it later, pretty boy."

"You're not supposed to act gay, just a little bi," Beth pointed out. "We want Davis to think he's got a shot at you, but if he hangs out in this place maybe he likes to watch girl on girl, too. Most straight guys do." Beth paused. "You all right?"

Keri didn't know how to answer. Beth's plan was just sinking in. She was supposed to act "a little bi" with Alex. Yeah, that was going to be a challenge. Her stomach reacted with the same queasiness she felt every time she thought about that woman. Trying to hide her anxiety with humor, she muttered, "Yeah, I just didn't realize I'd be losing my virginity twice tonight—my first undercover job and my first time in a swingers' bar."

Everyone reacted the way she hoped, with hoots of laughter. Steve slapped her on the back good-naturedly. "You'll do great. Who's going to tell the lieutenant she needs to look hot and put on a floor show?"

"Lucky me," Beth said, chuckling.

Keri kept her head down. Hot color had drenched her cheeks and neck. "What kind of backup will we have?"

"We'll use the two vans for surveillance so we can set up and not be seen. I'll give you the rest of the details at the briefing later, after I've spoken with the lieutenant."

"Hey, good luck with that," Steve called as she strolled away.

❖

"I'm doing what?" Alex raised her head from the surveillance reports she was reading. "It's not that I mind pitching in, but can't one of the others handle this?" She knew the real reason for her reluctance, and it had nothing to do with operations.

"Nobody else can do it, Alex. We need to make contact as soon as possible and this is our first real chance. It sounds like this scumbag likes to frequent alternative bars and watch women together. He's probably dealing out of there, too."

Alex groaned inwardly. It was difficult enough to work with Keri every day, keeping her at arm's length and fighting their growing attraction. But the reality of being alone with her in an environment filled with liquor, sexy lighting, soft music, and bodies in all stages of vertical lovemaking raised too many red flags.

Beth sensed her hesitation. "It's a one-time thing. Once the intro's made, you're out. I'm sorry to spring this on you, but I had to improvise."

She bit her tongue to keep from smiling. She knew Alex wouldn't have any tactical objections to the assignment. She'd worked undercover hundreds of times before. So her anxiety had to be about Keri. Beth played her final card. "She's probably feeling a little overwhelmed right now. It's her first UC assignment. She'll be nervous and we can't afford to have her blow this. I need you there to keep her on track and so does the team. This could be your chance to try out that mentoring thing you talked about."

"All right, enough already. I'll do it, but just this once. Now get out."

"You're a trooper, boss. We're meeting back here at twenty-one hundred hours." Beth blew an air kiss and ducked out the door just as Alex playfully hurled a small statute book across the room at her.

❖

Keri's entire wardrobe lay strewn across the bed as she surveyed her choice of outfits for the night. She had no idea what to wear. The faded jeans with threadbare patches beside the crotch and on both cheeks of her ass could possibly be considered sexy. She pulled them on along with a white Lycra T-shirt that stretched tightly across her chest and accented her small, athletic breasts. It stopped well above her navel, exposing several inches of tanned flesh between the shirt and the waist of the low-cut jeans. She added a short jeans jacket for the finishing touch and walked into the living room.

"Whoa, look out, druggies, here she comes." Kevin whistled and threw a pillow at her.

Keri snapped it from the air and threw it back. "Where's your ball and chain tonight, bro? Do you have a pass to be out by yourself?"

The two of them often joked that they used to bicker in utero. She'd never blamed her twin for her abuse. It wasn't his fault she was born female and their father saw her as a punching bag, but she knew Kevin felt guilty for not intervening.

From the worn sofa, her father held her mother's hand and glared his disapproval. "Are you really going out like that?"

"I'm on assignment, Dad. Don't worry, I'll be with Lieutenant Troy."

Bobby Morgan's eyebrows lifted, layering deep grooves into his forehead. "You tell her to keep the boys at least a hundred yards away from you."

Keri crossed to her mom, leaned down, and kissed the top of her head. "I love you, Mom. I'll be careful...and don't wait up."

"Have a nice time, dear," her mother said vaguely. Keri wasn't sure how much she'd taken in.

After reassuring everyone again that she would be fine, she waved good-bye and drove back to the office with her nerves bunching in her stomach.

Predictably, she was greeted with whistles and catcalls when she walked into the conference room twenty minutes later. She took off the jacket, slung it over a chair and spun in a series of 360-degree twirls across the length of the room. Concluding with a split to the floor, she gave her best Elvis imitation of "Thank yuh ver-uh much."

Alex watched from a corner chair she'd chosen for the briefing. Not only was Keri Morgan drop-dead gorgeous in the outfit, but she'd already won over the entire team with her personality and entertaining antics. She was the right choice for the job, however awkward the consequences were for Alex. It wasn't Keri's fault if her boss lost concentration every time they were in the same room.

Keri's final split left her kneeling in front of a pair of black cowboy boots with silver tips. She lifted her gaze from the boots to skintight black jeans that covered muscled legs and continued to the join of thigh and torso before disappearing under a bronze-colored blouse. A transparent pattern woven into the blouse revealed flashes of a white camisole underneath. Full breasts rose and fell with each breath and a steady pulse pounded on the side of the sleek neck. A square jaw and lips ripe for kissing brought Keri back to her senses. In a matter of seconds—seconds forever etched in her mind—she had followed the undulating curves of Alex Troy's body and thought of kissing her again. She made eye contact with Alex as she stood. "Nice boots, Lieu."

Alex's insides ached. The look in Keri's eyes seemed to brim with heat. Maybe they simply mirrored Alex's own desire or her fear. Something was certainly churning there, and the intensity rattled Alex's usual detachment.

Mercifully, the pager on Keri's side vibrated and she grabbed it, glad for the distraction. She read the display and recognized the code she'd given Chad. "It's showtime," she said aloud to no one in particular.

Beth held her arms out and waved everybody forward with her hands. "Gather 'round and let's go over the plan one more time." Beth turned to Alex. "You wanna go first, Lieu?"

The officers rolled their chairs closer to the table as Alex began to speak. "Our workup on Davis shows he's pretty clean, records wise, except for a blip on the IRS screen. Your surveillance has given us an idea of his patterns, but we need to find out about known associates. That'll come when we get closer.

"Today I received the lab results from the first four deaths of our college students. The report confirms that the drugs in all of their systems are from the same batch of ecstasy. I'm still waiting for the tox results from Stacey Chambers. I want everybody to utilize the utmost caution." Alex nodded for Beth to review the evening's operational plan.

"Lieutenant Troy and Morgan will be going into the club to make contact. The rest of us will leave first, find the best places to set up, get in position, and wait for their arrival. Neither of them will be wired, so I want surveillance as tight as we can get it."

The officers fidgeted in their seats, tired of the talk and ready for action, as Beth continued. "Rick and Paige, you'll be in front in the panel van. Take pictures if possible for later identification. Mike and Renee, you'll cover the back lot and alley in the blackout van. If Davis leaves, meets, or talks to anybody back there, I want to know about it. If we're lucky, this'll be a routine intel-gathering operation and our first contact with the target. Is everyone clear on their assignments?"

Everybody nodded.

Beth tossed a set of car keys to Alex. "She's Jane, you're Tarzan. Make us proud…and don't wreck the 'Vette."

Keri and Alex stayed in the conference room after everyone else had gone, waiting for the signal to proceed to the bar. After a few minutes, Alex cleared her throat and rolled her chair closer to Keri, her heart pounding faster in direct proportion to their proximity.

"Morgan, I know you're nervous, but you're going to do a great job. I'll guide you through it. Just follow my lead. If you have questions, I'll try to answer them."

Keri heaved a sigh. "What exactly do you have in mind for our floorshow?"

Alex had to smile at the irony of her situation. "Just act like"—she traced the strong line of Keri's jaw with her index finger, her eyes never leaving Keri's—"we're *very* good friends."

The current from Keri's body teased slowly up Alex's arm and dove directly to her core. Keri's blue eyes turned hazy and her nostrils flared as the pulse at her neck raced. Alex swallowed the burst of attraction that blocked her throat.

Intense heat radiated from the point of contact on Keri's jaw and through her body with lightning speed. She felt mesmerized by Alex's touch. The tenderness and intimacy of it belied the tough exterior Alex tried to portray. Keri held her gaze and felt as though she were looking into the soul of a woman saved. Her heart thumped against her chest. She heard the blood racing through her veins, headed toward the ache between her legs. It was the most exquisite pain she'd ever experienced. She prayed it would never end.

"It's a very intimate environment," Alex said. "Not like most bars, so prepare yourself." She ran her tongue slowly across her lips.

"Yes, I can imagine," Keri finally managed.

"Oh, you can?" Alex teased.

"I mean…Oh, hell, I don't know what I mean." Keri stopped. They were both kidding themselves if they wanted to pretend they'd have to fake some heat.

"Other people may ask you to dance, men and women. If they do, go with your gut."

"Right." The way Keri felt right now, she'd probably jump some stranger in the ladies' restroom out of sheer frustration.

"You'll be fine. Trust me." Alex couldn't remember the last time she'd said those words to anyone. The look in Keri's eyes told her that she did.

Beth's voice came across the walkie-talkie. "We're in position."

Keri stabilized her emotions and projected herself into the role she was about to play. She was this sexy woman's "date" for the evening but she was also going to send signals to men, hoping Sonny Davis would respond. She had to get him interested by projecting a bisexual persona. She hoped she was up to the challenge and wouldn't just come across as a lesbian hot for the woman she was with, even if that was the truth. And it was, regardless of the fact that Alex was her superior officer and that Keri still couldn't completely forgive the past.

What if someone asked Alex to dance? Keri couldn't leave the room in a jealous huff like she did a few days ago when she saw Alex with Helen. The thought sent her confidence into a nosedive. She'd fled because *she* wanted to be the woman on that table, arousing the same fierce reaction she'd seen in Alex. Pushing that thought out of her mind, she stood hastily and left the room, side by side with her boss. When they reached the car, Alex opened Keri's door. She did the same thing when they arrived at Shelly's and placed her hand in the small of Keri's back as they strolled toward the club.

Keri walked slowly toward the entrance, wanting to prolong Alex's touch for as long as possible. It felt so incredibly right. She had never been so turned on by a simple caress or so aroused by a woman's proximity. Everything about Alex excited her. Physically, sexually, and emotionally. The ache that coursed through her body made it clear that her feelings for Alex Troy had escalated to new and torturous levels. She wasn't sure which hurt more, her attempts to bury her physical cravings or the equally impossible attempts to conceal her feelings. As they approached the club door, Alex's hand slid down her back and brushed lightly across her butt. Before she pulled away completely, Keri caught her hand, gave it a light squeeze, and reluctantly released it.

Alex allowed herself to imagine that Keri clung to her hand out of uncontrollable desire. She wanted to believe her feelings were returned. She even wondered if she might have found the woman she was destined to spend her life with. Although the idea seemed absurd and the timing disastrous, there could be no other reason for her uncharacteristic lapses into professional unconsciousness and sexual fantasy.

When Keri released her grip, a familiar hook wrapped around Alex's heart and settled into place. She reminded herself this was work and any interest Keri displayed was just an act. A silent mantra echoed in her mind: Sonny Davis behind bars equals captain's bars.

Chapter Nine

Shelly's lacked the usual wall-vibrating rhythms, boisterous voices competing for attention, and oppressive smell of testosterone. The music was loud enough for dancing but it was still possible for people to talk. Small candlelike fixtures on each table lent an intimacy Keri found inviting. Here, among people of all ages and sexual preferences, the atmosphere was freeing and arousing, and she quickly lost herself watching the sensuous fluidity of women's bodies together. A familiar tightness grabbed her pelvis and she cast a sideways glance at Alex. The lieutenant was impossible to read, showing no discernible reaction to the steamy sensuality on all sides.

Keri had spotted Chad a few minutes ago but she'd delayed telling Alex, instead absorbing the sexual energy in the room. She forced her gaze to the curly thatch of black hair across the room. Sonny Davis. Chad had found him, and the two were talking. She tactically assessed her surroundings, noting exits and potential hazards. During her evaluation her gaze skimmed past a young blonde on the dance floor being caressed by a brunette. The blonde kept staring at Alex.

Keri placed her hand possessively on Alex's arm and leaned in close, speaking next to her ear to make herself heard above the music. "Our target's in the back and it looks like he has company."

She inhaled Alex's warm musk perfume and found herself not wanting to move. Her lips inadvertently touched Alex's earlobe and she felt the lieutenant shiver.

Alex stifled an involuntary moan that threatened to expose her desire. *I'm just horny*, she thought, *and God knows Keri's gorgeous.* Her hot breath sent goose bumps across Alex's skin.

"Let's find a seat." Alex indicated a table directly in Davis's line of sight.

They ordered drinks and waited for Chad to do his part. The blonde on the dance floor continued to watch Alex and when the song ended, she started toward their table. Keri couldn't allow another woman to touch Alex. That wasn't part of their plan.

Running interference, she placed her hand on Alex's knee and slid it slowly up her skintight-denim-clad thigh. "Would you like to dance?"

A series of vibrations shot up her arm as she registered Alex's heat. This was no time for an attack of nerves, she thought. The ploy had worked. The determined blonde had veered off in another direction, aiming her seductive stare at another woman. Alex's eyes were fixed on Keri's hand, which rested inches from her crotch. The look reminded Keri of that horrible night in the gym. She withdrew her hand so quickly it sent her beer flying off the table and skidding across the dance floor.

"Nice improvisation, Morgan. I didn't see that coming."

Keri jumped to her feet, horrified. Great. She'd drawn attention to them. What did it matter if someone asked Alex to dance? Weren't they supposed to blend in?

"I'm sorry." She snatched up a cocktail napkin. Before she could hurry to clean up after herself, Alex caught her wrist.

"Don't be. You've made an impression on our target." She nodded toward Chad, who was approaching their table.

With a cocky swagger, he picked up the beer bottle and handed it to the barman who'd approached to deal with the spill.

"Hey, ladies." Chad acted like a smooth operator. "You got his attention with that little touchy-feely show. Wanna play?"

"Why not?" Alex tried to erase the vision of Keri's hand teasing its way up her leg, leaving a trail of oversensitized flesh and inextinguishable passion. She'd silently prayed Keri would stop but wished she hadn't. She was just playing a part, Alex reminded herself, defending against the advances of another woman. But she was so damn good at it, Alex had experienced a wild thrill to be claimed so publicly. The thought that her pleasure-pain gave Sonny Davis even the tiniest thrill made her stomach lurch. She distracted herself with a sharp instruction to Chad. "By the way, Einstein, I'm Kathy and her name's Lynn. Remember that."

Three NFL-sized men and an accountant-type character were strategically positioned around Davis. Alex almost smiled at the predictability of the stereotypical vile henchmen. Two of the large men rose as she and Keri came closer.

"Sorry, ladies," one said, "I gotta pat you down. You understand." He lifted his hands in resignation, but the sneer on his face said he was enjoying himself.

"Whatever." Keri raised her arms.

The goon, a buzz-cut blond, took his time, slowly running his hands over Keri's body, squeezing and patting places that couldn't possibly conceal a weapon and leering at Alex as she stood by helplessly. The hairs on the back of her neck bristled and she thought about the woman Keri had hugged in the police parking lot. An uncustomary surge of jealousy clamped like a vise through her insides. The thought of anyone else touching Keri infuriated her, but someone like this guy, mauling and probing for the sheer hell of it, made her homicidal. She reminded herself this was business and there'd be payback soon enough.

When it was Alex's turn to be groped, she mimicked Keri's pose, inhaling deeply and waiting for the assault. Muscles throughout her body tensed as the unwelcome stroking around her breasts, between her thighs and down her legs seemed to go on forever. When the blond finally completed his task, Alex whispered, "Sorry about your penis."

With a confused look, the man withdrew and told Davis, "They're clean, boss."

Davis waved a fifty dollar bill at the waitress. "Get these ladies a drink."

Chad made the introductions and pulled up chairs for Alex and Keri.

Davis said, "Sorry about the body search." His full lips curled back over pristine, perfectly shaped teeth and produced a devastatingly handsome grin. With his smooth complexion and curly black hair, he looked like the proverbial Greek god. While they waited for their drinks to arrive, he introduced the four men at his table. The blond who'd searched them was "Fletch." A huge individual with no neck was "Hunk," and a scar-faced, dead-eyed sociopath had the nickname "Cappy." The brains of the crew appeared to be "Dolph," who had the nose and beady eyes of a rodent and wore a green leisure suit that had gone out of style two decades ago.

Alex flashed her most seductive smile while studying each man carefully and cataloguing every facial nuance. Davis cruised her and Keri at length through dark, menacing eyes, his expression heating as he took in the gentle curves of Keri's body and the slight tenting of her T-shirt from the air-conditioning.

"You two'd have to be swingers," he concluded finally. "You're too classy to be whores and too cute to be dykes…nothing personal. I like watching two women together as much as the next guy. Guess that's why I come here."

Keri felt the vein bulge on the side of her neck. She wanted to arrest this scum-sucking piece of filth right now for allowing his goons to handle Alex. Keri knew it had taken every ounce of her restraint to endure the mauling of her body by these misfits.

"So, Chad tells me you girls are looking to have some fun."

"Yeah, we like a little variety, too," Keri said, eager to close out the game now before anyone thought he could maul Alex again. "We'd like to get our hands on some—"

"Hot bodies," Alex completed, closing her fingers firmly over Keri's right knee. It was too soon to bring up drugs, and she was surprised that Keri had made such a rookie mistake. They needed to establish rapport with the group first.

"How come I haven't seen you here before?" Davis asked.

"Good question." Alex managed a small insulted pout. "I used to dye my hair jet black and wear it longer. Oh, yeah…and I was with a guy the last few times." She trailed a hand casually over Keri's hair. "I like to keep my options open."

Keri struggled to keep the incredulity from her face. Alex was a pro. She made undercover look easy. Davis was completely hooked. He smiled and scooted his chair closer to Alex, a look of pure sexual hunger in his eyes. Helen Callahan had the same look the day she'd tried to seduce Alex. But Keri wasn't about to let another socially challenged and morally deficient degenerate have his way with her boss.

Before she could react, a college-aged girl wearing what looked like a toga approached Davis from behind. Her eyes were pinpoints of dull light, her face pale and drawn.

The three large goons rose simultaneously. "I have to talk to Sonny," the girl told Fletch.

"He's busy right now and can't be disturbed. Whaddaya want?"

The young woman turned her back to the table and appeared to be whispering to Fletch. After a brief exchange, she walked toward the back of the bar. Fletch returned to the table, leaned down, and spoke quietly in Davis's ear.

Alex made a point of looking bored, hoping Keri would pick up on her cue. They needed to act like they saw strung-out teens in clubs every day. After another round of drinks, lots of bragging, and some small talk, Davis cleared his throat and rose nonchalantly.

"If you'll excuse me for a minute, ladies. Nature calls." He went toward the restrooms at the rear of the bar, Fletch close behind.

When they were out of sight, Keri said, "Sounds like a good idea. This beer's going right through me."

Hunk lurched in his seat but Keri turned to him. "I don't really think your boss'll be in the same place I'm going, unless you know something I don't."

Alex thought about stopping Keri but decided it might look too suspicious if she made a fuss. Instead, she resigned herself to letting Keri go and hoped she wouldn't blow the case by doing something stupid.

Keri leaned over, gave Alex a light kiss on the cheek, and whispered, "I've got a hunch I need to check on." She gave Alex's arm a reassuring squeeze and darted after Davis.

She slipped along the darkened hallway to the restrooms and listened at the men's room door—nothing. A sliver of light shown through a crack in the back door that had been propped open with a beer can. Keri ducked into the adjacent broom closet. The small space reeked of Clorox and stale urine. Her nostrils burned and her eyes watered as she focused on the voices from outside.

Davis's cordial tone had dissolved into piercing cold. "You've been told not to contact me in public—ever. You've got a source. If you want more product call him. And if you do anything like this again, you'll pay."

Keri couldn't understand the woman's low, whiny reply. When Davis opened the door to come back inside, he motioned to Fletch with an angry jerk of his head and said, "Take care of this shit," and reentered the club.

When she was sure Davis had time to be seated again, Keri darted into the ladies' room, washed her hands, and came back to the table shaking them and complaining about the lack of paper towels. Keri swept a quick, confused look around the table. Alex wasn't there anymore. Nerves bunched in her stomach. She'd sensed that Alex wasn't happy with her rushing away to the restroom alone, but this wasn't a one-woman show. Keri supposed she wanted to prove she had what it took to work undercover, too. Even though she wasn't wearing a wire, the contents of her report would be valuable to the investigation. She'd memorized everything she heard.

"Looks like if you want any of that tonight, you better get a move on, girlie." Davis laughed from behind her.

Keri followed his gaze to the dance floor, and something vile and bitter rose in her throat. Alex was with the blonde from earlier. One of the woman's hands rested on Alex's lower back almost touching the swell of her butt. She held Alex so tightly their bodies moved in unison. Her thigh was wedged between Alex's legs. With every step the stranger ground her hips into Alex's body.

Keri tightened her fists until her nails cut into the palms. She knew exactly where the urge came from, but she couldn't stop herself from swaggering onto the dance floor like she was going to make an arrest. She grabbed the hand that had migrated to Alex's butt and lifted it away.

"Excuse me, please." She met the blonde's startled gaze in a challenging stare.

The hook tightened around Alex's heart, pulling her closer to Keri. Everyone in the club vanished except the gorgeous woman standing before her. As the blonde released her hold, Keri's satisfaction was obvious. Looking like she'd won the prize, she pulled Alex into her arms, carefully insinuating her body where the blonde's previously rested.

"Let's keep dancing," she said. "Davis is still watching."

There was no awkward maneuvering for position, no hesitation in the sway of their bodies as they moved closer.

"Did you find out anything back there?" Alex asked before her concentration was completely lost.

"Maybe. I don't know." Keri encircled Alex's waist and her leg slid naturally between Alex's thighs. Keri had wondered, even imagined, how they would fit together. Now she knew. Perfectly.

The curves and contours of her shorter, more compact body

melded completely into the dips and swells of Alex's sleeker frame. Where she was soft and yielding, Alex felt muscular and firm. Keri's breath caught in her throat as she succumbed to the surreal feelings Alex evoked. She felt weak yet simultaneously infused with a tender strength. She had never experienced this level of arousal with anyone, had never believed it possible. She'd resigned herself to the mediocre stirrings of excitement with one-night stands. But this… She trembled in Alex's arms as the pulsing heat between their bodies grew hotter. Her breasts tingled and her nipples stood erect. Pressure gathered in her pelvis. Time and place evaporated into pinpoints of pleasure where their bodies joined. The occasional ache in her clitoris throughout the evening had turned into a constant hammering. She wondered if Alex could feel her wet, swollen clit pounding against her thigh.

For her part, it had been years since Alex *wanted* anyone to hold her this close, to feel her need, to know her vulnerability. Somehow Keri Morgan had managed to sneak into the protected places of Alex's heart when she least expected it. Their bodies swayed like they'd done this dance of intimacy many times. Keri raised her head from Alex's shoulder and looked up into her eyes. The distance closed between them, the warmth of their erratic breaths swept across her face, and Alex's muscles trembled. Keri parted her lips in welcome. She wanted this just as much as Alex did. Neither of them could hide it.

Alex brushed her moistened lips lightly across Keri's and stroked the hot flesh with the tip of her tongue. The connection was complete, the fusing immediate. Alex felt as if she'd straddled a lightning rod. Every nerve in her body sparked with long-suppressed passion. Her knees threatened to collapse. She pulled Keri closer to steady herself, and with a sharp intake of breath plunged her tongue voraciously between Keri's parted lips. The burning that spiraled up from her core fueled a kiss she wanted never to end. For just a second she had to possess this exquisite creature, to feel she truly belonged to *her*.

Just as Keri thought she would be consumed by her own passion and the intensity of their kiss, she felt Alex's body tense. Dropping her arms from Keri's waist, she stepped back. "I think we've been convincing enough for one night. Davis will assume we're getting a room."

Keri was momentarily stunned by the sudden change of direction and body heat. Her head felt dizzy and she looked around, readjusting to her surroundings. Alex took her hand and led her out of the bar, waving to Davis as they exited.

"Are you all right?" she asked when they reached the 'Vette. She held the passenger door open.

"I'm fine." Keri slid into the seat. "Did I do something wrong?" She couldn't stop the relatively insignificant question, hoping to forestall the more fundamental queries that screamed for answers.

"No, we made contact and it went well, overall." Alex rolled down her window to allow the cool night air to dissipate the heat that still simmered between them. "That was quite a performance in there. You did a good job."

"What makes you think it was a performance? I need to tell you—"

"No, you don't. We'll do the critique tomorrow." Alex drove out of the lot.

Keri squeezed the console until her knuckles turned white. She wanted to apologize for her Bogart behavior and the inappropriate touching. "This isn't about the operation."

"Then I'm *sure* it can wait." Alex knew she couldn't bear the verbalization of what was so plain on Keri's face. It was hard enough to remain focused on the job. She retrieved the walkie-talkie from the glove box and cleared all the surveillance units, then asked Beth to switch to the supervisory frequency. She clicked over and waited, painfully aware of Keri staring out the passenger's window.

"Go ahead, Lieutenant."

"Beth, meet me at Northeast Center."

"Sure, boss."

Alex switched the radio off and clutched the steering wheel, eyes on the street ahead.

"Why did you dance with her?" Keri's voice quivered.

"It was our exit strategy." Alex kept her tone even and free of emotion. "You did exactly what I hoped you would and it worked perfectly."

"But how did you know I'd be so...predictable?"

Her pained look made Alex want to reach over and hug her. "I think you know the answer, and this is not the right time to discuss it."

"Is it the physical touching you can't stand, or the intimacy?" Keri flinched as soon as she'd spoken. Alex had tried to end the conversation, and that was the smart thing to do. Only she couldn't let it go. One moment they'd been dancing and kissing like nothing else mattered, the next Alex had rejected her. She remembered Alex's withdrawal from her in the locker room and contrasted that to the blonde fondling her on the dance floor earlier.

Alex turned a hard, icy stare on her. "You're out of line, Morgan."

She parked in the shopping center lot and prayed for Beth to hurry. Her nerves were on edge and her resistance nearly nonexistent.

"I'm sorry," Keri blurted. "Please, let me stay on the team."

Before Alex could unleash the torrent of emotion Keri had tapped into, Beth pulled her vehicle alongside and cut her engine. Alex bit back the words she knew she would regret. She needed to get some distance.

"Keri, let's go." Beth jerked her head toward the vacant seat beside her.

Keri started to object but Beth's expression and Alex's silence stopped her. She waited until Alex's eyes returned to her, now misty with emotion.

"I'm sorry if I offended you," she stammered.

"Go home and get some sleep, Morgan," came the cool response. Alex's face gave nothing away. "You're still on the team."

On their ride back to the office, Beth asked, "What's going on with the two of you? Something happened...spill it."

Keri furiously stroked her lucky key ring and stared out the window. "It's like I don't exist beyond this assignment."

"It's not about you. Alex has a lot on her mind. This case can make or break her and everyone else involved. You included."

"It feels like it's more complicated than that."

"It's not personal," Beth said. "Alex doesn't know you very well and this operation means a lot to her. She won't forgive herself if Davis caused Stacey Chambers's death and she doesn't nail him. This isn't the best time to be digging in the boneyard and scratching at scabs."

"I know that kind of pain," Keri said. "No one gets to leave it behind."

"That's right. So let her deal with it in her own time." Beth parked and killed the engine. "Now...are you going to tell me what happened tonight?"

"Maybe tomorrow." Keri reminded herself that Beth and Alex were close friends, not just colleagues. She wasn't sure if she wanted to confide in a woman who would probably pass on key information to Alex. "I'm tired," she said, opening her door.

"Don't spend all night thinking about this," Beth warned gently.

"I hear you, Sarge, and you're right. There's no point losing sleep over things I can't change." With a quick good night, Keri left the car and walked dejectedly toward her Jeep.

Chapter Ten

While she waited for the team to assemble for the morning critique, Alex sipped coffee and pencil-drummed her desk. Her mind replayed last evening's disturbing events: Keri's hand sliding up her thigh; Keri's leg fitting perfectly into the Y of her body; Keri's arm around her waist and their breasts pressing painfully against each other's erect nipples. But most distracting was the consuming hunger of their kiss. She fought the urge to close her legs around the gathering heat. Alex hadn't felt so excited by a touch or a kiss since Helen. But Keri Morgan was probably just as dangerous as Helen, for different reasons—maybe even more so.

With Helen their connection had been all about control and sex. But Keri seemed genuinely interested in her feelings. And then there was the emotional hand grenade Keri lobbed into her lap before leaving her alone and aching in the car. Alex had never considered herself some sort of twisted masochist. But maybe she needed Helen's variety of rough physicality or the anonymity of strangers to feel alive. Perhaps she was incapable of the intimate connections borne of human kindness. Her history of it with women was certainly nonexistent.

Beth's laughter drifted down the hall, signaling the end of the formal lineup session. Alex headed for the conference room, imposing self-discipline so she could distance herself from thoughts of Keri.

After congratulating the team on their work last night, she asked Rick and Paige, "Did we get pictures of Davis's associates? I'm assuming they came in through the front."

Rick Jones cleared his throat and straightened in his chair. "Yes, ma'am. We got some pretty good shots of all four. Paige already put them in the system for comparison with known offenders."

"Great." Alex smiled. "Photos, plus the physical characteristics Morgan and I provided, should get us a hit pretty quickly. Anything from the rear surveillance, Renee?"

"Well, we're not exactly sure, Lieutenant. Davis and one of his guys came out back with a young girl for a few minutes. We couldn't understand the conversation. Davis looked pissed and went back inside the club. The other man left with the girl a few minutes later in a white BMW. He hadn't come back when we broke off. But we got the tag number and the vehicle is registered to Fletch."

Alex rolled to the coffee pot and filled her cup again. "All right, from the inside. Morgan, give everybody the rundown."

Keri avoided Alex's eyes as she began to speak. "The informant did his part with the intro. I think Davis bought it. You'll all be pleased to know the lieutenant is a good dancer."

The group erupted in a round of good-natured laughter.

Alex couldn't resist. "Yeah, but Morgan tries to lead."

The laughter finally died down and Keri said, "Chad told him we're interested in a big score. But we didn't push it. Let him make the first move."

"Morgan was out back for that meeting," Alex prompted.

"Yeah, I followed Davis. It was pretty intense. He threatened this young girl for contacting him in public and told her to call her dealer if she needed more product. That's probably as close to an admission of drug dealing as we'll ever get from him. Then he told Fletch to take care of 'this shit.' I don't know what that was about, but he was definitely not happy with the girl or his dealer. I'm pretty sure there was no exchange. He wouldn't be that careless out in the open."

This was the first time Alex had heard about the conversation behind the club, but she had to admit that it might prove useful. "You never know when all these little tidbits of information will fall perfectly into place. Everything is potentially valuable until we know otherwise." She motioned for Beth to take over.

"Okay, everybody get a car," Beth said. "I want us on Davis every minute. Don't make contact, just watch him and document where he goes and who he talks to. Keep in touch by radio. And remember, this could go on for days, weeks, or even months before we hear from him. It sucks, but don't get sloppy."

Alex nodded approval of Beth's plan, then added, "Sergeant, could I see you and Morgan before you head out?" She wondered why her voice sounded less than enthusiastic. Teaching was usually one of her favorite parts of the job.

Keri shuffled several feet behind Alex heading toward the office. Beth poked her in the ribs. "Drop it, kid. Whatever it is that's bothering you, just keep your eye on the big picture. If it's not about the job, it's not important right now."

"I've just got a feeling this isn't going to be pretty."

"Critique is part of the job, especially with someone new. Listen, stay cool, and try to learn something. Alex has been at this a while."

When they entered the office, Alex motioned for them to join her at the small table in the corner of the room. Beth sat between her and Keri, pointedly observing their failure to make eye contact. She gave Alex a quizzical look.

"Let's get started so you two can go to work." Alex wasn't about to let Beth have the floor. She knew her friend too well. "Morgan, is there anything else you'd like to say about your part in the operation last night?"

Keri looked over Alex's head to the blank wall behind her to avoid those hypnotic brown eyes. *Surely she doesn't want me to talk about what happened between us.* Keri wasn't even sure what did happen. "No, ma'am, I don't have anything else to add."

"Well, I have a couple of observations." Alex paused, remembering Keri's prickly sensitivity to professional feedback. "You're new at this, so don't take it personally."

She was forced to meet the younger woman's stare. The gentleness mixed with anxiety in Keri's eyes echoed in Alex's depths. She took a labored breath and heaviness gathered in her chest.

"First, as I think you can appreciate now, we need to be cautious about introducing the subject of drugs too quickly. That's a dead giveaway and besides, Chad told him what we wanted before we ever met."

"You're right, Lieutenant. I started to ask and probably would've if you hadn't put your hand on my knee." Keri stopped but the words had already made an impression. Alex's face flushed bright pink.

She cleared her throat and continued. "Second, it's never a good idea to go after a target alone, without a cover officer. When you followed Davis to the restroom, you put yourself in danger. I couldn't see you and couldn't have backed you up if something happened."

Keri's shoulders slumped but Alex knew she had to keep talking or she'd never finish. Even her sugarcoated critique seemed to wound Keri with each word. "It's my fault for not giving you more specific instructions. It was your first undercover assignment and unfortunately we didn't have the luxury of time on this one."

"I know I messed up, Lieu. I just want to get this scumbag." The room was closing in on Keri. She rubbed her sweaty palms across the cool fabric of her jeans-clad thighs.

"That's what we all want, Morgan, but patience and experience are our best weapons against this guy. As you said earlier, we can't rush him."

"I understand, boss. Do you want to replace me?" The words choked painfully from Keri's lips.

Beth slapped Keri playfully on the back and spoke for the first time. "Hell no, we're not replacing anybody." Acknowledging she'd overstepped, but showing no sign of remorse, she queried, "Are we, Lieutenant?"

"I'm not interested in replacing you at this point. We just need to be better prepared and more cautious in the future."

Keri thought the air around her seemed suddenly lighter. "Thank you, ma'am, I'll do better and I appreciate your being honest with me." She tried to smile but knew there was one more thing she needed to address with Alex Troy. "Lieutenant, could I have a minute when we're done, please?"

Beth sprang from her chair, as if on cue, and hovered at the door. "If you don't have anything for me, Lieu, I'll catch up with you later." Before Alex could answer, she disappeared, closing the door behind her.

"Fine," Alex replied through pursed lips. She fought the urge to follow Beth as emotional alarms vibrated through her system. "How can I help you, Morgan?"

"Lieutenant, I wanted to apologize. I shouldn't have—"

Alex stopped Keri with a vertical palm. She couldn't bear to relive the physical sensations as each word glided from Keri's inviting lips.

The thought dispatched delicate butterfly ripples to her clit that hit their mark with the ferocity of a sledgehammer. "It's not necessary to apologize. Whatever you did was part of the act and helped get us in with Davis."

"Right." But Keri couldn't leave it alone. She refused to accept that they could share a kiss so intense and walk away as if no connection existed. "And that crack I made in the car about touching. I just want you to know I wasn't trying to hurt you. If I was out of line, I'm sorry."

Alex felt her anger rise, the ever-present defense against all things emotional, but the sincerity in Keri's eyes stopped her usual outburst of indignation. "Thank you, I appreciate your honesty. Let's just forget it."

The knots in Keri's stomach grew tighter. Forget it? Would it be that easy? Alex's tone made it clear the conversation was over, but Keri sensed it was far from that. Sometime soon they needed to talk. Honestly. "Sure."

After Keri walked hesitantly out the door, the phone rang. Alex briefly debated not answering it so she could grab a quick breakfast, but the heavy weight of responsibility overtook her hunger. She scribbled a few notes, thanked the operator, and slumped against the side of her desk, trying to understand the possible significant of the message: *Please see Marilyn Carruthers at Granville Drug Rehab after 0800 hours. She has information about the Chambers death.*

Maybe this was the lead she'd been waiting for. Maybe finally someone knew something that could help the investigation. She stuffed the note in her pocket, grabbed her briefcase, and walked to her car.

❖

The Granville Drug Rehab office was located next door to the courthouse in an old gray one-story building. The location suited their clientele perfectly. They left court and reported immediately to drug rehab, and most never returned a second time. Alex had checked Byron Chambers's list of Stacey's contacts and found Marilyn Carruthers among the group of coworkers at the center. After identifying herself at the front desk, Alex was escorted to a small office at the back of the building.

A makeshift cardboard nameplate beside the door indicated the office of Marilyn Carruthers and Stacey Chambers. Alex's insides balked at the delicate handwriting she recognized as Stacey's. It bothered her that newbies were often relegated to the least desirable accommodations even though their enthusiasm usually surpassed the veterans'. She knocked on the door and a quiet voice asked her to come in.

Marilyn Carruthers introduced herself and motioned Alex to a chair. The young woman was Stacey's opposite, short and round, mousy-brown hair, unexpressive green eyes, and a voice that Alex had to strain to hear. The two of them had probably worked well together because they were so very different. Alex looked around the office trying to imagine Stacey working here.

The room was exactly as she expected: dated and dull. An old table served as a two-sided desk with straight-backed chairs on either side, scratched metal in-baskets at either end were piled high with files that threatened to topple over, and an institutional-green sofa against the wall sagged in the middle from years of use. The room spoke to the value placed on its occupants and their clients. Alex found it a sad commentary on the culture in general, and somehow insulting to the memory of a young woman she'd liked and respected.

"Your message said you had information for me."

Marilyn Carruthers looked conspiratorially around the room before answering. "It could be nothing, but the press release said any details might be of value." She waited for reassurance.

"That's right. You never know what could be helpful in a case like this. So, please, tell me what you know and I'll evaluate it."

With a sigh of relief Marilyn said, "Stacey was counseling an African American woman in drug rehab. They'd only been working together for a few weeks, but Stacey liked her and thought she had the potential to start over and make a better life for herself and her child." Marilyn stopped. She seemed reluctant to continue, as if embarrassed by revealing confidential information.

"Yes, and…?" Alex's impatience was getting the better of her. She fought an urge to take the soft-spoken woman by the shoulders and shake the information from her in one quick motion.

"This client not only used drugs, she also slept with the dealer for quite a while. She was finding it hard to extricate herself from that connection. The last time they talked, she told Stacey she was willing to testify against him if she could get protection."

Alex straightened in her chair. "Do you know when they had this conversation?"

"It would've been a few days before Stacey…" Marilyn's voice trailed off as tears gathered at the corners of her eyes.

"Stacey was a wonderful person," Alex reassured Marilyn in hopes she would continue. "She'll be missed by everyone who knew her." She patted Marilyn's hand and asked, "Did she say if she'd contacted anyone about this woman's testimony or made any arrangements to seek protection for her?"

Marilyn swiped at a loose strand of lifeless hair that fell across her forehead. "She just said they were going to talk to a friend of hers in Vice/Narcotics and set everything up after the community watch meeting. But then…well, you know."

Alex's throat tightened and she felt a pang of guilt rip through her. "Yes, I know."

It appeared a small light of recognition suddenly went off in Marilyn's eyes. "You were the person she was going to talk to in Vice/Narcotics, weren't you? I've just put it all together. She spoke of you often and with such high regard when she interned for you."

"Yes." Alex held back the surge of raw feelings that threatened to distract her from her purpose. "Marilyn, can you tell me this client's name or the name of the dealer?"

The woman's eyes lit up, "I can tell you both. She was Tiffany Brown. I'm not sure if that was her real name, but it's the one she used here and it checked out. And the dealer was Sonny Davis. He's supposed to be big time."

Alex wanted to reach across the table and hug Marilyn Carruthers within an inch of her life. This was the break she'd been waiting for. Struggling to contain her enthusiasm, she willed her voice to remain calm. "Is there anything else you can remember?"

"Not that I can think of. Stacey was so excited about helping this young mother and her child start over. It was going to be her first success story. She really loved this job and she was excellent at it."

"She was excellent at everything she did, from what I could see." Alex stood, shook Marilyn's hand, and started toward the door. "Thank you again for everything. Your information is important."

As she walked toward her car, Alex considered Marilyn's statement. She wondered what Davis's friends would think of him sleeping with an African American woman. His racist roots seemed pretty deep, except in the bedroom. If Tiffany had been sleeping with Sonny Davis, she'd probably have information about his contacts, his business schedule, how he replenished his stash, and maybe even where he kept the drugs. If he had realized that Tiffany wanted out and was talking to Stacey, he must have wanted to shut her up. Had he arranged for Stacey to be eliminated before she could go to the police with what she knew? A crack addict was easy enough to discredit, but a board-certified therapist, and a councilman's daughter to boot, wouldn't be so easily dismissed.

But if Davis had Stacey killed to keep her quiet, why didn't he kill Tiffany as well? Or did he? The first order of business was to have the team track down Tiffany Brown. If she was still alive, she could be the key to this whole case, of that Alex was sure.

❖

Keri hated the waiting—waiting for Davis to call for another meet, waiting to see Alex again, waiting for a chance to talk to her. Hurry up and wait. For the past few days the team had tailed Davis from bars and strip clubs to flophouses and back without learning anything significant, and no one could locate Tiffany Brown. Keri did her job, tried to keep the guys psyched, and pumped Beth for information about Alex. What else could she do but wait?

Her waiting came to an abrupt halt when Alex strolled into the lineup area. Everyone immediately straightened in their seats and the room seemed to crackle with excitement and anticipation. Keri never understood how Alex had such an effect on her troops, but it happened every time.

Keri's senses also sharpened but she was looking for something else, for some sign that Alex at least remembered their kiss. But there was no such indication. Alex avoided eye contact just as she'd avoided talking to her since that night, leaving Keri to think maybe she had just imagined it all, maybe she'd just wanted something magical to happen and her mind had played tricks on her.

"Sergeant Price briefed me on your progress," Alex said. "You've all done an outstanding job gathering information on Davis. I know it's been boring. Nobody likes grunt work, but I have a feeling that's about to change." She sat down at the head of the small conference table and continued. "Who has the intel on his associates?"

Paige Hunter, the shy DEA intelligence officer, shuffled some papers and said, "Yes, ma'am. Two have criminal records, two don't. James Fletcher, AKA Fletch, is Davis's right-hand man and they're childhood friends. He appears to be clean. Charles Randolph, nickname Dolph, has no record, but he's a suspect in three substantial fraud cases the Bureau is working. The victims in all three cases have either refused to cooperate or have disappeared."

Her partner, Rick Jones, spoke up with his country-boy charm. "And we all know what that means."

Paige grinned. "Now comes the hard stuff. Henry Watkins, AKA Hunk, is a former high school football star. He started using meth and ecstasy right after he graduated, and apparently supported his habit by committing armed robberies. He served three years at Crayton Maximum Security Prison."

"So we can assume quite a few criminal connections," Alex said pensively. "And Cappy?"

"Freddy Capanelli is also an ex-con. He served two years for assault with a deadly weapon with intent to kill, inflicting serious injury, and another year for attempted rape. The assault was on his then-girlfriend. He's a real nice piece of work. That's pretty much it."

Alex looked up from her notes. "What was Cappy's weapon of choice in the assault case?"

Paige flipped back through the file. "A 9mm Glock, which was never located, but three bullets were recovered from the victim and shell casings were found at the scene."

"Thanks, Paige, good work. Questions from anyone?" Alex waited, and when no one spoke, she continued. "We now have a pretty clear picture of Davis. His history, habits, associates, places he frequents, and where he might try to hide from us. How about Tiffany Brown? Does anyone have information on her yet? Do we know where she is?"

Keri tried unsuccessfully to meet Alex's eyes. "I spoke with my CI again last night and he provided a few names. People she knows and places she hangs out."

Alex nodded. "Follow up every possibility. We've got to find this girl before she turns up dead."

"Is there anything new on Stacey Chambers?" Beth asked.

Alex opened her case file and pulled out the autopsy results and toxicology report from the state lab. "I just got the reports back today. Stacey Chambers's COD was acute irreversible cardiovascular damage caused by a drug overdose. The tox report confirms it's the same as the ones found in the other victims and in the drugs we've purchased from Davis's dealers on the street—they're selling it as ecstasy, but the primary ingredient is PMA, not MDMA. It appears she probably ingested the substance in something she ate or drank at that meeting."

"I might be able to help with the how, Lieu," Steve Alston offered. "Our lab did a fingerprint analysis on the prints recovered at the scene. The drinking glass found next to Stacey's body had two sets of prints. One was hers and the other belonged to our missing witness, Tiffany Brown."

Alex considered this new information. It didn't make sense that Tiffany would intentionally give a spiked drink to Stacey. "Well, one thing is for sure, whoever this drink was intended for was intended to die. The dosage was so high there could be no other outcome. Were there any other prints of interest recovered, Steve?"

Alston scanned the report again before answering, "No, ma'am."

"Not exactly a smoking gun," Beth said.

Keri's undercover cell phone jingled to life as if on cue. She grabbed it off her waistband and placed it carefully on the table. There could only be a few possible callers, and Sonny Davis was the one she'd been expecting. "Everybody clear the area," Beth said. "Steve, hook up the recorder. If it's him, we want to be ready."

On Beth's cue, Keri took a deep breath and hoped she wouldn't sound as anxious as she felt. "Yes?"

"Yo, is this lovely Lynn who likes variety?" Davis's too-charming voice was unmistakable.

"Who is this?" Keri gave Beth a thumbs-up.

"It's your main man, Sonny. We met at Shelly's a while back."

"Oh, yeah, I remember now. What's up?"

"I was wondering if you and that hot little redheaded friend of yours were free on Saturday night. I'm arranging something special at the Gentlemen's Club and I sure could use some new scenery. Why don't you drop by?"

"Well…" Keri glanced toward Beth for the go-ahead, intercepting a sharp "ain't no way in hell" look from Alex. "I'm not sure if Kathy can make it, but I'll be there."

"Talk her into it. I'm partial to redheads. See you there." Then the line went dead.

Keri cringed at Davis's reference to Alex. She knew exactly what he meant, and it made her nauseous.

Steve pumped the air with his fist. "Yeah, now we've got a game."

"All right, guys, huddle up," Beth called to the group in the hallway.

Before the planning could begin, Alex got to her feet and asked Beth for a few minutes in her office. The sergeant didn't look at all surprised at the request.

"Steve, get a drawing of the location," Beth said. "Make coverage assignments and assess our vehicle situation. I'll be back in a second for the briefing."

Alex simmered with annoyance as they walked to her office. "You promised the last time was a one-shot deal," she said as soon as they were in private.

"At the time, I didn't know this was going to happen."

Alex presented the rational argument. "It's not appropriate for me to be a principal in an ongoing investigation. You know it as well as I do. I can't maintain objective oversight of the operation if I'm involved in it."

"Under normal circumstances I'd agree, but these aren't normal circumstances and Davis isn't an ordinary bad guy."

"I understand, but that doesn't help my dilemma."

Beth's stare was intent. "I think we both know your dilemma is more complicated than you want to accept."

Alex should have known Beth would call her on her feelings for Keri. The thought of spending time alone with her again, especially in the kind of scenario that weakened her will, tantalized and tormented her. She would never forgive herself if she blew this case because she couldn't be totally professional.

"We've got to be willing to bend the rules a little to catch Davis," Beth said. "Can you do that or should we just scrap the operation now and tell everybody to go home?"

"Don't be ridiculous. Of course I want to catch Sonny Davis. That's why I have to say no to this." She sighed. "You're right. It's complicated."

"You're worried about making the wrong move because Keri impairs your judgment?" Beth asked directly.

"Of course." There was no point pretending. Beth knew her too well.

"The wrong move is the one you're making right now," Beth said softly. "We have an opportunity, mostly thanks to you. How is it going to look if Keri shows up alone? More importantly, do you really think she can pull this off by herself? Is that a chance you're willing to take?"

Alex thought about Keri's impulsiveness and risk taking. This was a dangerous undercover operation. Davis and his thugs weren't stupid. One tiny misstep and Keri could not only blow it but place herself in serious danger.

"No," Alex said. "I can't take that chance."

"So, let's do this."

Alex nodded. "I just need to stay focused on the big picture."

"Thank you." Beth opened the door. Before she walked away, she said, "Everything will work out."

Alex didn't answer. Even if they managed to convict Davis and she got her promotion, she still wouldn't feel things had really "worked out" because she would be left wondering how to deal with Keri Morgan. If there was a successful conclusion to the Davis case, Keri would expect to join Vice/Narcotics permanently, and the chief would probably insist upon it. Alex would be stuck working with her indefinitely. How would she preserve her professional distance then?

She leaned against her closed door and cursed beneath her breath. As if that wasn't enough to unsettle her thinking, she now had to leave for a supervisor's meeting in Bedford, chief's orders. She knew who she could thank for that. Helen Callahan would expect her to stay overnight, since it was a five-hour drive, but Alex had no plans to be stuck in a hotel with her manipulative ex. Helen could go fuck herself, and Alex wouldn't be there to help.

Chapter Eleven

A lex claimed a seat at the mahogany bar in the Bedford Marriott lounge and idly cruised the new arrivals for a potential hookup. It had been too long since she'd allowed anyone to touch her body just for pleasure. Now she ached for it. Yet despite her cravings, nothing sparked. Her customary interest was absent. Her nerves already sizzled with fragility. Five hours on the road had failed to banish her fantasies of Keri. Instead she thought nonstop about the excruciatingly pleasurable dance at Shelly's bar and that unforgettable kiss.

Being away from home always made her melancholy for the things she'd left behind. This time, one of those things was Keri Morgan. She remained like a watermark in Alex's subconscious. Why was she so drawn to this woman that she couldn't get her out of her mind? Keri wasn't the first warm, honest woman she'd met, but none of the others had ever captivated her so completely. Alex wondered if she was simply needier now because of the changes in her life, or if those events had somehow changed what she wanted.

Other than her aberration with Helen, she'd always looked for brief, uncomplicated liaisons with women. Keri would never be one of those. Alex already knew that from just one kiss. Keri wanted more and if Alex were honest with herself, so did she. But the timing couldn't be worse. She wasn't ready for this, and maybe she never would be. Alex wasn't even sure if she was cut out for a long-term relationship with one woman.

She jerked the idea from her mind and placed her order for Stoli vodka and tonic. The handsome Latino bartender returned with her favorite cocktail a few minutes later and Alex knocked back a mouthful.

As warmth from the alcohol flooded her chest, she drove her thoughts to the other personal matter she was trying to ignore, her parents' house and the Trojan Horse.

Alex had reviewed the documents Norman had given her and was overwhelmed by the magnitude of her parents' estate. The stock shares themselves would be worth millions if she sold them outright. And the vacation homes were valued at several million. It seemed unfathomable that she could be the sole heir to such a fortune. What would she do with all that money—ever? But Alex had no specific feelings about being wealthy, beyond the numbing enormity of it all. She just couldn't grasp it yet. Her main concerns at the moment were expelling Keri Morgan from her thoughts before she became a greater problem and getting back to the case that would define her future.

Two task force members greeted her, looking tired and unhappy, obviously having made long drives themselves. Helen Callahan was conspicuously absent.

The DEA supervisor said, "Where's Callahan?"

Alex shrugged. "She hasn't arrived yet."

"She arranged this briefing in the first place," he said, confirming her suspicions. "What gives?"

Alex struggled to keep her face calm. She couldn't appear weak or ineffective to these men. It was so typical of Helen. Screw up and leave her the mess. But this time, whatever her game, she was toying with Alex's livelihood. The temptation to throw her to the wolves was strong. Alex didn't owe her shit.

"In all honesty, I don't know," she told her male colleagues. "I'm as surprised as you are, but Callahan seems to think the rest of us are just her cheerleading squad, or hadn't you noticed?"

She intercepted a startled look between the two men and smiled in satisfaction. It was out there now, the fact that she'd failed to stand by another female officer. They could interpret her antagonism toward Helen any way they wanted.

"Yeah, we noticed the attitude," the DEA supervisor said. "Jesus Christ. I left a search warrant on three meth labs for this."

Sounding equally disgusted, his companion said, "Get used to it. I've worked a few major cases with Callahan. If you want my opinion, she's a glory hog who gives her troops lousy leadership."

They sat down and ordered drinks, her new best friends. Over the next hour they took numerous trips to the buffet, discussed progress and strategies for the Sonny Davis investigation, and shared all the dirt they had on Helen. Both men were on the point of leaving when a briefcase landed in the spare chair at their table and a breathy voice announced, "I'm here."

"Captain Callahan." Alex stood and began gathering the files she'd referred to. "We were just winding up the meeting." Her two companions shook hands with Alex, grunted an obligatory farewell to Helen, and left.

When the men were out of earshot, Helen said, "Well, of all the nerve."

"I agree completely. How dare you schedule a meeting that wasn't necessary, five hours out of town, and inconvenience three people for your own selfish reasons? Since none of us knew what you really wanted, we discussed the case and adjourned." Alex gave Helen a scathing look and continued packing her briefcase.

A shocked expression skirted across Helen's face and disappeared just as quickly, replaced by the sultry visage of a seductress. She slid an arm around Alex's waist and whispered in her ear, "I'm certain you know what I want. You're the reason we're here and you knew it before you came."

The swell of heat that usually accompanied Helen's touch was noticeably absent, a fact that gave Alex great satisfaction. A line from *The Wizard of Oz* skipped through her mind: *Ding dong, the wicked witch is dead*. She stepped away from Helen's grasp and conceded, "Yes, I did. I decided it was time I stopped covering for you and started taking up for myself. Everybody sees through you, Helen. They know you're touting your own agenda for the credit and glory, and it's over. Stay out of this investigation from now on and out of my life."

"I can*not* believe you betrayed me to these *men*." Helen's face turned a bright shade of crimson as Alex's words registered. "Do you have any idea what you've done?"

"Of course. I told the truth. But more importantly, I stood up to you for the first time in my life. Never contact me again unless it's in a professional capacity." Alex turned and strode away.

Helen came after her, grabbing her arm in the lobby. "Alex, darling. Don't be like that." She stroked the hollow of Alex's cheek with her thumb and looked at her with those intense bedroom eyes.

Amazed that this woman still thought she could assume command of her life, Alex jerked free of her and said, "Touch me again and I'll bring charges. You're not in control anymore, Helen. Get used to it."

"Alex, you're not listening to me." Helen's words were like aspartame, sickly sweet and usually accompanied by hazardous results. "This is just a silly misunderstanding. I've missed you. Darling, can't we talk about this? I know it's been difficult for you."

Alex remembered those eyes on her body, those hands stroking and filling her with unbridled pleasure. Amazingly, the only sensation those memories evoked was distaste. "You're right. We do need to talk."

As if she'd been given a second chance, Helen's attitude changed from solicitous to in-charge. She steered them toward a love seat in a quiet corner of the lobby. "Mind if I get a drink?"

"Actually—"

"You don't expect me to have this conversation completely unfortified, do you?" Helen flagged down a passing barman and gave her order. Her palm was hot against Alex's leg as she kneaded the well-defined muscle in her thigh. "That's one thing I can always count on." She smiled up at Alex. "Even when we're fighting, your body still wants me."

Alex waited for the usual pulse to hammer in her crotch. Nothing. She drew a deep breath of relief. "Yes, Helen, we did have great sex," she said. "But it wasn't worth the price."

Helen flinched, but her recovery was almost immediate. "Will you ever forgive me? I'd like to make it up to you somehow."

Alex's mind flashed back to Keri. It had only been days ago that she leaned against Keri's chest as they danced, and listened to her heart pound. How could two women's touches feel so different and elicit such physically similar but emotionally diverse responses? Helen's calculating caresses only reminded her that their life together had been emotionally charged but substantively void. Keri offered something altogether different. She reminded Alex of life before Helen Callahan—love, possibility, hope—all the things Helen had denounced or destroyed.

"Helen, it's too late," Alex said flatly. "It's over." Her voice cut like a surgeon's knife, steady and sure.

Helen stopped, stared into Alex's eyes and dropped her hands into her lap. "You sound serious."

"I've never been more serious in my life."

The muscles around Helen's mouth tightened, but her eyes sparkled with challenge. Sparks of light flashed in her squinted eyes and her nostrils flared. Her gaze never leaving Alex's face, she taunted, "Like you have a better offer. Get real. Obviously she doesn't want you or you wouldn't be sitting here with your tail tucked between your legs, pretending we're saying good-bye for good. Let me guess, little Miss Innocent?"

Alex checked her rising anger, determined not to stoop to Helen's level. She got to her feet. "Here's your drink."

They were both silent as a waiter set the shot of bourbon on the low table in front of Helen.

"I'm going now," Alex said as soon as he moved away.

"Sure, you are." Helen downed the bourbon with one swift gulp and reached for Alex's hand. When she pulled away, Helen's shocked expression quickly turned to rage. "You have absolutely no idea what you're doing. Nobody walks away from me." As the distance between them grew, Helen's last desperate insult echoed through the hotel lobby. "After you've popped her cherry and get bored, don't expect me to be waiting."

Without looking back, Alex walked out the door and headed toward the parking lot, feeling Helen's hold on her heart and mind fall away.

❖

Steady rain, sharp lightning, and rumbling claps of thunder accompanied Alex on her journey back to Granville. As she drove, she relived Helen's shock and anger and smiled with sheer satisfaction. Finally their professional relationship could assume its appropriate place alongside the others in her life—no more important, no less. But it was the personal aspect that brought a smile to Alex's face. Helen's grip on her had ended, and Alex knew the change was permanent. She would never be affected by Helen again. The sway of her sexual prowess no longer existed for Alex. She wasn't excited or enticed in the slightest; in fact, thinking about Helen repelled her.

It was Keri's face that flashed constantly before her now, lips slightly parted, full and tempting. Alex wanted to feel those lips against hers, to have them explore and torment her body. She visualized Keri's firm body under her sliding, stroking, and screaming to orgasm. Alex imagined the lust and subsequent satisfaction in Keri's eyes as she came with Alex's fingers buried deep inside her. The image left her wet and weak. She tried to replace her fantasy with memories of past encounters and other lovers, but her attempt failed miserably, only increasing her craving for Keri.

She repeated the well-known admonishment that kept her at arm's length: Keri was a subordinate. Alex knew that fact alone could get her demoted or even fired. Such a breach of protocol was totally unacceptable. Yet she felt she'd go mad trying to contain her feelings and keep their contact strictly business. The hypnotic flapping of windshield wipers emulated the conflict in her mind: *It can work, no it can't, yes it can.*

Suddenly every encounter with Keri formed part of a larger picture that made sense to her, giving new context to her reactions. Her anger over the brunette's fondling of Keri in the police parking lot. Her conflict and procrastination about placing Keri on the task force. The electrifying results of Keri's first touch in the gym and their near kiss in the locker room. And finally that dance and their incredible kiss at Shelly's bar. Everything crystallized into pinpoint clarity. She was undoubtedly attracted to and sexually aroused by Keri, but there was more. No matter how professionally inappropriate or potentially painful, her feelings were inescapable. The unthinkable had happened; she was in danger of falling in love and she had no clue what to do about it. Her options seemed as clear as this dreadful weather.

Headlights from an approaching vehicle returned Alex to the business of getting home in one piece. They seemed to be the only cars on the road as she slowed to round Brighton's Curve. Rain pounded the windshield as jagged lightning dissected the night sky. Home was very close and she could hardly wait to relax in her own surroundings.

She squinted for visibility through the downpour. The oncoming car hit a puddle of water and hydroplaned out of control. Headlights suddenly veered into her lane of travel. She blew the horn but the vehicle continued its path toward her. Alex had only two choices: straight ahead into the lights or down the embankment.

❖

Keri was on her way home when the accident call was broadcast. Normally, she wouldn't have responded but there were no patrol cars in service and the accident involved personal injury. Even though she was no longer in uniform, she felt compelled to respond. She flipped the emergency switches and her unmarked car became a flashing, wailing chariot.

Cars jerked to the side of the road and intersections whizzed by as Keri negotiated the evening traffic, expertly shifting from gas pedal to brake, accelerating around the unobservant and slowing for the uncertain, just as her father had taught her when she was only ten. Lights created a spray of color through the heavy rain and coming night. As she approached Brighton's Curve, the traffic thinned out until there were no cars at all, much less signs of an accident. Maybe someone skidded off the road onto the muddy clay shoulder, righted himself, and continued on his way. Perhaps whoever phoned in was confused. They hadn't stayed at the scene, so perhaps there was nothing to see.

Keri positioned her car just off the shoulder of the road, grabbed her neon orange raincoat from the seat beside her, and pulled it on. Grumbling to herself and cursing the downpour, she retrieved her Maglite from its charger on the floorboard and sloshed her way to the steep embankment that gave way to Brighton's Creek fifty feet below.

Spiraling blue lights from her vehicle cast eerie dancing shadows through the saturated night. The sloping shoulder to the right of the roadway, once built up by gravel and rock, was now riddled with gullies. Pine trees and blossoming clematis covered the ridge leading down to the creek. As Keri splashed through standing water toward the apex of the curve, hairs on the back of her neck came to attention. Skid marks started on the pavement approximately twenty feet in front of her car heading toward the embankment. On the clay overhang, tire tracks continued over the edge of the precipice into the foliage below.

Keri peered over the side. A dark-colored full-sized vehicle was nestled precariously between two skinny pine trees about ten feet down on the side of the ledge. Keri couldn't tell if there were any occupants. If there were, they could be seriously injured and it would take a while to get them up the slick embankment. She began her hazardous descent toward the vehicle. The terrain seemed to shift beneath her tennis shoes. She'd have been happy for cleats and a tether but she settled for small shrubs that dotted the bank and prayed their rain-soaked roots would hold her weight.

"Is anybody down there?" She inched closer to the car and flipped on her Maglite to survey the stability of the vehicle's position.

She reeled at the sight before her. The car, a green Ford Crown Victoria, was wedged between the two small trees with its left front and right rear bumpers the only apparent means of support. Worse still, from the two antennas mounted on the trunk and the permanent tags, Keri realized with a sickening jolt that this was an unmarked police car. In the same instant she knew it was Alex's vehicle, and fear almost made her double over. Where was she?

Heat began to rise inside Keri's raincoat despite the chill that enveloped her. As she inched along the car, she clung desperately to a patch of kudzu that wrapped around the base of a small poplar tree. The flashlight in her right hand urgently intruded into the body of the vehicle, providing proof of its owner. A tan briefcase lay on the passenger side floorboard with the gold initials "KAT" gleaming in the stream of light. Keri had seen Alex carrying that case many times.

Terror gripped her throat as she tried to call out. Only a whisper escaped her lips. Steeling herself, she cried, "Alex! Can you hear me? Where are you?"

Rain beating against the side of the car was the only response.

Fastening her left arm around the pine tree at the car's front bumper, Keri leaned toward the driver's door and stuck her flashlight inside for one last look. At least Alex wasn't trapped in the car, injured and in need of medical assistance. A weakening dread passed through her as she took in a dark stain trailing across the upholstery from the driver's seat to the passenger door.

Without warning the rear end of the vehicle began to slide. Keri swung her weight toward the pine tree and wrapped her right arm around it for support. Her flashlight fell to the ground. The unmistakable sound of glass breaking and metal being crushed left Keri alone in the dark with no backup and no idea of Alex's location.

Keri clung to the lone pine with aching arms. She was soaked and couldn't see much, but she had to find Alex. She wasn't about to slide quietly down the slope. Using her left hand and foot, she made gouges in the hillside as she clung to the tree with her right arm. If she could make them deep enough to support her weight she could climb back out of this rain-drenched hell. Her fingers ached as nails cracked and broke away, but she still clawed at the muddy incline. As soon as tiny ruts appeared they filled with water and sloughed off down the bank. "I'm no quitter," she kept repeating to herself, digging harder.

"Officer, you down there?" A gruff male voice called from the top of the ridge.

It seemed to Keri she'd been hugging that pine tree for hours, calling for Alex. "Yeah, I'm here, but the car's a goner. There was somebody in that vehicle and I have to find her." Keri called back up the bank.

"Just hang on, lady. I'm the wrecker driver and you ain't findin' nobody till I get you outta there. I'll light up the place with my spots and drop you a line."

After what seemed an eternity the towrope appeared and Keri grabbed hold.

"Can you climb or do I gotta haul you up?" he hollered.

"You'll probably have to winch me out of here. The hillside is completely washed away down to the clay." Her muscles ached with tension from the ordeal. Her feet slipped, sending her belly first into the red mud and sharp undergrowth as she tried to leverage herself upward. *Please let me get out of here soon so I can find Alex. She has to be all right.* When she finally saw lights at the top of the rise, she reached out her hand and was drawn swiftly over the edge onto solid ground by the wrecker driver's massive bulk.

Beth Price and several uniformed officers and paramedics rushed to her side.

"Are you okay, Keri?" Beth's face registered concern as she gave her a visual once-over. "Let the EMTs check you out. You're bleeding."

"I'm fine, Sarge, really. It's just a few scratches. Look, this is important. That's Lieutenant Troy's car down there."

"Yeah, we know."

"I'm not sure where she is, but I think she may be bleeding." Beth's comment finally registered. "What do you mean, you know? We have to find her."

"Calm down, Keri. We already have. Or rather, she found us. She managed to crawl out of the car when it wedged against the trees before the rain got too heavy. She got to a house and the folks there called in just as she passed out. I think her ankle's badly bruised and she probably has a light concussion. She can't walk too well, but she's in my car."

Not waiting to hear the rest, not caring about anything except confirming Alex was all right, Keri sprinted to the sergeant's car, her legs suddenly adrenaline-powered. As she neared the vehicle the pale dome light shone on rain-soaked auburn hair and Alex turned to greet her through the open passenger window. She had a cut lip, and blood from a raised knot on her forehead covered the left side of her face.

"Oh, my God," Keri gasped.

"Do I look that bad?" Alex winced from an attempt to smile.

"God, I'm glad to see you." Keri reached hesitantly through the window, hand outstretched, afraid of Alex's response. Sensing no indication of withdrawal, Keri delicately outlined Alex's jaw with her finger. As she stroked Alex's face, their eyes met and held in an admission of mutual caring that left Keri drained of strength but charged with emotion. Her eyes clouded with tears, and she said hoarsely, "I've never seen anyone more beautiful in my life."

The words filled Alex's heart as her pulse pounded faster in her aching head. "Do you always say exactly what's on your mind, Morgan?" Her smile assured Keri that she was teasing. Noticing Beth's approach, she said more formally, "I'm really all right, Keri. But you look a little ragged. Do those scratches hurt?"

"Not really. I'll be fine."

"Keri, about the last few days—"

"The only thing that matters now is that you're here and you're okay. I know you need space when you're confused."

Alex frowned in puzzlement. How could Keri possibly know what she needed? And yet… Catching Beth's attention, Alex called, "Have the paramedics checked Morgan for injuries?"

"What about you, Lieutenant?" Keri tried to argue.

"Don't worry about the lieutenant," Beth said. "I'm taking her home right now. That's where she was headed when some idiot ran her off the road. She refuses to go to the hospital."

"Was this a hit-and-run?" Keri asked. "Did he make contact? Did you get a description of the car and driver?"

"It was a big, older model car," Alex replied. "I couldn't tell anything about the driver in the heavy rain. But I don't think it was intentional. The car just hydroplaned."

Beth patted Keri on the shoulder and directed her toward the ambulance. "Don't worry about it. The uniform guys have already broadcast an alert. They'll run it down. Now, go let the medics take a look at you."

Rain dripped off Keri's hair and ran down her back as she turned reluctantly from Alex and walked toward the waiting ambulance. "Sergeant, are you sure the lieutenant will be all right?"

"Absolutely, and so will you." As Keri climbed into the back of the ambulance, Beth muttered, "But I don't think it's the physical injuries either of you need to worry about."

Her comment was almost drowned out by another torrent of blowing rain, and Keri thought she'd probably misheard the faint humor in her tone.

Chapter Twelve

When Alex entered the lineup area late Saturday afternoon the assignments had already been made and the officers were preparing to leave. Her walk showed little sign of her ankle sprain. Even the cuts and bruises to her face and lip had almost vanished. She'd disguised the final traces with careful makeup. As the troops filed from the room, she handed Keri a razor-thin cell phone.

"Wear this."

Keri frowned. She'd expected to be wired. "It's a cell phone."

"And a transmitter. When the time is right, we'll be able to hear everything that's going on. It won't help us much in a noisy bar but we can send you text messages if we need to."

"You two get going and be careful." Beth patted Keri on the shoulder and handed her the Corvette keys.

Before Alex could speak, Keri said, "I know. Don't wreck the 'Vette. By the way, Chad called. He says Tiffany is running scared, but he can find her. It may take a few days."

"Good work," Beth replied. "Keep this up and you'll be my prize pupil."

Alex leaned toward Beth and whispered, "I'm going to need that weekend at the lake you keep talking about. And copious amounts of alcohol will be involved." She followed Keri toward the parking lot to get the 'Vette.

On the way to the club, Alex filled every minute with final instructions and reminders. She couldn't afford to indulge the attraction she felt toward Keri. "Your main purpose tonight is to entice Davis, make him feel comfortable, and make him want more. We wait for him to bring up the subject of drugs. Anything else would raise suspicion."

Keri responded with nods and mumbled acknowledgments. When she could no longer contain the need to be on a more personal level with Alex she asked, "You really liked Stacey Chambers, didn't you?"

Alex looked at Keri's profile as she drove, wondering how this young woman sliced through her carefully constructed façade to the very heart of her. "Yes, I did."

"What was so special about her? I mean, she worked for you. How did you get so close?"

"It wasn't really anything she did, exactly. It was more about who she was. Something about her attitude was contagious. She believed in possibility and wanted everyone to have a fair chance. She was incredibly hopeful and honest." As Alex described Stacey she realized that the same words could easily be said of the woman next to her.

"She sounds a lot like my friend Josh," Keri said. "He was a great believer in the potential of the human spirit. Any cause that came along, he was on board. I used to tell him that he was burning his candle too brightly, that he needed to slow down or he'd spontaneously combust. I had no idea I'd lose him so soon." Her voice cracked and she clutched the steering wheel tighter.

Alex reached across the seat and placed her hand on Keri's knee. "I know how you feel. We never expect to lose those bright spots in our lives, ever." Keri's pain and empathy struck an all-too-familiar chord, peeling away another layer of Alex's resistance. She withdrew her hand to refocus on the job. "Do you have any questions about our purpose tonight?"

Keri had plenty of questions but none of them were work related. In the five days since the accident, Alex's demeanor had been different. The professional barrier was still in place, but Keri felt somehow more connected to her personally. Some of the emotional separation seemed to have been replaced by a cautious watchfulness. Keri didn't really understand how or why the change had occurred, but it gave her hope for their future. She wanted to talk with Alex about what was happening between them but that conversation would have to be put on hold as they pulled into the lot at the Gentlemen's Club.

Alex watched Keri walk toward the entrance, feeling against all reason like she was leading the lamb to the slaughter. Keri wore black skintight leather pants and a red stretch top. It didn't take imagination to see the dips and curves of her body as she moved. Alex wanted to stop this whole process, start over, reconsider, and choose another primary officer. But it was much too late to back out now, and besides, Keri was doing a good job.

A waiting line stretched out the front door of the upscale club. Chad appeared from the crowd, whispered to the bouncer, and led them inside. "Sonny's been waiting for you." He pulled Keri aside, telling her, "I tracked Tiffany down tonight, but she won't talk to anybody but you. I told her she can trust you."

"Good, call me with the details tomorrow."

The dimly lit building vibrated with earsplitting music. High-beamed ceilings and painted concrete walls made it look like a warehouse that had been converted into a meat market for sexual predators. Scantily clad women balanced trays of cocktails and delivered them to eager patrons with a personal touch. Nude and seminude strippers gyrated on the raised performance platform vying for attention and tips. The atmosphere was heavy with smoke and the stench of stale sex.

Sonny Davis and his cronies held court in front of the stage watching the strip show. He had a woman on each arm. His face lit up as Keri and Alex approached.

"Hey, the girls I've been waiting for. Vodka tonic and beer, right? Get these ladies a drink, Amber," he cooed to one of his arm decorations and motioned to Keri and Alex. "Have a seat." He patted sleek cushioned chairs on either side of him.

Fletch rose beside Davis to pat the women down, but Davis waved him off. "They're fine."

The hairs on the back of Alex's neck bristled. She didn't like having Davis between her and Keri. The first rule of engagement was divide and conquer. Davis was a slick one, all right.

Davis gave Keri and Alex a quick up-and-down appraisal, then addressed Keri. "You've never been to a strip club before, have you?"

Keri looked away from the g-string-clad dancer humping a pole on stage. "What gave you that idea?" She blushed, embarrassed for Davis or Alex to think her inexperienced. She'd been in plenty of places like this, but never with her mind so singularly focused on one woman. If she was going to make this work, she had to get her head out of her pants and play her part.

"But you"— Davis turned his attention to Alex—"I bet you've seen plenty of naked women."

The way Davis leered made Keri want to use his pretty face for a punching bag.

Alex answered in a seductive tone Keri had never heard. "As a matter of fact, I have. My ex-boyfriend loved titty bars. It's the reason we finally broke up. He didn't know the difference between looking and touching."

"Too much of a good thing, huh?" Davis waved the other two women away and scooted his chair closer to Alex.

When their drinks arrived, Keri gulped down part of her beer more quickly than she intended and immediately felt the results. Watching Davis eyeballing Alex, she fought the urge once again to throttle him. Her head began to pound. She pressed against her temples and tried to focus on her surroundings. Tonight she'd detected a familiar bulge under Cappy and Hunk's jackets and the outline of an ankle holster under Fletch's pant leg. The men hadn't been armed at Shelly's. Her eyes burned in the smoky room and her vision blurred. She finished her beer in two gulps and caught a subtle warning look from Alex. Her meaning was clear. She and Keri weren't armed, a definite disadvantage when the men around them were. They needed to stay sharp and focused.

Davis snaked his arm around Keri's chair and leaned into her. "Ever think about doing that for a living? With a body like yours, you'd rake in the cash." He nodded toward the stage and slid a finger down the length of her arm.

Keri cringed inwardly but forced herself not to let it show. Davis's eyes held the glazed-over expectancy typical of drunk, horny, and demanding men. "Not really. I don't have the right moves."

"Maybe you just need a few lessons." He continued to stroke her arm as he watched Alex for a reaction.

Alex couldn't hear what Davis was saying, but from the look on Keri's face it wasn't anything she wanted to hear. Anger boiled inside, and she reminded herself that this was part of the job, no matter how disgusting. Her grip tightened automatically on her glass as she pretended to laugh at one of Fletch's off-color jokes.

When Alex returned her attention to Keri, she was being led to the dance floor by Davis. It took all her strength to remain seated and let the younger officer handle the situation. To do anything else would've blown their cover.

Sonny Davis slid his arm around Keri's waist and pulled her into his body. She felt the hard muscles along his chest and pelvis against her softer flesh and cringed. The urge to resist was almost unbearable.

"So how long have you and the redhead been together?"

"Not long," she answered, stealing a quick glance in Alex's direction to be sure she was okay.

"I bet she's hot in bed. She's the silent type that screams like a banshee when you fuck her. Am I right or what?" Davis rubbed his chest against Keri's breasts and backed her into a darkened corner of the dance floor.

A wave of disgust and anger churned in Keri's stomach. A knee to the nuts would probably get his mind off sex, but if she stayed focused there would be a bigger payoff than watching him writhing on the floor holding his balls. But her head was pounding like a jackhammer driving rivets behind her eyes.

"I get it, you don't kiss and tell." Davis slid his hands down Keri's back and pumped his hips forward. "My kind of woman, the kind that don't tell."

"And you're my kind of man, strong and sexy as hell. But don't you have an old lady?" The words almost hung in her throat as she allowed Davis to grind his pelvis against hers.

"Up until a couple of weeks ago. She thought she could fuck me over. Nobody fucks Sonny Davis without a personal invitation."

"I bet she's pushing up daisies somewhere in the des-sert." Keri's speech slurred and she wondered how one beer could have such an effect. She shook her head from side to side, which only served to make her dizzier.

"Not yet, but soon."

Memorizing Davis's words verbatim for future reference, Keri tried to sound sympathetic without being overly solicitous. "I don't blame you, man. Fuck a double-crossing bitch."

Sonny nodded. "I knew you'd get it. You're one of those broads that got a double dose of the loyalty gene."

"Damn straight." Keri nuzzled the side of Sonny's neck and almost puked at the strong taste of his aftershave.

"Look, I like you and your friend. We could do some serious business together. You girls can get my product into the women's scene around town. My guys can't touch those places. There're big bucks to be made with the dykes, all that disposable income and high drama. They're always in need of a fix of some kind. What do you think?" He emphasized the question with another hip thrust.

Keri's vision blurred and two grinning Sonny Davises smiled down at her. "I think you talk too much and don't take enough action. Bring it on. We can handle whatever you got."

Davis laughed and maneuvered Keri on the dance floor until they were in front of Alex's table. "I believe you probably can."

Alex watched Sonny rake his fingers through Keri's hair and trace the angle of her jaw to the edge of her lips. If he tried to kiss her, Alex knew she wouldn't be able to contain her rage regardless of the effect on the case. The fact that he was breathing the same air so close to Keri made her want to choke him with her bare hands. He squeezed Keri's upper arms, slid his hands behind her, and kneaded her back down to her buttocks.

The bulge in Davis's pants became increasingly obvious as he moved his determined strokes up and down Keri's body again, lingering on her butt. His eyes were glassy and unfocused, but it was Keri's expression that worried Alex more. The usual soft candor of her gaze had given way to a distant edge. The change could not have been caused by a single glass of beer.

Alex stood, checked her temper, and sauntered over. With a slight pout, she ran her hand up the inside of Davis's leg and crooned in her sexiest voice, "You're making me jealous, Sonny." She licked her lips and breathed on his face. "God, I'm so horny."

Davis dropped one hand from Keri's butt and hooked his arm through Alex's. "Well, bring it on. Your girlfriend and I were just getting things cranked up. I'd love to make it three-way. Damn, that would be hot and a great way to seal a partnership."

Alex let her fingers linger inches from Davis's crotch. "Hold that thought. Gotta use the restroom."

He nodded, his mouth agape.

Alex extended her hand for Keri's. "Come on, Lynn. After all that beer, I *know* you need to go, too."

Keri cast a slightly vacant look at Sonny, who slapped her ass and said, "Don't keep me waiting."

Alex slid an arm around Keri's waist and led her to the restroom. When they were safely inside the single-seat facility, she locked the door and pushed Keri against it.

"Are you all right?" She leaned into Keri's space and examined her face.

"Yup, I'm fine, boss."

"You don't look so great. Your eyes are glazed over, your face is flushed, and you're slurring like a drunk. I'm going to call this off."

Keri stared at Alex's hands that still gripped her waist. "You know, I think this is the third time you've touched me. They say third time's the charm."

Alex started to withdraw, as if she'd just noticed the touch herself, but Keri grabbed her hands. "Don't...I like the way it feels." She cupped Alex's hands on her narrow waist.

Sparks shot through Alex's body, bringing blood and passion to the surface. She'd felt like this before holding Keri—so very right. Yet the circumstances this time were horribly wrong. Keri's eyes were wide, her pupils constricted and cloudy with confusion or intoxication.

Keri leaned forward and framed Alex's face in her hands. "You are so fucking beautiful. All I've thought about for days was how it felt to kiss you." She licked her lips and moved closer. Alex felt hot breath against the side of her face and waited for the kiss. Keri's hands drew her nearer. Her body strained against the fabric that separated them. Urgency grew in the pit of her belly and the craving would not be still.

Keri whispered, their lips close enough to touch, "I was so afraid that night at Brighton's Curve. I don't know what I would've done if I'd lost you. Do you have any idea how much I care about you? How badly I ache for you all the time?" Her hands slid up Alex's sides, palmed her breasts, and thumbed Alex's taut nipples into hard pinpoints of sensation. "I need you so much. Please, Alex."

Please? No one had ever *asked* her to let them love her. She'd been told what she wanted plenty of times and taken when she wasn't sure what she wanted. But that simple word combined with Keri's skillful foreplay made Alex's resistance almost futile. Her body had given up already. She wanted Keri with every cell in her body, but this was not the time or the place.

Alex steeled herself against the loss she knew would hit the minute she broke contact with Keri and stepped back, forcing Keri to release her grip. "That's it. We're definitely out of here. Splash some water on your face. I'll make excuses to Davis. Meet you back at the table."

Keri shook her head, producing a light wave of dizziness. She turned toward the sink, scooped cold water in her hands, and buried her face in it. The shocking contrast of icy water on her skin did little to cool the burn that seemed to scorch her from inside out.

"Please don't call it off, Alex." She lifted her hands away from her face and turned around. Alex was gone.

❖

When Alex exited the restroom, the house lights were on. She was so angry she stood in the shadows and took several deep breaths. *How dare that scum-sucking bastard drug one of my officers?* She waited for Keri, returned to the table, and asked Dolph where she could find Davis. He motioned toward a private lounge area in the back.

She followed his directions and found Fletch and Cappy standing in front of a door that led into a private dance room. "I need to see Sonny."

"Can't right now. He's busy." Fletch nodded toward the door. She could hear raised voices coming from the room.

She sighed in phony disappointment. She helped Keri into a chair and said, "Wait here a sec. I have to make a call, then we're leaving."

"You're going somewhere?" Fletch asked with an edge of suspicion.

"Yeah, we are." Alex gave him some attitude. "We were all set to party, but some asshole slipped something in Lynn's drink and now she's getting sick. Ruined the whole fucking night for us."

"Sonny won't be happy."

Alex flipped out her cell phone. "You can tell him I'm real disappointed, but what's a girl gonna do? I guess we'll hook up another time."

Fletch absently waved her off, turned his back, and motioned a dancer over with his other hand. Alex saw her opportunity while Fletch and Cappy played grab ass. Walking away with the cell phone to her ear, she kept an eye on them. When they were fully preoccupied and no one else was paying attention, she ducked into the room next to Davis's. She let her eyes adjust to the darkness. The smell of spent passion from a single sofa in the room wafted to her nostrils and made her nauseous. She inched closer to the adjoining wall and placed her ear to the cheap divider.

"What the hell's your problem, Tiffany?" Davis's voice boomed.

A scared, female voice answered, "I don't know what you're talking about, baby."

Davis made a disgusted noise. "I heard you were going to the cops on me."

"Ain't no way, Sonny. I swear it. I got my baby to think about."

Davis's voice had the edge of barely controlled anger. "Then what the hell are you doing hiding from me?"

Tiffany's voice trembled as she tried to explain. "I wasn't hiding from you. Haven't you heard about that dead woman, the councilman's daughter? The cops are after me about that. Ask Cappy where he found me. I was getting a bus ticket to get my baby out of town. I can't take no murder rap."

"Why would they think you had something to do with that?" Davis's voice still sounded skeptical.

"That's what I'm saying. Word on the street is she was poisoned or drugged and I was there. That's all I know. You gotta help me, baby. We were good together. You know it."

Davis's cruel laugh vibrated through the walls and Alex shivered. "Ain't that justice for you? That damn drink was meant for you. I thought you were informing on me. I had one of my boys passing out drinks at the meeting. You must've given it to the Chambers girl. There was enough in that thing to kill a horse."

Tiffany started crying. "I can't believe you tried to kill me. I swear, Sonny, I never double-crossed you. I love you, baby."

"We'll see about that. I don't have time to deal with this shit now." A loud thump against the wall startled Alex back into the corner of the room. "Cappy, get your sorry ass in here."

"Yeah, boss?"

"Take Tiffany to my safe house on the east side and stay with her. Don't let her out of your sight. If you lose her, it's your ass. Got it?"

"Sure thing, boss."

Alex had heard enough. Her muscles tightened with loathing for Sonny Davis. His comments were not only incriminating, but they just might be the final nail in his coffin in Stacey's case. She peeked out the door, saw that Fletch was still occupied with the dancer, and headed back to the table. Keri was sitting with Hunk and Dolph, looking like a dejected child.

"Lynn, we have to go." Alex's tone left no room for argument. She helped Keri to her feet, arms around her waist, and guided her to the front door.

"Hey, where you going?" Dolph called after them.

"Some sick fuck put something in her drink. We'll party another time," Alex shouted back, already halfway across the room.

When they returned to the car, Alex radioed for a marked unit to stop Cappy's car when it left the club. It was to look like a routine traffic stop. When they found Tiffany Brown, they were to arrest her on suspicion of murder. Under no circumstances was she to be allowed to post bail. If there were any papers on Cappy, they were directed to serve them; if not, to release him. She told Beth what she'd heard between Davis and Tiffany. She wanted Steve to take a sworn statement from Tiffany before morning. She also told Beth that she'd take Keri home. Her instructions were for Beth to pick Keri up the next day.

Clear of the club, Alex drove in silence and fumed inside. First thing tomorrow, Beth would get Keri to the hospital for a blood test. Confirmation of drugs in Keri's system would be essential, even though they'd never be able to prove who actually spiked her drink. She thought of Josh's death and knew Keri would go ballistic when she found out about her own drugging.

Alex knew it was her fault. She was responsible for keeping things under control. It was her job to anticipate anything. Her focus should've been strictly on Davis and his associates, not wandering to Keri and worrying about her. She'd failed the operation, her experience, and most of all, Keri. Costly mistakes were often the result of mixing business with pleasure.

Keri shifted toward the console and leaned her head against Alex's shoulder. Her condition seemed to have deteriorated since leaving the club. She looked up through bloodshot eyes and said, "I'm really sorry. I messed up, didn't I?" She stroked Alex's arm, let her hand rest over Alex's on the console and entwined their fingers.

The delicate caress raised goose bumps that raced to Alex's center and exploded into heat. *This is exactly what I was just kicking myself for*. But still she didn't stop Keri.

"I've got to tell you something, Alex." Keri's voice wandered and slurred. She released Alex's fingers and placed her hand on Alex's thigh. "It's important."

Alex's breath caught in her throat. "Save it for another day. You'll be glad you did."

Keri's head was spinning, but she continued, "I'm not sorry I touched you. I wanted—"

"Don't say any more. Please, Keri."

"I've been having these feelings ever since I met you. We both know I'm no good at hiding how I feel." All of a sudden a dim light went on in Keri's head and she struggled to sit up. "Omigod, am I fired?"

"No, you're not fired. You're just a bit drunk, so I won't hold anything you say against you. Is this your house?"

Keri pointed to the John Deere mailbox with her father's name on it. "Yep, that's me, country bumpkin Keri Lynn Morgan. You can let me out here. I don't want to wake my folks."

"I'll make sure you're safely inside."

Alex helped Keri up the steps, through the screened-in porch, back door, and into her bedroom. The smell of fried chicken filled the house and reminded Alex she hadn't eaten since breakfast. It was easy to picture Keri in the modestly furnished farmhouse caring for her parents with the loyalty and hard work such a place inspired.

Keri's small bedroom was fairly nondescript with the exception of a hand-knitted comforter at the foot of her bed and two framed pictures on the dresser. One photograph was her mother, apparent by Keri's striking resemblance to her. Her mother was pinning her badge on at the graduation ceremony from the academy. The other was a handsome young man with jet-black hair and blue-gray eyes.

Noticing the direction of Alex's gaze, Keri said, "That's Josh, my first true love. No sex, but love just the same. I was closer to him than my own brother."

Alex flinched as she imagined Keri in anyone's arms but hers.

Keri continued, her words becoming more slurred. "He died a year ago, too. 'Member I told you a fuckin' doper slipped him an overdose at a frat party? He didn't even do drugs." Her blue eyes turned stormy as she stared at the picture.

Alex knew this was the reason Keri needed so desperately to be on the task force. It was about revenge. She'd gotten her own powerful lesson about revenge from Helen. It could serve as a motivator but also led to poor judgment. She hoped Keri would not fall prey to bad decisions she would later regret.

Keri looked away from the photograph and snickered. "How about that?" She stripped down to her thong without the slightest hesitation or embarrassment. "I got you into my bedroom on our first date."

Alex stared, openly admiring Keri's strong body and resisting the temptation to touch her, just once, to feel that hot silky skin respond to her searching fingers.

"Wait. I'll be right back." Keri steadied herself along the furniture and hallway to the bathroom. She returned a few minutes later smelling of soap and toothpaste. She jumped into the four-poster bed and snuggled under the covers.

"Are you okay?" Alex sat on the edge of the bed, trying desperately to suppress her desire.

"I'd be better than fine if you'd do me one little itsy-bitsy favor." Keri's head felt like someone had blown insulation in through her ears.

"And what's that, Officer Morgan?" Alex asked as she tucked the covers around Keri's neck.

"Kiss me. Every time I see you, that's what I want." She grinned like a kid asking for an ice cream before dinner.

The request burned through Alex. More than anything she wanted to say yes, but that would be totally selfish and very unfair. "Go to sleep, Morgan. You've had a rough night."

Keri wanted to object but she couldn't speak anymore. She felt too sleepy to move, or talk, or reach out. Alex was so close, but she felt far away. As Keri drifted into a deep, inebriated sleep she thought she felt Alex's cool, soft lips against her burning forehead. With a sigh of contentment, she gave in to the fog closing on her mind. Alex liked her. The thought made her smile.

❖

On the drive home Alex called Beth. "I want you to make sure Morgan gets to the hospital tomorrow for a blood test. I want her checked for drugs, especially roofies. I know it's Sunday but it has to be done tomorrow ASAP."

Beth wanted details.

"She was out of it and I want to know why. I think somebody put something in her drink. On your way, ask her about tonight. See what she remembers. Make her be specific."

"You got it, boss. You're still coming up to the lake tomorrow, right? We've still got a couple of days off with the holiday on Monday."

"You better believe it. I need a break."

As Alex drove, Keri Morgan's face and near-naked body refused to leave her mind. She'd been unable to resist a single, light kiss to Keri's forehead after tucking her safely into bed. Would Keri remember the kiss or any of the heart-wrenching comments she'd made on their way home? *I know I'll never forget.*

CHAPTER THIRTEEN

Keri stood in the shower and allowed the cold stream of water to assault her body into consciousness. She'd slept through the alarm, which she didn't remember setting, and was still in bed when Beth called and said she was coming to pick her up. Her head felt like it was filled with steel wool, cold and abrasive and unable to produce discernable memories of the night before. As she pulled on her jeans and T-shirt, she tried to remember where she'd left her car. How had she gotten home? She peeked into her mother's bedroom, smiled at the peacefully sleeping frame, and rushed to the unmarked police car in her driveway.

"I thought you had today off, Sarge."

"I do, but before I go you and I have to talk." Beth waited for her to settle into the passenger seat then began the inquisition. "What happened last night?"

Keri toyed with the idea of making something up so she wouldn't sound like a total incompetent but opted for the truth. "I have no idea, Sarge. The last thing I remember clearly is drinking a beer in the club. I have some fuzzy images but nothing specific after that. Did I blow the case?"

"No, Alex called it off. She thought you might've been drugged. We're going to get you tested right now."

For the first time Keri noted the concern in Beth's voice and her death grip on the steering wheel. Her own skin started to flush as anger boiled to the surface. "You mean one of Davis's cronies slipped something into my beer?" She thought of Josh and could barely contain her emotions. "That son of a bitch. I'll—"

"Let's hold off on the threats until we know for sure. If this thing happened, we'll make it right. You're not alone, Keri." She paused for a moment, her expression thoughtful. "Listen, I think you need to take a couple of days off."

"No, I'll be fine. I'm just a bit fuzzy this morning."

Beth shook her head. "Go back in the house and throw some clothes in a bag. You're coming out to the lake with me."

"The lake?"

"You heard me." Beth tapped her wristwatch. "They're expecting you at the hospital. You've got ten minutes. We'll leave town right after they're done with you."

Keri couldn't think of a reason not to go. When she'd talked with Pat a couple of days earlier, she'd even suggested some time off to get away from Alex Troy, just to think about things. And the personal invitation meant a lot coming from her sergeant. Flattered, Keri said, "Thanks. I don't know what to say."

As she hurried away to collect some clothes, she heard Beth mumble something. It sounded like, "Don't thank me just yet."

❖

Keri sat in the waiting room and mentally plowed through the last twelve hours. Someone had to have drugged her because one beer had never affected her that way. She remembered drinking the beer and then piercing brown eyes boring into hers while strong hands encircled her waist. Maybe it had been Alex. The touch had seemed gentle. It felt like Alex's touch—but how could she know?

A flash of memory poked at her, a firm arm around her waist supporting and guiding. Her frustration grew as she was unable to discern real events from fuzzy images. The pulse at her temples pounded fiercely the more she tried to recall. A light tap on the shoulder startled her, and she looked up at a nurse.

"Officer Morgan?" The young woman motioned her to follow.

When they reached one of the examination rooms at the rear of the facility, Keri sat on the bed and followed instructions. The nurse tucked Keri's arm under hers, applied the blood pressure cuff, and slid a thermometer under her tongue. Her gentle touch brought another image to mind. Keri's hand was resting on Alex's, their fingers entwined. Fiery heat spread through her body. The feeling was so intense, then and now, she knew it was real.

"I don't know what just happened, but your pulse and temperature just spiked. Are you feeling okay?" The nurse removed the thermometer and inadvertently touched Keri's lip.

The sensation spiraled directly to her core and she remembered "*Kiss me...*" Alex's surprised face and tempting lips were very close to hers. She *had* actually asked Alex Troy to kiss her last night. And she was just as certain Alex had declined. Keri would definitely remember if they'd kissed.

"I'm all right," she finally responded to the nurse. But she wasn't at all sure if that was true.

"Okay, I'll be back in a minute to draw your blood for the test." The young woman left her alone with her disjointed thoughts and confused feelings.

Keri sifted through the evening's events again and felt Alex's warm hands stroking her arms, her firm grip closing around her waist, and her lips a breath away from kissing hers. Shifting uncomfortably on the examining table, she clamped her thighs around the painful ache, then slipped her hand between her legs and closed her eyes. She imagined Alex cupping her sex, feeling the evidence of arousal that soaked the crotch of her jeans, sliding her fingers along the sides of Keri's pulsing clit and stroking slowly up and down.

Pressure built like a hungry beast in Keri's center. She had never wanted anyone so much. Placing her other hand over the one that tormented her, Keri squeezed and imagined Alex's lips, full and wet like the flesh that throbbed between her legs. All she needed was one kiss from Alex and she'd come. She needed that kiss desperately.

A light knock at the exam room door jolted her back from near orgasm. She rubbed her hands briskly over her jeans-clad legs and tried to regain her composure. "Come in," she croaked.

As the nurse prepared to take a blood sample, Keri took deep, calming breaths. She had almost brought herself to orgasm in the hospital while fantasizing about her lieutenant. When had her feelings completed their gradual change from distrust and caution to attraction and longing? Reluctantly, Keri relived that confrontational interview with Alex once more. Her feelings were intense, but not the same as before. The outrage and righteous indignation had faded. This time, she could isolate Alex's words and nonverbal responses from her own defensive reactions. Alex had phrased her questions very carefully. In retrospect, none of them sounded accusatory, simply pointed and probing like any good investigator's.

Alex had been hand-picked by the chief to conduct the investigation and had simply been doing her job. It was a high-profile case with serious allegations against Keri and her partner. And Keri hadn't made it easy for Alex to determine the facts. Her answers had been evasive and emotional. Even a rookie knew what that suggested—deceit.

But she hadn't been dishonest, had she? Keri replayed the scenario in her head: arriving at the scene of a fight call, running to the rear of the apartment, and finding her partner, Brian Saunders, lifting a handcuffed suspect to his feet. She had seen the injuries to the suspect's face and head and had assumed the other combatant was responsible. Brian told her a white male in his twenties had fled the scene as he arrived. Keri believed he had followed proper arrest procedures, but she hadn't been at the scene to witness what happened, and the other suspect was never found. The injured man claimed no one else was there.

Watching the nurse move around the room, Keri wondered if she'd missed something that night. All she really knew was what Brian told her. And she trusted him. What if he'd misled her? She'd staked her reputation on his word and not her own observations. There was a possibility that her loyalty had been misplaced. Maybe there were facts she didn't have. Common sense and work experience suggested Alex must have known all the details by the end of the investigation, if not during their interview. Of course she would never discuss the case, but Keri began to think she'd misjudged her. Her own behavior had been immature and unprofessional.

The thought made her cringe. No wonder Alex seemed uneasy around her. She probably owed the woman a huge apology. Alex didn't create the problem with the use-of-force investigation, and Keri had to stop blaming her for it. The more time she spent around the lieutenant, the less she seemed like the ladder-climbing opportunist Keri had imagined. One thing was for sure, there was much more to Alex than a hard-nosed cop. Keri hadn't imagined the compassion and deep feelings on Alex's face when they talked about Josh and Stacey. The more she saw of that sensitive, caring woman, the more she wanted to see. And that wasn't all Keri wanted. The few times they'd touched, their bodies seemed to fit so perfectly she couldn't imagine holding another person. So far she'd managed not to show her growing attraction for Alex. She wondered if she could keep that up much longer.

The nurse turned from her workstation and snapped latex gloves onto her hands. "If you're ready, we'll get this done." She corded a length of rubber tubing around Keri's bicep and stuck a needle into her bulging vein.

As the tube filled with her blood the reality of why she was in this place returned to Keri. She'd been drugged. She didn't need a test to prove it. The effects on her body and memory were definitely not the result of the single beer she'd consumed. It could've been much worse. She could've ended up like Josh and Stacey—young, promising, and dead.

Keri thought about the things she'd regret if her life had ended last night. The list was long and the weight of it settled in her chest. She wouldn't be able to nurse her mother through the terrible disease that ravaged her mind and body. The rift with her father would go unresolved and the scars would never heal. She wouldn't find justice for Josh or become a real narcotics detective. The blot on her career from the use-of-force investigation would remain forever. Alex Troy would always believe she was a dishonest and unreliable officer. And, with an agonizing stab of sadness, Keri realized she would never make love with Alex. She wanted that, and more, with all her heart. The connection between them was hard to explain, but she felt it in every fiber of her being. She wanted a chance to explore that connection. Keri wasn't sure when it happened or how, only that everything had changed and the possibilities called to her as powerfully as the primal urge to mate.

❖

Alex navigated her old Mercedes coupe along the mountain roads leading to Beth and Tammy's place on Poplar Lake in Virginia. The two-hour drive gave her plenty of time to think about Keri and what she should do about her feelings. Maybe she'd talk to Tammy this weekend, if she didn't lose her nerve.

As she drove, her sunroof allowed the distinctive smells of

freshly plowed earth and strewn fertilizer to permeate the car. Cows and horses dotted the pristine countryside grazing on short grass and hay bales. She'd forgotten what being in the real country looked and smelled like. Nearing Beth and Tammy's house, Alex thought the drive had passed too quickly.

A border of Leyland cypress lined the driveway into Beth's cedar log cabin, producing the illusion of a hidden gateway. The two-story house sported a wraparound porch and rested at the bottom of the drive. It was silhouetted against the sparkling waters of Poplar Lake and appeared to be floating.

Tammy stood on the porch motioning her toward the open side of the two-car detached garage. Alex pulled inside, grabbed her overnight bag, closed the garage door, and walked toward her friend's partner. A small butterfly-bush garden adorned the side yard along the walkway. Tammy's ferns hung from the porch corners, variegated fingers beckoning Alex to enter, as inviting as their owner.

"It's great to see you, Alex." Her name always sounded so sensual coming from this willowy strawberry-blonde. Tammy gave her a full-body hug and they walked into the house arm in arm. The smell of baking bread permeated the homey interior.

"It's really good to be here," Alex said.

Tammy replaced her overnight bag with a frosty drink. Lifting her own glass, she toasted, "Here's to weekends."

Alex took a big sip. It'd been months since she'd had one of Tammy's special concoctions—vodka tonic with a hint of peach schnapps. The effects were immediate. "Strong, as usual." She smiled gratefully. "But much appreciated."

"Beth told me you were injured in a wreck. How are you?"

"I'm fine, just a few bumps and scrapes."

"Sit and keep me company while I finish this salad. Catch me up on police department gossip." Tammy gestured to the counter that separated kitchen and dining areas.

"Can I help with anything?" Alex asked.

"There's nothing to do. The bread is baking, salad is making, and Beth should be along anytime now. She'll put the steaks and chicken on the grill later. Besides, you're a guest."

"I thought she'd be here by now. Sorry, I didn't realize a trip to the hospital would tie her up this long, but then it is the weekend."

"Relax, Alex, and try to forget about work for a while."

Alex surveyed the interior of the house and sipped her drink. She was invariably impressed with Tammy's unique ability to make the natural log walls come alive. Patchwork quilts adorned the vertical surfaces and loft railing adding to the feeling of warmth and comfort. Dazzling displays of refracted light were masterfully directed through stained glass fixtures and window ornaments.

Their home exuded such an ambience of serenity that Alex felt embraced by love each time she entered. The confines of work and the burdensome task of self-protection slipped away as Alex allowed herself to relax.

Tammy put an immediate end to her respite. "So, Beth tells me you're interested in someone."

"Don't ever repeat that to anyone, please." Alex tried to be angry, but she knew Beth was coming from a place of caring.

Tammy continued calmly chopping vegetables. She gave Alex one of her most reassuring glances. "You need a life beyond the vicarious pleasures of your friends. We've been worried. We want you to be happy because we love you."

"If that's not my cue for some free counseling, I've never heard one." Alex propped an elbow on the counter and rested her chin against her hand. "Tammy, I don't know what to do. I admit I'm attracted to someone, but there are too many obstacles. For a start, I work with her."

Tammy changed to her therapist voice. "Then she must be struggling with some of the same issues if she's attracted to you, too."

"Sometimes I think she is, and God knows she gives me some interesting looks. But I'm not sure I could offer her the life she wants, if she even knows what that is." Alex watched Tammy's knife slice the vegetables with the precision of a master chef.

"What do you like about her?"

The stormy conflict Alex often felt dissolved into a calm that made her smile. "I think it's a combination of her vitality and tenderness. She's so eager to experience life and she does it with such sincerity and reverence. I guess I'm drawn to that. Sometimes I feel so…jaded, being around her makes me remember…"

Myself. Alex fell silent, startled by the thought and thankful she had kept it to herself. Tammy raised her eyebrows. "There's something else, isn't there?"

"Yes." Where to begin? "This will sound strange, but it's like she's a pain eradicator."

"I don't think I've ever heard that one before."

"She senses when I'm hurting and tries to make it better. I swear I can feel it being drawn out of me, but it doesn't seem to weigh her down." Alex paused, uncomfortable to be speaking so candidly about feelings she still didn't fully understand herself. "I don't even think she knows she's doing it. Sounds stupid, huh?"

"Not at all," Tammy reassured her. "It's sort of like my job. Learning to feel and respect the pain of others, but not being crippled by it. Otherwise, I couldn't function."

"But Keri—that's her name—has never had that kind of training," Alex said.

"So, she learned the hard way. She lived through pain and survived."

"I've got no right to dump my garbage on her. She deserves better than a battle-scarred lesbo like me."

"Oh, Alex, don't," Tammy said impatiently. "You're one of the best, most kindhearted people I know. You're just afraid of being hurt again and that's normal."

Alex heaved a heavy sigh. "Then there's the work thing. I can't get involved with somebody on the job, especially not a subordinate."

"That's the least of your worries, love," Tammy continued. "Work situations change all the time. You could find other interests. This woman could decide the force isn't for her and move on. Don't let your job stand in the way of a chance for happiness."

Alex thought of her parents' business and her father's wish for her future. "Maybe you're right."

"I think you should let yourself be open to possibility. That's all." Tammy gave Alex's hand a loving pat and said, "Come on, let's relax."

She led Alex from the kitchen to the rocking chairs on the covered porch overlooking the lake. For the next hour or so they talked, laughed, drank, and caught up on current events and relived old memories. Warmth from her surroundings coupled with the stimulation of two vodka tonics tamed Alex's stress and loosened the worries of work.

"You and Beth are so lucky," she mused, looking out toward the water. "I mean to find each other. A relationship like yours is rare. You complement the good and 'needs improvement' areas of each other's lives beautifully."

"Yeah, we've been together years and I still love her so much. Sometimes it feels like I've been drugged."

Alex caught a sharp breath at the offhand remark. She couldn't believe she hadn't thought about Keri's tests for at least an hour. She was so relaxed and comfortable that work seemed a lifetime away. She took out her cell phone but Tammy immediately announced her objections.

"Put that away. If there's bad news at work, you'll hear soon enough."

"I guess so. Maybe I'll take a sunset dip. I love this time of day."

Alex moved to the deck railing and gazed out at the lake, not really seeing the beauty in front of her. Tammy was right. All too often she pretended to take time off and ended up working. In the end, her body, mind, and spirit had suffered. This time she wanted it to be different. There was too much at stake. She had important things to think about and she wanted to give herself the mental space to do so.

The walkway to the dock virtually sprouted blooming black-eyed Susans and petunias. A woman would have to be a nurturer to spend so much time on landscaping at a vacation home, but that described Tammy perfectly. Her deep concern for everything living transcended her role as a therapist. Maybe a therapist was exactly what Alex needed to sort out the jumble of emotions that battled inside her. She wasn't having much luck by herself.

❖

Ten minutes later Tammy heard the crunching-gravel approach of her partner's car and then Beth hurried toward the house. A second woman emerged from the passenger side.

"Honestly, honey," Tammy greeted Beth at the door. "I still think you should've told them both. Alex is going to kill you for playing matchmaker."

"I know, but some things are just worth the risk." Beth grinned sheepishly.

"Get down to the dock and tell Alex so she's not completely blindsided."

"I will as soon as I introduce you to Keri," Beth grabbed Tammy in a bear hug and nibbled playfully on her ear.

"Don't think for one second you're fooling me, Beth Price." Tammy's lips met Beth's and parted when she needed to breathe. "I love you."

The lusty look in her eyes told Beth it was as true then as it had been the first time they kissed. "I love you too, babe." She opened the door wide and urged Keri, "Come on in. This is Tammy, my partner."

"It's so good to meet you, Keri. Beth has told me a lot about you."

Keri seemed surprised, but she returned Tammy's enthusiastic hug and said, "Thanks for the invitation. I was so excited when Beth asked me to come up. I need a break."

"You're so welcome. Sit, please." Tammy motioned to the bar. "Can I get you a drink?"

"A beer would be perfect." Keri thought about her last beer and almost reconsidered.

Tammy handed her a bottle of Michelob, then pulled steaks and chicken from the refrigerator. "How are your folks doing?" she asked as she worked. "Beth tells me you live at home to help them out."

"The doctors say my dad can live to a ripe old age if he does as he's told, but he can be stubborn. He doesn't understand about heart problems. My mom is slowly deteriorating. Alzheimer's. It's sad to watch. One day she seems like her old self and the next she's gone."

"It's a terribly difficult disease for the patient and the family. I'm so sorry." Tammy asked, "What's this I hear about you getting drugged?"

Keri's beer stopped halfway to her lips. "I still don't know what really happened with the target. Beth gave me the sanitized version." Keri's hesitation and sad blue eyes hinted at wounds old and new.

"The operation went well," Beth said. "And you're doing a great job. Now if you'll both excuse me, I need to take care of a few things." She dropped a kiss on Tammy's cheek and vanished up the stairs.

"I'm sure this assignment means a lot to you," Tammy said as she seasoned the steaks.

"Yes, it's a big opportunity." Keri enjoyed talking to someone outside the police community and for some reason she felt comfortable with Tammy even though they'd just met. She had a sense that Tammy could understand her need to prove herself in a job that was often unrewarding and thankless. "I don't want to let anyone down."

"I can't see that happening," Tammy said. "You're obviously a caring and devoted daughter and I hear you also have the potential to be a top-notch narcotics officer."

"Thank you." Keri scraped the moistened label from her beer bottle and looked everywhere in the room except at Tammy. She wasn't sure why it felt so strange to be complimented, or why she assumed automatically that Tammy was just being nice to her partner's colleague.

As if Tammy had read her mind, she said, "For what it's worth, Beth really does think highly of you or she wouldn't have invited you out here."

Embarrassed to be so transparent, Keri said, "I'm sorry. I guess I'm just shaken up after what happened last night. I should have been more careful, or at least known I'd been slipped something. Instead, I have to be…rescued by my boss."

"And you'd rather impress her, huh?"

Keri laughed. She could feel guilty color washing her face.

"I see." Tammy's gaze was very direct. Too direct for comfort. "Alex has that effect."

"You know her." Keri felt silly. Of course Tammy knew her partner's best friend.

"Not as well as Beth does, but we're both very fond of her." Seeing something shift in Keri's expression, Tammy said, "You seem bothered by her, or am I imagining it?"

After a long silence, Keri replied, "No, you're not imagining it. Alex and I have some history. I behaved badly, and…I guess I just want her to give me a chance."

"Alex is one of the fairest people I know. I'm sure you have nothing to worry about."

If only it were that simple. Keri sighed. She took a deep breath as tears welled up in her eyes. Without thinking, she said, "I wish I didn't care so much." She lowered her head instantly. How indiscreet could she get?

Tammy wasn't stupid. "You're attracted to Alex?"

Keri looked around desperately. "I should be helping with something. Where did Beth go?"

"I think she went down to the dock." Tammy glanced out the window, concerned that Beth hadn't returned. Hopefully she'd had time to run interference with Alex.

"Great. Mind if I join her?" Keri picked up her beer from the counter. "I've got a suit on under my shorts. I was so excited about taking a swim tonight."

"Be my guest. It's beautiful at sunset." Tammy walked outdoors with her. "But tell me something first. Do you care about Alex? I mean, personally."

Pretending seemed pointless. Keri placed her hand over her heart and let out a halting breath. "She just fills me up, Tammy. I never thought I'd feel this way about anyone."

"Then I have some advice for you. Tell her."

Keri's eyes locked onto Tammy's. "I don't think she wants to hear."

"Maybe she doesn't know what she wants." Tammy sounded very serious all of a sudden. "In life, we don't always get second chances. Go with your heart, Keri. That's the best advice I can give you."

"Then I'll take it," came the soft reply.

"There's something else," Tammy said. "I'm sure you've noticed the place settings for four. Alex is down at the dock."

Startled, Keri backed up. "How—"

"I think Beth's trying to do a bit of matchmaking of her own, but she should've told you."

A sparkle drove the uncertainty from Keri's eyes. "Then I'd better not disappoint her," she said with a hint of mischief. "Wish me luck."

Chuckling, Tammy said, "I do."

Just as Keri walked away, Beth came bouncing out the back door. Tammy shot her a pleading look. "Tell me you've warned Alex about our fourth guest."

Beth shook her head. "I was just going down there now."

"Too late." Tammy eyed her lover fondly.

Comprehension dawned on Beth's face. "Where's Keri?"

They both looked toward the dock. "On her way to a close encounter of a weird kind," Tammy said.

Chapter Fourteen

Alex adored the peaceful stillness that preceded night, those precious minutes between twilight and dark. At the edge of the dock she dropped the towel she'd grabbed from the cedar-sided boathouse and sat down. Dangling her feet in the water, she watched the sunlight withdraw with a splash of color behind a veil of pine and poplar. Tall guardian pines surrounded the cove, which was far enough off the main waterway to make passing traffic unobtrusive. Encouraged by the combination of beauty and tranquility around her, Alex allowed herself to feel everything she'd been fending off recently.

The anger she felt over the injustice of her parents' untimely deaths rose in her as it often did, uninvited. This time Alex didn't push it down. Her stomach tensed and emotion built in her chest. Small tremors rose from her midsection and escaped her lips with a whimper. She didn't want to hold back any longer. It hurt too much. She could feel it inside, eating away her life. Soon her shoulders were shaking uncontrollably, her wails echoed across the cove, and her tears fell unbidden.

She had no idea how long she'd been crying when she heard footsteps, alerting her that Beth had arrived for the sunset performance. Without turning, she said, "Sometimes it's just so hard to keep it all inside. I don't want to be the strong one anymore."

Standing behind Alex on the dock, Keri felt like a voyeur infringing on an intimate moment. What now? Should she announce herself or just wait quietly to be noticed? She opened her mouth to speak but was silenced by a compulsion to experience this heart-wrenching soliloquy, the betrayal of all she thought she knew about Alex Troy.

Alex drew a sobbing breath. "I wonder how my life would be today if I hadn't fallen in love with Helen Callahan, if my parents hadn't died so early, if I hadn't become a cop."

"Oh…I'm sorry, but…" Keri stammered.

Alex whirled around and came face-to-face with a blushing, swimsuit-clad Keri Morgan. Her mouth fell open. "Where did you come from?" She turned away and grabbed the edge of her beach towel, attempting to wipe her watery eyes.

Keri had never seen such hurt in their depths. "I'm so sorry to interrupt. I didn't know you were…"

Alex shook her head. "Please, don't."

The intensity of Alex's pain grabbed Keri and pulled her in. She closed the distance between them, sat down, and placed her hand on Alex's shoulder. "We're off the job." She tried to console her, knowing she couldn't possibly erase what she'd just heard. "If nothing else, I'd like to be a friend."

Alex's pride felt bruised. Embarrassed by her outburst, she struggled to regain control but couldn't. She'd never allowed herself to acknowledge the suffering or grieve the losses completely. Somehow she knew it had to come out now or she'd forever be a prisoner.

Keri watched tears pooling in Alex's swollen eyes as a progression of anger, fear, pain, and surrender clouded her features, battling for dominance. Instinctively avoiding eye contact, Keri wrapped Alex's shaking frame in her arms, bringing their bodies together. She couldn't help the joy that came over her as she understood what she was finally seeing, the person behind the public façade. "Let it go. I know it hurts. You're safe with me, Alex."

The soft whisper released another torrent of emotion. The years of psychological restraint shattered. More cries of unbridled anguish escaped Alex's lips as waves of tears tumbled down her face. The soothing sound of Keri's voice combined with the gentleness of her caress made Alex believe she really could finally be free. For the first time in years, she allowed herself to be comforted without fear of payback.

After a long time, she said, "I don't know what's happening to me." She took a deep, labored breath. "My emotions are all over the place and everything hurts."

Alex's sporadic breathing created invisible fingers that stroked Keri's neck and the swell of her breasts. She fought the physical responses threatening to overtake her, sensing Alex's deeper need. "It happens to everybody."

"What happens to everybody?" Alex sniffed.

"I call it the monster mash."

Alex's body jerked as a low chuckle sounded in her throat. "Care to elaborate on that highly technical term?"

"It's the sad stuff we bury, hoping it'll go away by itself. Problem is, it doesn't. It gets bigger, uglier, and scarier until it feels like a huge monster that's going to crush us from the inside."

Alex released the small sobs fighting their way up from her chest. "I didn't get to tell my parents good-bye."

"I'm so sorry."

"Then there was Helen," Alex choked out. "She once threatened to shoot me, but I stayed with her anyway. What an idiot."

"Shh…" Keri rocked Alex in her arms, finally understanding the terrified look in her eyes that dreadful night in the gym. Such intense pain. Damn Helen Callahan for hurting her.

"I don't know how I could let someone do that to me. I'm a cop. I know better."

"Alex, it's not your fault. Like a friend once told me, people can fool us sometimes, but we still have to trust. I know how it feels."

"How did you get to be so wise?"

"I'm a fast learner. And I'm convinced life is worth the effort."

They sat huddled on the dock as the full moon rose between the trees, casting its silver luminescence across the water. Intermittent periods of calm and restlessness racked Alex's body as the wellspring of tears ebbed and flowed, but she marveled at the incredible peace she felt in Keri's arms. As she began to feel more comfortable, she recognized a desire to remain there forever. A voice in the back of her mind asked if Keri could be the one.

Keri hadn't felt so needed for a long time. Sometimes when she held her mother, she felt the same draining she sensed in Alex. Her mother was dying, and Keri understood that part of Alex was also dying, a part Keri hoped she'd never have to revisit. Holding Alex felt so natural and right. She'd imagined how close they could be, but not in this context. She'd just assumed their physical longing would be answered before the emotional, but she much preferred this. She cherished the intimate glimpse of Alex's life and inner self she'd been allowed to share.

She finger-combed Alex's thick, auburn hair and lowered her head to inhale the remnants of a light floral shampoo mixed with musk perfume. The fragrance invaded her senses, creating a memory that would be forever Alex. Massaging the back of Alex's neck with small circular motions, she placed a light kiss on the top of her head.

Alex drew back slightly. "Keri…" What she wanted to explain, she wasn't exactly sure. "I'm sorry you found out about…me. Especially like this. I trust you'll use discretion."

Their eyes locked and Keri felt herself moving toward Alex's slightly parted lips.

Alex allowed herself to look beyond Keri Morgan, the officer, acknowledging the unspoken between them. The chemistry was too strong to ignore. Gazing into Keri's eyes, she was overcome with desire. Longing ripped through her and seared into her soul. She'd seen this strength and compassion before, but refused to consider its implications. Such levels of empathy and nurturing could never be faked. This was a woman deserving of trust and love.

Alex's brain screamed for her to stop, but as Keri came closer and her breath washed hot across Alex's face, she knew she was lost. All she wanted was to kiss her, to hold her and feel everything that came afterward, whatever that might be, for however long it lasted. Right now, her body demanded contact.

The feathery brush of Alex's lips initially tickled Keri's. She wondered if they'd touched at all until a jolt of electricity shot to her core, forever welding her soul to this woman. A splash of color flashed behind her eyelids. Her nipples grew hard and painful. Pressure built between her legs, straining for release. She grew light-headed as Alex's mouth demanded more. Never had Keri imagined a simple kiss could release so many feelings—tenderness, compassion, desire, need, hunger, craving, love, and an animalistic willingness to do or be anything Alex Troy wanted. She prayed this would never end.

Alex slid her arms tighter around Keri's naked waist. Everywhere their exposed flesh touched felt like a volcanic explosion followed by liquid fire burning its way to the river flowing between her thighs. The gilded moonlight cast shadows across their entwined bodies. Their kiss deepened, as did Alex's need. She refused to stop for air as her breath, ragged and hot, escaped in erratic spurts.

"Hey, are you two down there?" Beth's voice shattered the charged air around them.

Alex withdrew as if stricken. She stared at Keri, her eyes hazy with desire, mouth open and lips swollen. Breathing in short, uneven gasps, she traced the angle of Keri's jaw with her finger, then rose as though her legs were leaden.

"We can't," she said simply.

"Why?" Keri felt the distance between them grow with every breath Alex took.

"Because I want it too much." Without looking back, Alex walked away and climbed the stairs toward Beth.

Keri was unable to speak or move. She felt as if she'd flown too close to the sun, energized by the rays but ultimately burned by the intensity. She sat motionless as chirping crickets, buzzing mosquitoes, and the gentle lapping of waves against the dock invaded her oversensitized faculties.

She would never forget these life-changing minutes, the lingering fragrance of Alex's perfume, the creamy look and feel of her naked skin, and the burning points of contact as they touched. The silken texture of Alex's lips stayed with her. So, too, the way her tongue filled Keri's mouth and stroked her from the inside and the connection she felt so profoundly to the essence of her being.

A few minutes later, Keri knew she had to go after Alex and refuse to accept the dismissal of all they might have. Frantically she rushed up the bank of stairs toward the cabin. As she reached the top, a car spun out of the gravel driveway. It felt like a piece of her heart was dragged behind on the pebbly surface.

❖

"I fucked up." Keri buried her face in her hands.

"Don't be so hard on yourself." Tammy tried to reassure her, sensing the pain that radiated from her.

"But I did. One minute she was telling me about her parents and Helen, crying and letting me hold her, and the next minute she was gone."

A short pause followed while Tammy and Beth exchanged a disbelieving glance. Then Tammy asked quietly, "She told you about Helen?"

Keri recounted the conversation. She felt bad for talking about those private moments, but she needed to vent.

"So why do you think you messed up?" Beth asked. "It sounds like the two of you shared something special."

"Until she kissed me. No, that's not right. I kissed her. I mean, I'm not sure how it happened." Keri shook her head to loosen the passionate haze that clung to the memory. "We kissed and…it was so different, soft and hot at the same time. Listen to me, I sound like a cliché. I don't even have words for what I feel."

Beth gave her an encouraging pat on the leg. "You sound like a woman in love."

"I've never been that turned on by anyone in my life. I wanted it to go on forever. I wanted to make…" Keri's skin tingled and flushed with her recollection and the interrupted thought. She knew she should feel uncomfortable telling her most intimate feelings to people she barely knew, but the emotions just seemed to pour from her of their own volition.

"Isn't this a good thing?" Beth asked.

Tammy shook her head and smiled at her well-meaning lover. "Except for one little detail, honey. Alex isn't here. So we're not sure how *she's* feeling about all this."

"If there's one person in this whole screwed-up world I know, besides you, my little cupcake, it's Alex Troy, and believe me, she's crazy about Keri."

Lowering her eyes, Keri shook her head. "I don't think so. She told me it couldn't happen and just walked away. She didn't even look back."

Keri couldn't contain the tears any longer. They rolled down her face, unwelcome and unending. She didn't resist when Tammy held her.

"I know it hurts," Tammy soothed as Keri nestled into her shoulder. "But try to remember it's not about you."

"She's right," Beth said. "Alex is struggling with her own feelings right now. Give her some time. She'll work it out."

❖

Alex's drive back to Granville was riddled with self-recrimination and outbursts of disbelief. *What was I thinking?* She couldn't believe she'd told Keri all those things about her life. And *then* kissed her. Again. Keri, a subordinate. And the kiss was so perfect and the feelings that flooded her body so intense, she wanted to stay in Keri's arms forever. Though Keri's intent had not been sexually motivated, she had aroused feelings in Alex, physical and emotional, that no one ever had. Alex supposed on some level she was running away from that realization. She'd only just found her legs after Helen. She didn't want them to crumple beneath her all over again.

Beth had tried to convince her to stay and talk things through with Keri, but she wasn't strong enough to do that and she had to make some serious decisions before she took that risk. She couldn't look at Keri and pretend she didn't care. But she needed time and distance to reassemble her defenses and rehearse her justifications before she could convince herself they should stay apart.

The arguments were pretty straightforward. To fraternize with subordinates was a violation of departmental policy, not to mention a federal offense for sexual harassment. Add to that the same-sex component and things could get really messy. All it would take was one pissed-off employee she didn't transfer or promote or evaluate to their liking and she'd be in deep trouble. Just the hint that they were involved could be dangerous for both of them.

But the minute Keri saw her she'd know Alex was falling in love with her. That could not happen. Alex wasn't even sure she could be trusted to be discreet. She had no defense for her actions, unless being under the influence of love counted. She'd never be able to look Keri in the eyes again. And what beautiful eyes they were. *I'm so screwed.*

Chapter Fifteen

Alex paced her office and struggled to concentrate on the surveillance reports she'd been holding for the past two hours. The words ran together and Keri Morgan's face stared out at her from every page.

Their kiss still burned her lips and carved a path of desire through her body that was too demanding to ignore. With each memory of it she grew weak and wet, a gut-twisting hunger so strong that self-pleasuring had failed miserably to satisfy it.

Beth's distinctive three-tap knock sounded at her door.

Alex had been waiting for her. "Come in," she called, setting aside the file she'd been reading.

Beth took the seat beside her desk. "What's up, Lieu?"

"It's time we made those buys we were talking about before my accident. We have enough on his street-level dealers now, and if we can get Tiffany Brown to repeat what I overheard, we can put him away."

"I agree. Let's do it," Beth said. "We've linked two of the dead students who still had the drugs on them to specific dealers."

"Good, so we can compare their product to the evidence, and move on up the supply chain to Davis."

"Want me to have Morgan call her informant?"

"No, he's been hanging out with Davis. It won't look right to have him make a buy at the bottom rung."

Beth hesitated. "What about sending in Morgan herself?"

"That's out of the question," Alex said.

"Why? Chad has already set up a cover for her, and Davis knows she's in the market. If we ran this as a buy-bust we could arrest her, then she could call him and ask for help."

Alex considered the possibility for a few seconds. Davis had called "Lynn" to check in on her after the roofie incident. Maybe a strategy like that would flush him out into the open. But it could also shut down their options. She had a better idea, one that made her uncomfortable, admittedly. But it was time she left her personal feelings at home when she came to work.

"No, I want to keep Morgan playing him along until he'll supply her directly," she said. "We need to set this up as a routine bust and work a personal angle. There are other officers who would have been suitable for the task force. Bring in one of those." Thinking ahead, she asked, "Do any of those dealers have a lot of enemies?"

"A couple spring to mind." Beth's initial puzzlement gave way to comprehension. "I see where you're going with this. We collar one of them and circulate a story on the street that someone with a beef set him up?"

"Exactly. We can use Chad to spread a rumor once the bust goes down."

"There's a risk Davis will be rattled and lay low," Beth cautioned.

"Maybe for a short while," Alex conceded. "But it's just another day at the office for guys like him. Busts are inevitable. Lose one dealer, replace him with another."

"Such as Chad?"

Alex ordered herself to think like a future Vice/Narcotics captain. "Actually, the ideal candidate is Lynn."

Beth looked startled.

"You said it yourself," Alex continued. "Davis knows she wants in, and he wants to impress her. What better way than to bypass the middlemen and offer her a spot on his crew?"

"It's risky." Excitement filtered through Beth's tone. "But smart thinking, boss."

"We'll just have to see if he takes the bait," Alex said. "Set up the initial bust ASAP. We need to move on this before that particular batch dries up on the street."

While she waited for the arrangements to be made, she called Chief Lancaster and updated him on their progress and the latest plan.

After a long conversation about the Chambers case and reminders about Alex's promotion prospects, he let her go and Alex headed for the conference room.

Beth greeted her at the door. "We're ready, Lieu."

"Who's making the buy?" Alex asked.

"Tony Reese. He's a savvy street officer but new enough not to be easily identified. He knows what we need and how to get it done."

"Yeah, I've seen some of his arrests. He knows narcotics. Good choice, Sarge."

As Alex took a seat, she made eye contact with every officer in the room, gathering courage to meet the deep, probing ones at the end of the table. When she did, tunnel vision overtook her and the questioning look in Keri's eyes was all she saw. Her heart lurched and pounded rapidly against her chest. She wanted to gather Keri in her arms and take her home, not get her further involved in this dangerous case.

Keri's breath caught in her throat. Had it only been two days since they kissed by the lake? It seemed so much longer. Too long. Every muscle strained to make contact. Every nerve vibrated with the memory of that kiss and the proximity of their bodies. She still couldn't believe Alex had decided to put her career first and wasn't even willing to sit down with her and talk about what was happening between them. Although she'd accepted Beth and Tammy's advice to give Alex time, she couldn't help but be hurt.

"Folks." Beth waved the team into silence. "The lieutenant would like a few words."

Alex cleared her thoughts. She had no idea how long she'd stared at Keri before Beth spoke, but she needed to get her act together before people noticed. "I don't usually say this in the course of a drug investigation, but this one's personal. Davis drugged one of our own and he's got to pay. We're going to do a buy-bust on one of Davis's dealers so we can match his product to the drugs that killed Stacey Chambers and some of the other young people. Officer Tony Reese from the western division will make the buy. Later, when Davis starts to feel the lost cash flow, we'll see if we can place an officer inside his operation." Alex looked at Keri. "Is Chad still on board?"

Keri nodded, forcing thoughts of the weekend from her mind. "If the money's right, he'll do anything."

"Good. The minute the buy is complete, we'll do the takedown.

Officer Reese will be wired. He'll be arrested, too. If we're lucky the dealer we arrest will call Davis for bail or help, another connection."

Rick Jones asked, "Any special location you got in mind for the buy?"

"Chad could give us some suggestions," Keri said. "He knows the area Davis's men work and could find a spot near our target dealer, but not too contained."

"Good idea." Alex smiled. Keri was still engaged and in the game. "Just make sure he knows it's to be a fairly open public place, well lit. I want us to be able to control access and egress. Anything else? Sergeant Price?"

When her question was met with silence, Alex concluded. "Morgan, check with your man. When you and the sergeant are satisfied with the location, we'll reconvene for assignments."

The rest of the team moved around the conference room making preparations for the buy. Paige double-checked the cell phone transmitter and receiver. Renee wrote the beginnings of the raid briefing on the chalkboard, date, primary officer, and case number. Mike got fresh batteries for everybody's walkie-talkies and Maglites, while Rick made a fresh pot of coffee. Steve checked vehicle availability and made equipment assignments.

Alex watched the officers interact as they worked, joking and helping one another. They'd developed respect for each other's talents and came together as a formidable team. That didn't happen often with a multijurisdictional group. Politics and egos often hindered interagency cooperation. She was proud of their performance.

Her thoughts turned to Keri Morgan and her part in the investigation. Her informant, Chad Williams, had made contact with Davis immediately possible. Keri had handled herself well in a new kind of assignment and taken direction easily. It wasn't her fault that her lieutenant had developed an innocent crush on her that blossomed into…something stronger. Alex knew she couldn't continue to work with her and not speak of her feelings. In the past she'd easily compartmentalized her emotions, but now it was a struggle to remain detached for even short periods of time. She would be thankful when this case reached its conclusion.

"We've got a location," Beth informed the group eventually, "the Food King on Hanover Drive. It's in a strip mall with enough activity to provide good cover. The potential for civilian involvement should be minimal. Keri, finish the diagram while I partner everybody up." She sat and scribbled quickly on a yellow legal pad.

Keri moved to the chalkboard and sketched the location, along with all points of entry and exit. When she finished, Beth rose, plugged in the team assignments, then said, "Lieutenant, you and Keri can back us up, in case we need extra help. Keep an eyeball on the west side. I want the two of you out of sight. Since you've been the initial contacts with Davis, I don't want to take chances that any of his goons could ID you."

Keri cast a quick look at Alex but stood, put on her low-rider holster, and slid into her flak jacket as the other officers did the same. She wondered how she'd survive in such close proximity to Alex without talking about what happened at the lake. Her feelings bounced around like the steel ball inside a pinball machine. She knew they were both thinking about the incident on the dock, but she also knew they had to stay focused. Drug takedowns were very unpredictable. Anything could happen.

Beth had briefed her on the lieutenant's plan to insert her into Davis's organization as his new dealer. It had never occurred to Keri that she'd actually be inside the drug business on her first undercover assignment; officers more experienced than she had been discovered and killed attempting just such assignments. She thought about Davis pawing her at the club and wondered if she could keep up the pretense of liking this moral degenerate long enough to arrest him. She would have to be consistently persuasive in order to carry out the plan. Alex seemed convinced that she was up to the task. That confidence shored up her doubts. She could do this. She refused to fail.

❖

Four hours later, after the bust went down successfully, Keri stepped inside her glass-enclosed shower and adjusted the water until it was as hot as she could stand. The pressurized spray caressed her tired shoulders and back with welcome fingers of heat, fingers that reminded her of Alex's long, firm hands and their sensuous motions. Her center twitched and her stomach coiled into a knot of sexual tension. She closed her eyes and tilted her head back as silky sheets of warm water slid down her torso. Turning, she enjoyed the sensation on her chest and stomach. An involuntary moan escaped her lips, witness to the desire building inside.

What would it be like to make love with Alex? Keri allowed the liquid caress of the shower stream to wash over her arms, across her breasts, and down the flat plane of her stomach. Touching herself, she imagined Alex's hands on her as they had been at the lake, warm, soft, and needy. She palmed a breast in one hand, teased the nipple with her thumb, and pressed her other hand against the hunger low in her belly. She relived the touch of Alex's lips against hers and curled her fingers into the silkiness between her legs. Her pelvis bucked forward at the first touch, exquisitely torturous. She knew it would only be a matter of seconds before she came. And she also knew she would not be able to keep from screaming Alex's name. She thanked the gods that her parents were out of town for a few days, before she returned to the growing pressure in her body. Clinging to the side of the shower, she stroked faster, but something wasn't right.

Distracted, Keri opened the shower door and stuck her head out. The phone in her bedroom was ringing. Her first thought was Alex. She grabbed a towel and bolted from the bathroom. *Don't hang up, don't hang up.* They needed to talk. Alex had been pleased with her work today, but her demeanor had been all business, not the slightest sign or indication that they'd shared anything personal.

Just as she reached for the phone, it stopped ringing. Keri snatched it off the cradle, "Hello, hello." Dial tone. "Damn." She dried herself, wrapped the towel around her, and retrieved the message from voicemail. When she heard Alex speak, her heart and her clit pounded with the same beat.

Keri, it's Alex. I wanted to… A pause. A heavy breath. *I think things went well today.* Another eternal hesitation followed, during which Keri prayed that Alex would say something to acknowledge their personal connection. *I really just wanted to thank you for your work today and make sure you're okay with the next phase of the operation. I know it's throwing you into the deep end of the pool, but I know you can do it. Well—I guess that's all. Good-bye.*

Keri listened to the message over and over, trying to read something into the words and tone that wasn't there.

❖

Alex stared at her cell phone. What a coward, she thought. She was parked outside Keri's house, opposing thoughts battling in her head. She had tried to go home but that didn't work. Now she was sitting here like a teenager in heat or a demented stalker, trying to get up the courage to knock on Keri's door.

What would she say, anyway? Nothing was any different. Nothing had changed except her apparent level of sanity. It would still be nuts for them to start a relationship. The only good thing that could come of it would be sexual release. And while she felt she'd explode if her needs weren't satisfied soon, that didn't seem like a good enough reason to risk this case and her career, not to mention Keri's. The negative possibilities were numerous and well engrained in her mind. Alex turned the ignition, put the car in drive, then slammed it back into park.

She just couldn't leave. This whole situation was getting out of hand and interfering with work at a critical time. They had to talk. She'd run out on Keri at the lake without an explanation. The woman deserved an honest answer to the questions Alex saw in her eyes daily. She had to understand that a relationship was out of the question. Direct, simple, and final. Alex exited the car and walked slowly to the door, rehearsing her speech with each step.

When the door opened almost immediately after her knock, she stood staring at Keri, who wore nothing but a towel, her hair wet and falling into ringlets around her face. Tiny patches of moisture seeped through the fabric and it clung to Keri's body, igniting a hot throb in Alex's body that screamed for attention.

Keri stepped wordlessly aside, and Alex couldn't remember any of the sensible things she planned to say. She walked in and looked around questioningly.

"They're out of town for a few days."

Alex kicked the door closed behind her and pulled Keri into her arms. Her lips were on Keri's before she could take a breath, hungry and demanding. Their kiss deepened, her tongue probing the inside of Keri's mouth, sucking in the salty flavor of her. She backed Keri to the wall and pressed their bodies together, cursing the fabric that separated them and rubbed painfully against her swollen flesh. She wedged her leg between Keri's thighs, humping like a rutting animal. Her blood boiled with a desire to strip her naked and devour her where she stood.

Keri pressed against Alex's shoulders and backed her off enough to take a deep breath. "Alex, baby…"

The soft endearing words were like soothing music to a savage beast. Alex looked into Keri's lust-clouded eyes. "I'm sorry. I didn't mean to…I mean, I've never been like this before." And it was true. She loved sex, but this was more, much more.

Keri gently outlined Alex's bottom lip with the tip of her index finger. She loved seeing her like this, vulnerable and out of control. It meant Alex trusted her and that meant everything. "It's all right. I just needed to catch my breath." She cupped Alex's face in her hands and feathered her lips with light kisses. "God, I love your lips."

A slight involuntary tremble followed by intense heat rose from Alex's core. Her pulse pounded and her breathing became more erratic. Feelings and needs she'd been suppressing surfaced with such ferocity she could hardly contain them. She took Keri's hand, brought it to her lips, and imparted to each digit a slow, sucking kiss.

"Oh, Alex, I want you so much. I never thought this day would come." Keri sighed, moving her breasts back and forth against Alex's. "Please, take me to bed."

Alex took Keri by the hand and led her to the bedroom. As soon as the door closed behind them, she ripped the towel away from Keri's body. She needed to touch flesh soon or she felt she'd melt into a puddle of bodily fluids. "My God, you are more beautiful than I imagined."

She placed her hands over Keri's naked breasts and kneaded the soft flesh into puckered mounds of arousal. Keri moaned softly and arched her back to give Alex greater access. She was so open and trusting, so willing to give herself without reservation. Alex dropped to her knees. Sitting on her feet, she leaned back to take in the full exposure of Keri's body, nipples hard, olive skin tinted with heat, and the light tuft of dewy hair at the apex of her thighs. She pressed her face against the warmth of Keri's abdomen. "You make me crazy."

Keri breathed in a raspy staccato as Alex's fingers teased her nipples. "I hope that's a good thing."

"You have no idea how much I need you." Alex rose, kissed Keri again, and led her to bed. As Alex removed her own clothes, Keri's appreciative gaze danced from one body part to the next. Her eyes were misty with tears when Alex lay gently down beside her.

"Are you okay?" Alex asked.

Keri wiggled closer, entwined their legs, and stroked the side of Alex's face. "I just never thought I could be so moved by the sight of another woman's body. Just looking at you turns me on."

Her moist tongue teased Alex's lips, softly tracing back and forth, up and down as passion built between them. Alex's breathing increased and desire twisted her insides into pulsing knots. She wanted to ravish Keri, to immediately relieve the burning pain of desire that tormented her. At the same time she enjoyed the teasing and loving attention to her body.

When Keri's searching tongue began a slow entry into her waiting mouth, Alex could stand it no longer. She sucked her in, desperate to feel the warm, probing presence inside her. Hungrily, she allowed herself to be filled and drank of the sweet exchange between them. In and out, Keri's tongue stroked the inside of her mouth and Alex's pelvis pumped the air in response, the blessed tightening already beginning inside. Hot hands explored Alex's breasts and began a slow agonizing descent.

"Will you let me make love to you?" Keri whispered. Alex's mind flashed to the last woman who'd made love to her and who sought to control her, mind and body. She stopped Keri's hand midabdomen and looked into Keri's eyes. The gentleness and love she saw there turned her grip on Keri's hand into a caress. She knew she could trust this woman with her body, her mind, and even her life.

"You can do anything you want to me," she said. "But please make it soon."

Keri stroked the slight dip of Alex's abdomen and inched toward her pubic mound. She knew that if Alex could trust her with her body, there was also a chance she would trust her with her heart as well. Alex's body rose to meet her, but Keri slid her fingers down to stroke the join of thigh and torso instead. Alex moaned in agony and shifted to make full contact.

"You're killing me...please." Alex drifted into a red haze of passion. She thought of all the times she'd lusted for this woman, of her sensuously full lips, of her kisses that could suck the life right out of her, of her butt in jeans crossing the parking lot at work, of her touch in the gym, of her body in wet, see-through shorts and T-shirt. Her desire spiraled out of control. She craved this, with this woman.

Keri slid her fingers into the damp hair between Alex's thighs, closed around a handful of tender flesh, and tugged gently. The quick flicker of pain transformed to pure pleasure and leapt through Alex's body. "This is torture."

A chuckle sounded from the woman beside her. "I thought you liked things the hard way, Lieutenant."

Alex tried to laugh, but the stroking between her legs increased and all that came out was a whimper. "Just this once, I'll take fast and easy. I can't wait any longer."

"Tell me what you want, baby." Keri shifted on top of Alex and rubbed their bodies together in full contact. "Tell me."

"Jerk me off until I'm ready to come, then I want you inside me."

Keri shimmied her hand between them, moved her fingers slowly into the moist folds hooding Alex's clit, and captured her rigid flesh.

"Oh yes." Alex's body begged for release as her moan clung to the air like a fog. Her thrusting hips pounded against Keri's hand as the tugging on her distended tissue intensified. "Yes," she pleaded, "that's it." She pumped faster. "Don't stop."

Keri scrunched down slightly and straddled Alex's thigh, watching as Alex's face flushed and her legs began to shudder. "Come for me, darling."

Alex tensed when she felt the evidence of Keri's arousal wet and hot against her naked flesh. The pressure in her pelvis ached for release. She reached for Keri's breasts and stroked them in time to her thrusts. "Now, baby, go inside me now," she cried as the initial tremors began. With Keri's fingers buried deep inside her, she let go. Time crawled as she trembled with rolling waves of orgasm. She couldn't remember a climax that had lasted so long, or felt so complete and freeing as this one. She knew her release was much more than physical. Her body quivered as each tiny shock contracted and released around Keri's fingers. Pent-up fluids and frustration rushed from her and bathed her partner. She wrapped her arms tighter around Keri as she continued to ride her thigh.

She could tell that Keri's release was imminent and wanted nothing more than to feel her surrender. Keri's body rocked back and forth and short bursts of air escaped her lungs between moans. Alex felt her stiffen, and heard a low growl escape from her lips as she collapsed on top of her.

They lay quietly in each other's arms for several minutes. Eventually, Alex shifted and nestled Keri's head against her breast, combing her fingers through Keri's tousled hair. Only two words came to mind. "Thank you," she said. But those two words didn't begin to cover her feelings.

Keri raised her head and stared into her eyes. "I love you, Alex Troy."

Oh, my God. Alex knew the fire threatening to consume her was too intense to be anything but love. She burned for Keri, ached for her with every ounce of her existence. *When did it happen? I'm totally undone by her, so why can't I tell her I love her?* Maybe it was because she'd soon be sending this woman into the jaws of death. How could she declare her love and do that to her? And what happened if she didn't come back? The thought sent shivers through Alex.

"You don't have to say anything. I just want you to know how I feel," Keri said. "And it's not going to change, no matter what happens."

Alex snuggled deeper, warm and comfortable. She owed her so much. Keri had given herself completely and in so doing, allowed Alex to do the same. But more importantly, she'd demonstrated that it was possible to give and express love freely without expectations. Her faith amazed Alex.

They spent the night making love until they collapsed in each other's arms exhausted. Alex didn't want to talk or think about anything else. She wanted to touch and experience everything possible about Keri Morgan in one miraculous, delicious, all-consuming night. Because after tonight, she had no idea what came next.

Chapter Sixteen

A lex twirled her pen and jabbed question marks onto a blank yellow page as Beth briefed her on the interview and booking of their dealer from the night before.

"He refused to give up his source, but we got a good enough sample from the buy to make a comparison with the others. Chad called Davis and he sent someone to post our snitch out. Overall, it was a great night." Beth eyed her mindless doodling. "Are you listening?" No response. She tried again. "Keri Morgan."

Alex's head came up immediately. "What? What did you say about Keri?"

"I knew it. You're gaga over her. Want to talk about it?" Beth couldn't suppress a smile.

"No, I don't." It was bad enough that she spent every waking moment thinking about her and every sleeping moment dreaming about her. She absolutely did not want to talk about Keri. Besides, Beth had probably already guessed from the look on her face that they'd slept together. "I've already said enough as it is." Alex dropped her pen onto the notepad. "We have work to do. Let's go to lineup."

As soon as they entered the conference room, Beth said, "There's only one new item on the clipboard today. Homicide squad's got a body found behind the abandoned warehouses on Phillips Avenue. A young black female. It appears she was tied up for a while, then shot. I'll pass the picture around. If anybody knows this girl, contact homicide detectives." She passed the photo to Renee and kept talking. "Our next move with Davis is to prepare for the actual buy from him. We'll need Chad to—"

"Oh, my God!" Keri cut Beth off. "The son of a bitch killed her."

Alex felt the hairs on the back of her neck bristle. "Morgan, do you know this girl?"

Keri looked at Alex, her eyes circles of disbelief and horror. "It's Tiffany Brown, our witness and Davis's ex-girlfriend. I saw the picture Steve took of her when he interviewed her." She passed the picture to Steve. "Look."

"Yep, that's her. Somebody must've screwed up. She was supposed to be held without bail." He sighed. "But we don't know for sure that Davis had her killed. We'll need proof."

"Davis was pissed," Keri said. "He admitted to me that she'd be pushing up daisies soon. And you heard him, Lieu. He told her he meant for her to get the drink that killed Stacey. Do they have a time of death?"

Beth checked the alert. "Nothing here about it. They recovered a bullet at autopsy, but no weapon at the scene. Go talk to the homicide detectives when we break lineup and tell them what we suspect. Let them know they can't identify you as the source of this information yet because you're still undercover. But they at least need to check it out."

Alex felt the level of tension rising in the room. "Okay, folks, let's not get ahead of ourselves. Davis may be connected to this murder or not. All we have now is circumstantial evidence and a strong gut feeling. Let the homicide guys do their job on this one. We need to stay focused on our objective, nailing Davis for drug distribution and the other deaths."

"We have to be even more cautious," Beth said. "No one takes unnecessary chances." She stared directly at Keri. "Where are we on lining Davis up?"

"Chad's had a conversation with him. He's pissed about the arrest. I think he's about ready to deal."

Alex looked at Keri. "Is Chad's cover still intact?"

"Davis doesn't have a clue." Keri smiled with pride. "He's called me a few times since the strip club. All he can talk about is getting hooked up for that threesome he wants. I've been playing it cool."

"Good. So all we need is for Chad to put the idea in Davis's head that there's one surefire way to get you interested. Davis won't see it as permanent, just a means to an end." Alex considered the timing of the bust and Davis's apparent willingness to deal with Keri directly. He seemed anxious enough. It was now or never. "Tell Chad to set it up. If even the slightest thing feels off, tell him to drop the conversation. I don't want Davis getting suspicious."

"So, what if Davis calls me and makes an offer?" Keri asked.

"Set up a meet on neutral territory—not his house, not a public place—in case there's…trouble." Alex couldn't bring herself to say the word that initially came to mind: gunfire. The thought gave her chills.

"I'll take care of it, Lieutenant." Keri's eyes met hers and the look bored deeply into her.

Beads of perspiration formed between Alex's breasts and legs where Keri's lips had so hungrily fed. Alex dropped her gaze to Keri's hands and the pulsing in her clit soared painfully. The sparkling glimmer in Keri's eyes said she knew exactly what Alex was thinking. She licked her lips and grinned. Alex knew she was playing with fire but she couldn't help herself. It was like she'd had her first hit of cocaine and was forever addicted. She had to feel that high again—and soon.

She rose on weak legs. "Let me know when you have anything further. And contact homicide ASAP and fill them in." She walked toward her office to consider her growing uneasiness about the case. Her insides knotted with apprehension. She wondered if she was losing her analytical and tactical skills or if this was the price she paid for becoming emotionally involved.

❖

"He called," Keri said, standing just inside the doorway of Alex's home office. They'd spent the past two nights together, getting very little sleep, reveling in the passion that burned hot enough to consume them.

Alex sat hunched over her desk, her firm, full breasts peeking from the unbuttoned sides of an oversized denim shirt. Keri was amazed by the wave of desire that swept over her like a hot shower. She wouldn't have thought herself capable of such feelings a few days ago, but now they were ever present and unstoppable anytime she was in Alex's presence. She loved the time they'd spent together and tried not to overanalyze it. She could hardly believe her luck at being with such an amazing woman. Alex had turned out to be everything she could have hoped for—warm, loving, open, honest, and crazy about her. But Keri was also confused about what was going to happen next. She'd decided to live in the moment, give herself completely, enjoy Alex fully, and just wait. The fact that they hadn't talked about what was happening between them nagged at the back of her mind, but she dismissed the avoidance as inevitable. It was bad timing.

"He wants to meet in a couple of days," she said.

"That's great news." Emotions warred inside Alex. What if something went wrong? *I can't let her go.* "Did he say anything incriminating?"

"No. He's too smart for that." Keri crossed the room to lean against the desk.

"This is it, then." Heavy lines creased Alex's forehead. "Are you sure he doesn't suspect you?"

"As sure as I can be. He said I can bring Chad and he asked about you, but I said you had to work strange hours this week."

Alex's insides felt like she'd swallowed tacks. Her future in the department hinged on this case and all she could think about was Keri. Things could go so badly wrong on a drug bust, she felt paralyzed. She reached for Keri's hand and fought to tame the butterflies in her stomach. For a few seconds, she allowed her gaze to flicker hungrily over Keri's body but she carefully avoided her stare. It was a struggle to think about work; Keri's presence was too professionally disturbing and too emotionally and physically arousing. Alex knew they shouldn't be doing this. She felt weak for allowing it. But a part of her had rebelled so powerfully against the constraints of the past year that she had not been able to restrain herself.

Looking around the office Keri noted again the unadorned walls and meager furnishings. She took a seat across from Alex and scanned the metal desk. Her eyes came to rest on a photograph beside Alex's computer of a handsome, gray-haired man with a fiery redheaded woman.

"My parents," Alex replied to the unvoiced question. "They died a year ago in a plane crash. We were very close. My father was like a best friend to me. Laughter was our favorite form of communication. I miss them both a great deal." She stopped, intrigued that she had wandered off on yet another personal tangent with this woman. *What is it about Keri Morgan that makes me want to spill my guts in the most intimate way?*

"He has a kind face."

"He was a kind man. Thank you."

"And you have that same fire in your eyes that your mother did." Keri felt her confidence lift when Alex's skin flushed with color. There was no retreat to the impersonality of their work relationship, at least momentarily.

"That's exactly what my father used to say. He marveled at being able to survive a household with two redheads." Alex looked from her parents' picture back to the papers on her desk. "I apologize for my digression, Keri. I should be asking how you're feeling about the assignment. Are you ready for this?"

Keri's palms felt sticky and a pulse throbbed painfully between her legs as she allowed herself to stare openly at Alex's slightly parted lips and her peekaboo breasts. "Yes, I'm ready. I know this is important to everybody, especially you. I won't fail you."

The promise in Keri's eyes blinded Alex to everything but her presence. "Of course the case is important, but I care more about you."

The flash of caring on Alex's face made Keri realize the risk they were both taking by pursuing their relationship. For her it had already gone too far. She couldn't imagine her life without Alex in it. The feelings that had been awakened in her could never be satisfied without her. Keri felt her very essence was entwined with Alex's like the double helix of DNA. There was no going back. Pretending to be professional colleagues would rip her heart out. She'd do *whatever* it took to keep Alex in her life. Her last thought stopped her musings. *Would* she really do *anything* not to lose Alex? She knew at that moment that the answer was yes—even if that meant giving up the job she loved.

"I'll be careful, Alex, but I plan to make this guy pay for every vile and disgusting thing he's ever done. I know you're worried about me. But there are no legitimate grounds to stop me from doing this without sabotaging the case."

But how can I protect you if you won't let me? Tormented by a desire to protect Keri at all costs, Alex said, "At least promise me there'll be no cowgirl heroics."

"Alex, the only way to stop me is for you to admit personal motivation, and you won't do that." Surprised by her own audacity and sudden assertiveness, Keri added, "Please, let me do my job."

Tears clouded Alex's vision as she tried to focus on Keri's face. "I couldn't live with myself if anything happened to you. Do you understand?"

Their eyes locked and melted into pools of liquid longing.

"Yes, I do understand." Keri rose and came around the desk toward her. She took Alex's hand and pulled her to her feet. The air between them crackled. "I won't have you feeling guilty for giving me this assignment. It had to be this way, don't you see?"

Alex spoke around the emotions that choked in her throat. "But I wasn't talking about just now. I wanted to say that I—"

Keri brought a finger to her lips. "Don't say it. Not just yet. I couldn't be responsible for my actions if you did. But thank you for letting me see that look in your eyes again. It'll get me through this case." She squeezed Alex's hands, leaned forward, placed a light kiss on her cheek, and turned to leave.

Alex eased her drained body back into her chair, passion making her weak. "Do you always say exactly what's on your mind?"

"Yes, and that's one of the many things you love about me." Keri flashed her magnetic smile and Alex felt it sweep over her like a warm breeze. "I'm going home now."

"Okay, get out of my office and get ready to catch me a bad guy... and be safe."

"Thank you. And don't worry. Nothing will keep me from you now." She flashed Alex a disturbingly seductive smile and exited. She wasn't sure her legs would carry her through the door.

Listening to her lover's departing footsteps, Alex was bombarded with guilt. She'd lost all objectivity and control. This had never happened to her on the job. What was going on? The reply was becoming more frequently the one she wanted to hear: *I love Keri Morgan*. She allowed herself to give voice to the notion again and prayed that it would be okay.

At work she had struggled to remain aloof and in control, while nightly she and Keri made love until their bodies or a new day forced them to stop. She pulsed with an almost debilitating ache to feel Keri's hands on her constantly, stroking her tender breasts, sliding her strong fingers into the moisture between her legs. The frustration in her body demanded relief that only Keri could provide. They couldn't hole up in Alex's home forever, ignoring the world outside, yet that was exactly what happened when they were together. Alex knew she had to define her relationship with Keri and figure out how they could be together after this case was over. One thing was certain; she wanted to be with Keri more than anything in her life.

Alex had experienced another side of Keri Morgan, the determined young woman who stood up for her beliefs and wasn't afraid, regardless of the consequences. Alex's concentration was admittedly off, but two things she knew without a doubt—Sonny Davis was dangerous and Keri was going after him virtually alone. She understood the driving force behind Keri's obsession with this man, but she also knew it could get her seriously injured. Wishing she'd never chosen Keri for the task force, she looked toward the ceiling and shook her head. If she believed in prayer, now would be a good time to start.

Chapter Seventeen

"Earth to Morgan." Beth waved her arms.

"What? Sorry," Keri said. "I guess I was somewhere else."

"Girl, you shouldn't stand around naked in a police locker room. Don't you know you could get molested? Then who'd you call to take the report?"

After a couple of dry runs of the takedown scenario in the muggy night air, Keri had decided to shower before her drive home. She hadn't heard Beth come in as she stepped from the tile surround and toweled herself. "That doesn't sound like such a bad idea at the moment," she said.

Beth didn't bother to hide a snort. "You didn't hear a word I just said, did you?"

There was no use denying the obvious. "I'm sorry, Sarge. I was distracted."

"Is that what you're going to say when Davis has a gun to your chest?" Beth discarded her uniform shirt. "Am I going to have to call this whole thing off?"

"No," Keri insisted. "I know what I need to do."

"Then get your head out of your ass or you won't be on this team anymore. Trust me on that. No arrest is worth getting an officer hurt."

"I'll get it together. I promise." Keri tried to shake herself free of the worry she'd seen on Alex's face last night. She wanted so much to hold and reassure her that everything would be fine—with the case and with them.

Beth hesitated. "You know she cares about you, right?"

Keri tried not to give herself away. If anyone in the division found out what was going on, she and Alex would both be taken off the case and Alex would be brought up on charges. In a neutral tone, she said, "Yes, I know."

"Good. She wants to see you." Beth turned on the water and stepped into the cubicle, throwing her towel over the door. "Don't stay up all night. You need to be fresh tomorrow."

Keri stared after Beth as she disappeared into the shower. Was it possible that she knew about her and Alex? Would Alex have confided in her? Keri decided that would be too risky at this point and dismissed her suspicions. Beth was probably just trying to make her more comfortable for the sake of the investigation. Calling, "See you tomorrow, Sarge," she closed her locker door and headed down the hallway to Alex's office.

Alex met Keri at the door and offered her hand, something she seldom did with subordinates. The need to touch her was too great. "Come in."

The softness and warmth of Keri's hand shot up her arm and settled around her heart. *My God, I love touching you. Standing right here, just like this.* Her insides felt like she'd swallowed BBs. Her future in the department hinged on this case. But she couldn't hope to remain focused while she was in such turmoil. Things could go wrong quickly on a drug bust, and she was about to send the woman she loved into the bowels of hell with a predator. Few other professions required such sacrifice. Was it really worth it?

She released Keri's hand and looked at her for the reassurance no one else could provide. Interlocking her fingers into a white-knuckled fist, she said, "Don't take any unnecessary chances tomorrow. Don't make any assumptions with this guy. He's dangerous."

Keri squeezed her legs together to stop the trembling and the inevitable ripples of excitement that claimed her every time she stood within feet of Alex. She never tired of the charge she got from their proximity or of the changes in Alex. The cool distance in her eyes had been replaced by a smoldering look of longing. Her professional bearing slipped a little whenever they were close, just enough for Keri to notice. It pleased her to be the cause. The single-minded dedication that once defined Alex Troy now included her, and Keri found that very arousing.

The days and nights they'd spent together had brought Keri more joy than she'd imagined possible. Touching Alex, feeling her excitement rise, tasting her, hearing her screams of pleasure and pleas for more, and watching her face as she climaxed would be forever etched into her memory. She wondered if Alex held such memories of her, when they were apart, of how she felt as they made love.

She placed her hands on top of Alex's and unlocked her clenched fingers. "I promise I'll be careful." As she brought Alex's fingers to her lips and kissed them tenderly, she was aware that if something went wrong tomorrow this could be their last day together.

Alex was flooded with mixed emotions as she watched Keri kiss her hands, then step back, assuming a supervisor/subordinate posture. The woman standing before her was no longer the insecure, confused officer of three years ago. The underlying pain that Keri had tried so hard to cover with humor was no longer reflected in her blue eyes. Alex wanted to believe that she was part of the reason for this transformation. The time they'd spent together had certainly changed how Alex saw herself. Keri had said she loved her. But Alex feared that she would accept that love into her heart only to lose Keri, like she'd lost everyone else who loved her. Tomorrow Keri could be gone forever and it would be her fault for putting her in this ungodly position.

"Will you come home with me?" Alex held her breath and waited for Keri's answer.

"Of course I will."

"It's just that I can't bear not being with you tonight."

"You won't have to. I'll see you there in thirty minutes."

❖

How can anyone breathe this air? Keri coughed as the musty-thick mildew smell clung to and choked her as she entered the room. Narrow slits barely eye level with the sidewalk served as windows, allowing only a dim oozing film of light to squeeze in like a hazy appendage.

On one side of the bare-walled flat, undefined figures squirmed and moaned on the single piece of furniture, a box spring mattress on the floor. Visual affirmation was not necessary. Those guttural sounds betrayed the primitive attempts of a man to satisfy himself at a woman's expense. Her voice, heavy from weight or intoxication, barely cracked the periodic stillness between his sucking breaths and vulgar expletives. Why didn't they see or hear her come in? This had to be a drug-shooting gallery or a flophouse for prostitutes.

"Move your ass, you sorry whore," the man puffed.

Cautiously Keri edged closer to the mattress, careful to remain in the darkened corners. As her eyes adjusted to the dimness she saw a huge hand with puffy swollen fingers grabbing the side of the mattress. Greasy sweat beaded on the massive naked body and oily blond hair matted against his head as the man humped and panted atop the pitiful-sounding creature. Keri's stomach churned and convulsed at the grotesque sight.

The only visible sign that a woman existed underneath the enormous mound of flesh was a pale gray, lifeless arm dangling off the side of the mattress. Needle tracks marked and discolored the entire arm and the back of the hand.

"Is this bitch dead or what? I want some action here." The man panted, red-faced from exertion. Turning his attention slightly toward a figure lurking across the room, he continued, "If this is the best you can do, I want my damn money back."

A silhouetted form shuffled from the darkness and grabbed the woman's outstretched hand. With expert precision the cigarette-stained, dirty-nailed digits wrapped her upper arm with rubber tubing and forced a needle into her bulging vein.

"Now, that should help. Give the man his money's worth, Alex." He laughed and retreated into the shadows.

Did he say Alex? Keri struggled, frozen in place. She anguished in paralyzed silence. Could this possibly be *her* Alex? Could it be the gorgeous, statuesque woman she loved, reduced to such desperation? How could this possibly have happened?

One final disgusting grunt sounded as the obese ogre finished his cruel invasion and rolled away from the woman. Her face, though vaguely familiar, was unlike anything Keri had seen before. Lethargic, listless eyes gazed out from bloodshot and bruised sockets. Dry, cracked lips mouthed inaudible words. A once firm and active body lay crumpled in an emaciated heap. Keri's anger enraged and weakened her as she realized this mass of human degradation was indeed the remains of a once-vibrant Alex Troy.

Simultaneous with her realization, a wicked, gut-wrenching laugh echoed from the corner. A yellowish green haze illuminated the silhouette. Keri's attention was riveted on a mound of dirt on which the figure stood. She strained to shield her ears from the vile laughter and run from the horrifying image, but she was incapable of motion.

"Welcome to your worst nightmare, pig," the voice sneered, spraying saliva in her direction. As he spoke the mist cleared around the raised platform and up to his unexpressive face. Sonny Davis stood irreverently perched on her mother's grave. "I've got your mother and your worthless lieutenant at my feet, and you have nothing. Face it, bitch. You're out of your league."

The words penetrated Keri's heart like red-hot steel. The throbbing in her temples neared explosive proportions. Fists clenched, she summoned all her courage and strength and made a crazed dive for Sonny.

"I'll kill you, you—" Keri yelled.

"Keri, wake up. Honey, you're having a bad dream." Alex wiped at the perspiration that covered Keri's forehead and chest. "Are you okay?"

"What the fuck?" Keri looked around, momentarily disoriented, until she saw Alex beside her in bed.

Reaching for a bottle of water on the nightstand, Alex offered it to Keri. "Have a drink and tell me about it." She placed the bottle back on the table and snuggled Keri into her arms.

"It was my usual nightmare, chasing bad guys and fighting to arrest them. Superhero type stuff like that." Keri tried to laugh off the sense of dread that persisted in her gut.

"Do you have nightmares often?" Alex stroked her cheek tenderly.

"Well…" The truth was she never had bad dreams, but this one hit close to home. Her mother and Alex were the two most important people in her life and she'd thought about them a lot lately. Maybe it was all just getting mixed up with the work stuff and coming out as a nightmare. She refused to accept any other possibility. Her mother was safe at home and Alex would never let anything like that happen to her and neither would Keri. Davis would have to kill her first.

"You're worried about tomorrow?"

"No."

"You're a terrible liar, Keri Morgan."

Keri was overcome with the sweet sensation of being truly known by the woman she loved. She kissed Alex lightly on the lips but the caress instantly deepened into more.

"We should really get some sleep, baby." Alex tried to employ reason but her efforts failed miserably as Keri's lips claimed hers again.

"Not now, please, Alex. I need you."

Alex could not deny Keri. She never had. Tonight would not be different. They made love as if it were their last time—raw and needy, then soft and reverent. Then Alex held Keri as she drifted into sleep, her head against Alex's breast. She prayed this would not be their last night together.

❖

Alex left for work twenty minutes after Keri. When she arrived she slipped up the back steps of Vice/Narcotics and made her way to the conference room without being seen. The room was filled to capacity with agents from the other task force agencies. There was one notable exception: Helen Callahan. Everyone was focused on Beth, who stood at the front explaining the raid plan.

Alex spotted Keri's curly chestnut top and her legs threatened to give way as she watched Keri assume center stage. Blood pounded in her veins and grew warmer. Her mouth and lips felt parched as she remembered the soft eagerness of Keri's mouth last night, Keri's hands caressing her face and filling her most private places. She experienced anew Keri's voracious appetite as they made love into the early hours of the morning. Her back stung from the nail marks Keri had left when she screamed to climax. Alex's insides boiled with a passion she'd never imagined. She felt herself grow damp as she watched Keri discuss questions. Her demeanor was one of honest humility; she was open and willing to learn. There wasn't the slightest indication of arrogance or ego. The more Alex watched, the more she wanted Keri, in her arms, in her bed, in her life.

Keri detailed the layout of the warehouse and surveillance area she'd drawn on the worn chalkboard. She thought of Alex's commitment and derived strength from the visual. Her presentation covered all the necessary details of location, time, quantity of purchase, and procedure regarding the anticipatory search warrant.

"Will you be wired?" This question came from one of the DEA agents.

"Yes. I'll have the cell phone transmitter. Sergeant Price and Steve Alston will be monitoring. If I get in trouble the abort signal is 'I'm outta here' and they'll call in the backup team. The signal to move in will be when I say the dope 'looks like good stuff and we have a deal.' Is there anything else?" Silence greeted her last question, so Keri sat back down.

Alex opened the door and stepped into the room. All eyes focused on her, waiting for final instructions. She visually acknowledged each person.

Keri's pulse raced and her palms dampened. If only she could look into Alex's confident brown eyes, she knew she'd be all right. The bad dream had shaken her confidence and concentration. Making love with Alex had helped relieve some of the anxiety, but the nagging images from the dream seemed almost prophetic. Today's tasks only compounded her nervousness. She had to appear confident and in control at the briefing, and more importantly she had to *be* in control for the buy. But pride and something stronger filled her chest as Alex moved to the center of the room. She didn't try to stop the smile that burst across her face, just thinking about lying in her arms.

"Folks, you've worked hard to get to this point and tonight it pays off for us. All I ask is that you remember our three main priorities— everybody goes home safely, Davis goes to jail, and we get the dope. We've got a good operational plan, let's work it." Alex nodded to Beth.

Beth gave out the team and location assignments she'd prepared. "Everybody be in position by eight o'clock tonight. The buy is scheduled for ten."

Keri felt Alex's eyes on her as she secured the cell phone transmitter to her belt. When she looked up, the cinnamon brown warmth covered her like a caress. Her hand went automatically to her midsection to calm a nagging hunger that had nothing to do with skipping lunch. She inhaled deeply to steady her breathing, her eyes never leaving Alex's. Worry transformed Alex's face; her gaze darkened, lines creased her forehead, and her eyebrows knitted closer together.

Keri smiled, gave a mock salute and said, "Don't worry, boss. And take care of Sarge, will you?" She walked out of the room.

Alex felt part of her insides unravel as Keri disappeared through the doorway. Her sixth sense tugged at the back of her mind. Something bad was going to happen tonight. Her instincts were never wrong about that. She wanted to throw herself between Keri and danger, to confess her love and beg for a chance to explore the feelings this young woman aroused in her. Instead, she watched her one chance for love walk away, ready for the deadly situation that Alex herself had approved.

Chapter Eighteen

Keri hated dealing with informants, especially Chad. He'd always been just a petty thug, but there was something unnatural about a guy who'd sell his mother for a buck. He was barely a step above Sonny Davis on the ecological hierarchy. At least he didn't sell drugs to schoolkids and pimp women's bodies for his own amusement. She just wanted him to hold it together long enough to meet Davis. She'd handle the rest.

As they skirted along Phillips Avenue toward the industrial district in Chad's old rusty Chevy truck, Keri solicited more information about Davis's operation. She knew Steve and the backup teams were listening and could adjust for any new intelligence she obtained.

"Will Sonny be alone or will he bring his entire crew?"

"He usually takes Fletch or Cappy with him wherever he goes. It depends on his mood. He does some sick shit when he's in a dark mood." Chad took a long pull on his cigarette and blew the stream of smoke out the driver's window.

"Does he usually have a lookout when he does business?"

"At least one of his guys is there, sometimes two." Chad was about as helpful as a paper fan in a heat wave.

"Does he carry a weapon?" Keri rubbed her feet together, feeling the cool leather of her ankle holster, comfortable it was sufficiently stocked and concealed.

"No. He leaves the dirty work to his goons." Chad scratched his head nervously and blew cigarette smoke out the window.

"Okay, when we get there, let me do the talking. Stay close but don't interfere unless I tell you to do something. Got it?"

"Sure, sure, I got it." Chad's upper lip glistened with perspiration.

"We're pulling up to the building now, guys. There's a white BMW out front, license GPR-4371, two occupants. No other vehicles or subjects in sight," she said for the waiting officers.

Keri looked at the huge warehouse and a shiver ran up her spine. "Hey, guys, wasn't Tiffany's body found near this warehouse?"

The building was surrounded by similar-sized structures, all dark and apparently empty. Surveillance wouldn't be easy. Any cars or people in a place like this would seem suspicious. She hoped the advance teams had found good cover and close by.

Two blocks away behind another empty warehouse, Alex, Beth, and Steve Alston were positioned in the surveillance van, monitoring Keri's transmissions. At Keri's last comment, Alex turned in her seat and stared at Beth.

Oblivious to Steve Alston behind the steering wheel, she said, "We've got to get her out of there. These bastards probably *did* kill that girl, and Keri's next."

Beth shifted her eyes toward Steve. With her calmest expression, she said, "She knows the abort code and she knows how to take care of herself. She'll be fine."

Alex lowered her voice. "You'd better be right about this."

As Keri and Chad exited their vehicle and approached the BMW, Chad's forehead beaded with sweat despite the mild temperature. Keri regarded him impatiently. "Will you chill? You're going to blow this whole deal."

Davis opened the passenger door and stepped out. Cappy unfolded himself from behind the wheel, his jacket hiked up over an automatic weapon. Keri was immediately glad Chad was with her, bad habits, sweat, and all. Davis's usually clear eyes were bloodshot and leering, as if she stood before him nude. Bile rose in her throat.

"Hey, baby, come on in." He motioned toward a small door leading into what appeared to be an office space of the warehouse.

Cappy ran ahead, fumbled with a key, unlocked the door, and held it open. "You watch our back," he yelled over his shoulder to Chad, then slammed and locked the heavy metal door behind them.

Keri's cop intuition sensed serious trouble. Alone with two thugs, one of whom was obviously armed, in an abandoned building without backup was definitely not good. She scanned the area for escape routes, telephones, and potential weapons. There were no weapons in sight and no one else in the room that she could determine by sight or sound. The only point of entry was the door they'd come in through, not even a window. Keri remained wary and cautious as she stepped farther into the space.

Cappy started toward her. "I gotta search you." If he found the ankle holster, it was all over.

"What? You don't trust me even now, Cappy? I'm hurt." Keri paused for effect. "I get it. You just want to cop another feel, right?" She walked toward him with her arms outstretched in resignation. "Feel away, if you're that hard up."

Davis waved Cappy off. "F'get about it. She's clean." He slid an arm around Keri and directed her to a dark-stained sofa in the center of the otherwise empty room.

Keri contained her disgust. "This isn't my idea of a fun party place. I've got the cash."

"What's your hurry, baby? Why don't we kick back and get to know each other better? I don't usually do this myself. But you're special."

"Any other time I'd love to," Keri lied smoothly, "but this is business. I don't like to mix my business with my pleasures."

"Well, if you promise to come back for the pleasure part later." Sonny grinned and signaled Cappy toward the back of the office.

"Oh, you'll see me again." Keri managed a sideways glance, trying to appear friendly without puking.

Cappy took a knife out of his pocket, flipped open the blade, and stooped down in the corner of the office space. With a couple of quick wrist flicks, he pried up a loose board and reached under it. When he pulled his hand out, he clasped a brown paper bag in his fist. He offered it to Keri.

She accepted the bag, reached in, and took out one of the tape-wrapped bundles. Taking the pocketknife he offered, she cut a small hole in the packaging and dipped her pinkie in. As she raised the white powder to her mouth, the distinctive acrid taste of cocaine bit her tongue and brought tears to her eyes.

"Yeah, this is good stuff. I'd say we've got ourselves a deal," she said.

Outside, Keri's words crackled through the receiver. "Okay, guys. That's the signal. Everybody move in." Beth radioed the other units. "Go, go, go! Get the ram and pry tool on that door now!"

The hairs on Keri's neck stood at attention as the stale room swirled around her. Seconds crawled. She suddenly couldn't think of another thing to say to Sonny Davis besides "you're under arrest." Just being in the same room with him made her skin crinkle with loathing. She ached to exact a little cop's revenge for the despicable atrocities he'd perpetrated on so many innocent people with his drug peddling. If backup didn't arrive soon, Keri was certain she'd lose control.

"What's the matter, honey? You look a little stressed. Why don't we sample that fine nose candy you just bought?" Sonny jeered, easing his slimy tentacle of an arm around her shoulders.

"Police! Open up, search warrant!" a voice announced from behind the door. Heavy pounding accompanied the subsequent demands for entry.

Finally! Keri's shredded nerves crystallized into trained, automatic responses. She shoved Davis away and pulled the baby Glock 9mm from her ankle holster, yelling, "You're under arrest, Davis." From the corner of her eye, she saw Cappy reach for the holster at his waist. She leveled her gun at his chest. "Freeze!"

He pulled the weapon out.

"Don't make me shoot you, Cappy."

He raised the weapon toward her. The pounding continued behind her, followed by three sudden earsplitting booms. Cappy fell in front of her, a crimson stain covering his chest and the floor beneath him.

Sonny Davis's face paled momentarily, then glowed a brilliant red. His eyes bulged beyond their socket capacity as he lunged toward Keri. "You're a damn narc, you little bitch. I'll fucking kill you."

Keri sidestepped his swinging fists and glanced at Cappy. He didn't move. Police procedure dictated that she couldn't shoot an unarmed man, so she reholstered her weapon and set herself for Davis's next charge. Adrenaline coursed through her system. She felt invincible and so ready to whip his ass.

Davis steadied himself and rocketed a right hook toward Keri's head. She anticipated well. His fist sliced the air and threw him off balance. Keri locked her hands together and brought them back over her right shoulder. She knew she'd only have one chance. As he lunged toward her again, she stepped forward and smashed him in the face with all the force she could gather. She jolted from the sudden impact and rejoiced in his corresponding wail.

Simultaneously an excruciating pain slammed her chest. The room faded to black.

❖

The commotion continued from the surveillance receiver—shouting, cursing, and then three unmistakable sounds, gunshots, followed by flesh pounding flesh. A tremendous crash reverberated off the tin walls of the van and faded into silence.

"Shots fired! Repeat, shots fired," Beth announced on the radio.

Alex clutched the walkie-talkie in her hand until her fingers ached. She felt the blood drain from her face. Chills racked her body but she was sweating profusely. The possibility of life without Keri flashed before her eyes.

I knew something terrible was going to happen. I should never have let her go in there alone. This was my responsibility. If anything happens to her, I'll... She couldn't let herself go there. In a voice devoid of emotion she said, "Steve, get me mobile—now."

Steve gunned the gas pedal and headed toward the warehouse.

Beth grabbed the mike. "Any unit on the scene yet, advise."

No response. Alex's fingers tightened around her walkie-talkie as if she could squeeze some life from it. Keri had to be all right. The universe wouldn't play such a cruel joke—give her hope only to have it shattered. Every muscle and nerve in Alex's body contracted as time dragged like a slug.

Police and ambulance sirens wailed in the distance. Alex's anxiety about the operation and her fear for Keri skyrocketed.

"Hurry!" Alex urged Steve, her nerves raw.

The drive seemed to take an eternity. Worst-case scenarios horrified Alex for the remainder of the trip. Skits of torture, forced drug use, rape, and mutilation violated her logic and challenged her training and procedural knowledge. Visions of Keri bruised, beaten, and bleeding scrolled through her mind like a bad movie, ending only as Steve sounded their horn and tugged on the wheel to miss a patrol car that braked suddenly in front of them.

Police cars and two ambulances already littered the lot when they arrived, their flashing lights casting ominous shadows across vacant buildings. The scene reinforced Alex's worst fears. So many emergency vehicles in the same place meant only one thing—something had gone terribly wrong and Keri was in the middle of it.

She scrambled out of the van and sprinted to the warehouse door just as an officer pried the metal frame off its hinges. Alex drew her weapon, crouched, and scanned the interior of the building. The main facility was empty. She focused on the small enclosed office in the back and motioned for officers to cover both sides. Moving directly to the door, she violated the first rule of entry procedure by standing in front and kicking it open. Procedures be damned. Keri was in there and she could be hurt.

When the door flew back, Alex's worst nightmare flashed before her eyes. No one was moving. The space reeked of gunpowder residue and blood. Keri was lying on the floor. Fresh red blood pooled under her head and streamed into the center of the room. Panic choked Alex's first attempt to call out and hot tears stung her eyes. She forced down the bitterness in her throat and tried again. "Medic!"

Alex ran to Keri and cradled her head in her lap. "Keri, Keri, talk to me." *Oh God, please don't let this be happening. I'll do anything, just let her be okay.* She checked for injuries, feeling Keri's scalp and body to determine where the blood had come from. "Keri." No response. Alex felt her own life draining away as she felt the weak pulse in Keri's neck.

Paramedics rushed to her side. "Lieutenant, we need to take her now." Alex didn't move. "Lieutenant, let us help her."

Beth knelt down beside Alex and placed her hands over Alex's where they rested on either side of Keri's neck. "Alex, you need to let these guys get Keri to the hospital. Now."

It was as if Beth had slapped her. Alex's head snapped up. "Right, of course." She moved away but watched the medics closely as they assessed Keri's condition and loaded her on the ambulance. "How is she?"

One of the attendants responded, "I'm not sure, but I can't find any obvious injury. I don't think the blood is hers. We won't know anything further until we get her to the hospital."

"Go now," Alex ordered and started toward a marked patrol car.

Then she stopped and looked back at Beth. "Will you take care of things here?"

"Of course, get going. Keep us posted."

❖

As Keri lingered between consciousness and oblivion she heard a familiar voice but couldn't focus. She drifted back into the darkness.

"Here you go, Officer." The nurse directed Alex to a small exam room. "She's right in there. You can go on in."

Alex watched her own trembling hand reach for the door. Weakness consumed her body and rendered her almost incapable of movement. She was usually impervious to the unmistakably rich smell of blood mixed with antiseptic scents of Betadine and alcohol, but today her stomach lurched into spasms and she moved the door far enough to step inside. She fought the desire to rush to Keri's bedside and gather her in her arms. Her next impulse was to find Sonny Davis and kill him in the most painful and humiliating manner possible.

Keri's beautiful olive complexion was pale and ashen. Red, bloodshot circles surrounded the unopened eyes and deeper crimson splotches formed on her cheeks and arms.

"How is she?" Alex asked.

Renee Siler rose from the chair beside Keri's gurney and stepped back as Alex approached. "She's going to be all right, Lieutenant. There's a possibility of a concussion. She hasn't regained consciousness yet."

Alex made eye contact with Renee. "Why did it take so long to get into the building?"

"Lieutenant, we were there within seconds. The minute Keri gave the signal we were on that door with the battering ram and a pry tool. No one knew it was a reinforced metal door. By the time you arrived, we'd already been working on it for a while."

Alex carefully studied Renee's face for any indication of deception. Seeing none, she relaxed a bit. "I just hate it when we miss details like that, details that get someone hurt. Sorry. Didn't mean to jump you." She looked at Keri's pale face again. "Renee, would you mind waiting outside?"

When she heard the door close quietly behind her, Alex dragged the aluminum and plastic chair closer to Keri's side and took her hand, relieved to feel the warmth. She caressed the helpless fingers, bringing them to her lips for a single, lingering kiss. Her heart pounded hard against her chest, each beat more painful the longer Keri remained unresponsive.

Keri struggled to open her eyes. A warm, soft hand held hers. "Keri…" a feminine voice whispered. "Please…" There was a definite sense of urgency in the tone. Alex's face came into focus.

"I've never been so happy to see anyone in my life." Keri managed a weak smile. "What happened?"

"Don't worry about that," Alex said. "You got him. You were all three out cold when we got in. You had the wind knocked out of you, maybe a concussion. It took forever to break down the metal door." She still held Keri's hand, stroking the smooth skin, unwilling to release her grip.

"So I did okay, huh?" Keri grinned, her eyes never leaving Alex's.

"You did great." Alex paused. She couldn't contain her feelings. *You have to know. I've waited too long already.*

"What's wrong, Alex? We got the bad guy, the drugs, and I'll be fine."

"I need to tell you something. This probably isn't the best time or place, but it can't wait." The tightness in Alex's chest began to loosen as she looked into Keri's eyes and prepared for the most important words she'd ever say. "I'm—"

The door of the small examining room burst open and Bobby Morgan hurried to his daughter's bedside. "Are you okay, girl?" He was oblivious as Alex released her hold on Keri's hand, rose from the chair, and back stepped out of the room while Keri's eyes begged her to stay.

Keri's pulse pounded in her temples. Was it her injuries or the simple knowledge that Alex was about to say something that would change both their lives? Torn between her desire for Alex and the need to reassure her father, she watched Alex fade from the room like a fantastic dream she prayed would never end.

"What happened? Are you going to be all right?" Bobby self-consciously patted her hand while surveying her face and arms. "Who did this to you?"

"Daddy, it's going to be fine. It was just a little scuffle, no major damage. Trust me, he's worse off than I am. You taught me to take care of myself, remember?"

Bobby Morgan's face seemed to darken and the well-worn lines of his face thickened. "Yeah…" He looked away, unable to meet her eyes. "I'm sorry about that. I've been trying to tell you for a while now."

Keri had never seen her father look so vulnerable and ashamed.

"I should've never laid a hand on you. It takes a sorry man to beat a woman, especially his own child. And I should've been there for both of you when your mother was…" Bobby's eyes grew misty and he lowered his head, stuffing his hands into worn jeans pockets. "Can you ever forgive me?"

Keri rubbed her father's flannel-clad arm. "Dad, we all do things we regret. It's important to learn from them and do better. You've done way better."

Bobby bent down and hugged her awkwardly. Keri felt the moisture of his tears against her neck. She knew he was sincere, but it would take a long time to rebuild her trust completely.

After a few seconds, he straightened. "Well, guess I better go fill out the paperwork. I wouldn't do anything until they let me see you. Besides, there's a bunch of cops out there waiting to get in here. I'll be back soon."

When he opened the door, most of the task force came pouring in, everybody talking at once. Keri half listened, responded periodically, and constantly watched for Alex, but the lieutenant didn't return. After offering congratulations and a few jabs about how to take down a suspect, everyone except Steve and Beth left.

"I'm lying around like I don't have anywhere to go. I've got to get out of here. My job's not over yet. I need to debrief Chad and interview Davis." *And find Alex.*

"Hey, wait up, cowgirl," Steve cautioned. "We can handle the rest of the show. You've done more than enough for one day."

Beth's voice was stern. "You're not going anywhere, young lady."

"And just why not, Sarge?" Keri asked. "No disrespect intended, but if I recall I just made a drug arrest and I have follow-up to do."

"Have you forgotten that you haven't been discharged from the hospital? Besides, we have a whole team of officers who can process a suspect, execute and document a search warrant, and tag and bag evidence." Beth gave Keri a stern gaze.

"Sergeant, please don't do this. I need to see it through. I've been primary on this case from the start and it's only fair that I finish it. Please, I feel fine. I promise to take it easy. You can even send Steve to baby-sit if you'd feel better."

"If it's any consolation, Sergeant, I'll look after her." Steve offered his best cherubic smile, which brought a grin from Beth. "We just need to question the guy for a few minutes. I can do all the paperwork."

"Let it go right now, Steve. We've all got enough on our plates tonight."

He took the hint and headed back to the waiting room.

Before Beth could follow, Keri asked, "Where's Alex? I need to see her. She was about to say something when my father came in."

"She gave me instructions to take care of you and then left."

"But…" Keri's heart and mind screamed for the woman she now knew loved her. She was certain of it. "Then please let me finish this case. If I can't see her, I have to be doing something meaningful."

Beth seemed to understand the pleading look in Keri's eyes, the need for distraction fueled by the desperation of passion. "You can go on three conditions—you're released by the doctor, your father approves, and you take Steve with you. Oh, make that four. You deal with Alex's wrath when she finds out I let you do this."

"Deal." Keri gave Beth a weak smile, "And I promise to take it easy."

After a long chat with her father, a consultation with the ER doctor, and another private session with Beth, Keri got dressed, and she and Steve headed back to the station to confront Sonny Davis.

❖

When Keri and Steve walked into the small interview room, Sonny Davis lunged across the table and shouted, "I'll kill you, you damn bitch."

Fortunately for him, the shackles restricted movement beyond a threat, denying Keri a reason to go after him again. "Back off, you drug-dealing, flesh-peddling, bottom-dwelling piece of slime," Keri countered, pleased with her verbal skills in spite of the nauseating headache.

"Fucking dyke," Davis mumbled.

Steve balled his fists and started to rise from his chair. Keri knew what came next. Her partner was very protective. She placed her hand on his shoulder. "Steve, he's not worth it. Let it go." Turning to Davis, she said, "You know, Sonny, if you're the alternative, being a dyke looks pretty good."

Steve erupted in laughter as Davis's face turned splotchy with anger. "The good news, scumbag, is that you're not injured. The bad news is, you're not injured. Now you're ours." He read the Miranda warnings to Davis and waited as Keri pulled a chair close to the table.

Keri spread her notes out on the table between them. "Let's talk about your case."

"I got nothing to say to you about nothing, bitch."

"Not even if it could help you?" She hoped Davis wouldn't talk. The thought of cutting him any slack for any reason made her insides churn.

He eyed her. "I might have some information that you want. But you have to be willing to work with me." Davis leaned back in his chair and stared smugly at Steve.

"I can't make you any promises. Does it pertain to an ongoing case?"

Davis stroked his stubbly beard, leaned back in his chair. "I think you'd call a dead girl an ongoing case. But I have to get immunity on this one."

"Keep talking." Steve encouraged.

"It's about a young girl that got iced a while back. Does that sound familiar?"

"You'll have to be more specific than that," Steve answered, feigning indifference. "No details, no deal."

Davis looked around the room, seeming to weigh his options. "This one was found behind a warehouse."

Steve scratched his head and played dumb. "What warehouse?"

"Near the one we were at tonight. God, you cops are thick sometimes. What I'm saying is somebody popped a cap in her. She was getting too nosy for her own good. Got what she deserved."

Keri's head pounded harder and the blood in her veins started to surge. The cause of death for Tiffany Brown hadn't been released. Not even the newspapers had gotten hold of it yet. Davis was definitely involved.

"I just put it all together myself. Cappy took her out."

His sneer sent Keri over the edge. Visions of the young woman's body, cold and lifeless, flashed in a tormenting slide show. The thought of her orphaned child was too much. "You slimy bastard." Keri made a grab for Davis's throat.

This time it was Steve's turn to intervene. He positioned himself between Keri and Davis just as she lunged.

"Fuck you, bitch." Davis laughed. "You can't touch me and you know it."

"Let me show you how to kill somebody, you piece of garbage." Keri tried to push Steve out of the way, aching to wipe the smirk off Davis's face.

"Morgan, stop. He's trying to bait you."

Davis's bulging eyes changed from mocking to defiant. "Did you see that? She tried to kill me."

"I didn't see anything, asshole." Steve put his arm around Keri's shoulder and eased her into a chair. "And by the way, all deals are off the table. You'll be charged with the original drug offenses and several counts of murder and conspiracy to commit murder." He opened the door and motioned a uniform into the room, instructing. "Go ahead and process him for us, heavy on the bond. We've got all we need tonight."

Keri stared unfocused at her hands. After a long pause, she said, "I don't know what came over me. I wanted to kill him with my bare hands. I've never lost control like that before."

"But you didn't touch him. You stopped. We all lose our cool from time to time. You had to stop me from doing the same thing earlier. It happens."

The words registered slowly. "Thanks, Steve, you're a good partner and friend. I'd like to go home now. Please."

"Sorry, partner, no can do."

"What do you mean? I'm exhausted and my head is pounding like a bass drum."

"Have you forgotten my promise to Sergeant Price? I told her I'd take care of you. I don't want that woman on my case. I'm taking you home with me for observation. Cindy won't mind."

"I'm fine, really. My dad will be worried sick."

"I'll call and let him know you'll be staying with me and my wife tonight. He wouldn't want you to drive all the way out there at this hour anyway."

"Okay, you win." But her heart wasn't in it. What she really wanted was to find Alex, talk to her, hold her. Where was she?

Keri felt like weeping. Alex's mood shifts made no sense to her, least of all now. She felt a fresh wave of anger consume her, but this was deeper than her outrage at Davis. This was personal and almost debilitating. The case was over. She couldn't understand why Alex would abandon her now.

❖

Alex drove for hours, replaying the horror of seeing Keri unconscious and bloody. When she finally stopped it was dawn and she was at the cemetery. Her parents' shiny granite headstone caught the early light and cast her reflection back at her. She looked tired, her hair wild and windblown. She dropped to her knees, rubbed her hands across the smooth surface of her parents' grave marker, and remembered her childhood and their life together. Burying another loved one was not something she ever wanted to experience again.

There had been no doubt that her parents loved each other and her. Every decision was made jointly. Vacation time was a family affair. Each meal was for talking and sharing with each other. Problems were merely opportunities in disguise. Alex had been trained to seize those opportunities and turn them into advantages. She was taught that personal character and integrity were more important than money, and love trumped everything. Had fifteen years with the department so colored her thinking that she'd forgotten those valuable lessons?

No doubt being a cop was dangerous. It came with the territory. But that worst-case-scenario thinking that went with the job bled over into her personal life. She was always looking for what could go wrong and how quickly, never for the positive side of a situation. No wonder her relationships failed. Girlfriends expected her to come home, leave the job at the door, and become a loving, sharing, and fully engaged partner. Instead she'd learned to compartmentalize her feelings about the everyday atrocities she saw at work and she'd built a containment wall around her heart to keep out the pain. But that method of self-preservation had also kept her separate from feelings of joy, intimacy, love, and true sharing. Alex had allowed pride in her work to become her fulfillment. She'd even come to believe there was something missing inside her—the capacity to connect fully and love completely. She hadn't thought herself capable of such feelings, until Keri Morgan proved her wrong.

This courageous woman had reached in and untangled her twisted thinking. Keri had made her look at the fuzzy logic she'd always applied to her life. She'd demonstrated how easily one heart connects with another if it's allowed. Her complete honesty and vulnerability had broken down Alex's defensive barriers. It was those qualities and her seemingly inexhaustible capacity for love that Alex adored.

She thought of that as she knelt at her parents' graves. Keri had not been killed or even seriously injured. She had survived and Alex had been given another chance—a chance to get it right. Her heart filled with uncontrollable love and an urgency to tell Keri her feelings. She recalled her father's one wish for her: to be happy. Everything else would follow, he always said. She hoped he was right because she refused to let another day go by without the woman she loved at her side.

Chapter Nineteen

Keri wasn't sure which caused more frustration, the concussion from last week or trying to decide what to wear to the celebration dinner. She pondered her choices, transfixed by her naked reflection in the full-length mirror. Five outfits lay strewn around her bedroom. She'd ruled out a dress as too formal. *Beth said to be casual.* She finally decided to keep it simple with a pair of black pants and a red top. Her goal was to be well-dressed but not overdressed.

Bruises on Keri's cheeks and arms from the arrest of Sonny Davis had almost completely vanished. Her brilliant blue eyes had regained their luster after some much-needed rest, and the recurring headaches had disappeared. Nightmares occasionally haunted her attempts at sleep, but she had the consolation of knowing Sonny Davis would never touch anyone she loved again.

Every day of her recuperation, Alex had called to check on her. She visited a couple of times and officially met her parents and brother. If either of them thought it strange that her lieutenant was taking such an interest in her recovery, they never mentioned it. Not once during that time did Keri and Alex discuss anything personal. But it felt personal. Alex was attentive and nurturing in a way Keri had never seen. Still, the things that weren't said hung heavily between them.

Keri appraised her body as she prepared for the final meal before the guys all returned to their respective assignments. She stroked her naturally curly hair, which managed to bend and curve in the directions she wanted for a change. She applied an ample supply of mousse and fashioned her hair into a wet look, but even those attempts to conceal the prematurely gray strands that emerged and exposed themselves proved useless.

With a scrutinizing eye she examined her body, almost perfect, except for a small roll of baby fat around the waist. The areola surrounding her nipples appeared milk chocolate and deepened to dark when aroused. Stroking taut abdominal muscles, she allowed her fingers to follow a natural path to the soft triangle between her legs. An involuntary gasp escaped her as her fingers aroused her insatiable longing. Anyone would love to enjoy her sexually, but her needs went much deeper than sex.

Visions of Alex at the lake crept into her mind. Holding Alex's body close to her own and the undeniable heat brought Keri's hand once again to her own aching flesh. The softness of Alex's lips and the hunger of her smoldering kisses made Keri wet with the deepest desire she'd ever experienced.

She slid her fingers inside the silky moisture and stroked her firm, demanding clit, then collapsed onto the bed. Her rubbing intensified as she replayed their kisses and lovemaking over and over and surrendered to the tantalizing ripples of pleasure emanating from her pelvis.

Alex's tongue darted in and out of her mouth and stroked from the inside secret places her fingers now desperately probed. Harder and faster she pressured her burning flesh until the much-needed explosion of gratification engulfed her. If only Alex were here. Keri gasped for breath. Keri needed her so badly, her attempts at self-satisfaction proved useless. All she could feel was the hunger that Alex Troy had awakened.

❖

As she drove to Malone's Steakhouse, Keri's mind reeled from earlier thoughts and conjured up more. She wondered what it would be like to make love to Alex without worrying that it could be their last time. What would a life with this complex woman be like? She imagined every aspect of their lives together: where they'd live, where they'd work, their friends and family. All the things other couples took for granted, Keri prayed for with Alex. And she knew in her heart that someday it would happen. As soon as Alex accepted the fact that she loved her.

After she parked, Keri sat in front of the restaurant and watched some of the team members go inside. She was so nervous. Everybody would be talking about the case, their case. She could handle this, no problem. She knew what the problem was, though—seeing Alex again and not knowing if her feelings, the feelings they never discussed, were the same. Her insides quivered.

"Well, are you coming in or what?" Beth's tap on the car window startled Keri. "Someone told me you were sitting out here. What's up?"

"Just thinking…and feeling a little sad that it's all over." Keri mustered all her courage and exited the Jeep.

"God, you look hot, I just might keep you all to myself," Beth teased. "You're asking for it in that getup. Black and red is so sexy. Is it for anyone special?" An immediate rush of adrenaline made Keri's pulse leap. She couldn't be sure if it was from Beth's obvious appreciation of her outfit or wondering how Alex would respond.

When they entered the restaurant, all the team members were present except Alex. Three vacant seats awaited them at one end of a long table in the private dining room. Beth deviated from her norm and took the seat at the head. She motioned Keri to sit on her left. The table decorations were a cowboy motif, the team's idea of paying homage to Keri.

As she joined the group they immediately wanted details about the case. This was the first time they'd all been together since the arrests, and they were anxious to hear her account of the incident. Each time she recounted the story her whole career was validated again. Even Internal Affairs had rubber-stamped her shooting of Cappy and cleared her for active duty in record time.

After a while, the discussion turned to the absence of Lieutenant Troy, an unusual development, everyone agreed. The dinner had been her idea and she was footing the bill. Surely she wouldn't stand them up.

The hovering waitresses had already refilled everyone's drinks twice when the door opened and Alex walked in. She wore tapered black pants that caressed her firm buttocks and thighs and a crisp white cotton shirt. The slight trace of gray highlights, mixed with the basic amber of her neatly trimmed hair, made Keri draw a long, shaky breath. She loved that distinguished look. What a striking woman and how comfortably she entered the space, even an hour late. She possessed a powerful sexuality that was palpable from across the room, and Keri was drawn to it. Without realizing it, she stood, staring, and their eyes locked. Neither of them looked away. It was almost as if an arc of electrical current sparked between them.

Alex was not prepared for Keri's breathtaking appearance. She had seen her half-naked in a bikini and completely nude in bed, but nothing had equipped her for this sight. Keri's tailored black silk pants clung to places Alex longed to explore. A red Lycra shell cupped her small, firm breasts, revealing the absence of—or necessity for—other support. Brown wavy hair hung loosely around her shoulders, highlighting her olive complexion and startlingly blue eyes. What made her even more seductive was the fact that she had no idea about her natural appeal. Such understated beauty demanded attention.

Eyes followed Keri's movements wherever she went, but she was oblivious to it. Alex's desire rose as she headed to the vacant seat opposite Keri. *I have to hold it together through dinner...at least.* "Good evening, folks. I'm so sorry for being late. I had to make a stop at the lab on my way." Alex waved several papers in the air as she took her seat.

The team waited with practiced patience, except Beth. "Let's have it, Lieu. What's in there, a nice fat, juicy bonus for everybody?" Cheers sounded as the officers expressed their agreement.

"You wish." Alex unfolded the papers as she spoke. "These are the lab results from the homicide investigations of Tiffany Brown and the other college students. I haven't even seen them myself."

The room grew suddenly quiet as Alex relayed the information to her team. "The weapon used by Freddy Capanelli to shoot his girlfriend two years ago is the same weapon used to kill Tiffany." Applause, fist pumping, and high fives accompanied the announcement. "There's more. The blood found on the sofa in Davis's warehouse, the same warehouse where we made our drug buy, matches the victim's."

Steve Alston stood and held his drink in the air. "I propose a toast. Now that is what I'd call a kick-ass investigation. We went after a doper and came up with a murderer." Glasses clanked together in celebration.

Alex added the final details. "When the homicide guys picked up Fletch and threatened him with murder charges, he sang like the proverbial bird. He admitted that he told Cappy and Hunk to take Tiffany to the warehouse. The three of them went back later and worked her over to see if she'd told us anything. She didn't tell them about her statement, guys. Then Cappy went back later to finish the job. The 'brains' of the outfit, Dolph, was the one who paid a street dealer to poison Tiffany at the community watch meeting where Stacey Chambers died, and the dope we recovered has the same characteristics as the drugs the college students overdosed on. The DA's office has agreed to bring multiple murder charges against all of them. Our boy Sonny and his whole gang are goners. Big-time."

Alex had one last comment before she could relax and enjoy the evening. She stood and tapped a fork against her water glass. "Guys, just one more thing, if I may." The room once again quieted. "I want to thank each of you for the outstanding job you did on this case. You have proven that officers from different agencies can work together. It took all of you to make this investigation so successful. If the opportunity presented itself, I'd choose each of you again. I'm proud of you and wish you all the best as you go to your next assignments." Alex felt pride start to swell in her throat and finished quickly. "That's all I have. Thank you."

The officers applauded and cheered as Alex sat down. Then Beth rose at the head of the table. "Wait just a minute. That's not all." She held her glass in the air. "I propose a toast to the next captain of the Granville Police Department, Alex Troy."

Each officer toasted her promotion and filed by to shake Alex's hand. Keri was the last in line. When their hands came together, Alex held firmly and lowered her voice. "This would not have been possible without you. What you did, all of it from day one. Bringing Chad into play, your creativity and fast thinking. You made it happen. I'm very proud of you, Officer Morgan."

Keri blushed and joked, "And what about my dancing skills? Admit it. I made you look good."

Alex was grateful for the levity. "That you did, Officer Morgan. That you did."

When she took her seat, she did so with a huge sigh of relief. The assignment was finally over. At least for now, Keri no longer worked for her.

Keri's pulse quickened as Alex smiled across the table at her. It was that same magnetic smile with something extra. Alex's eyes were soft and hungry and swept over Keri like a lover's touch. She felt it in her depths. When the tip of Alex's tongue slowly rimmed her lips, Keri gripped the napkin in her lap and pressed it into her tightening pelvis. She was oblivious to the other officers eating and talking around her.

Alex's meal sat before her untouched. The hunger clawing inside her could not be satisfied with food. She slipped her foot out of her right shoe and raised her bare foot to the seat across from her. *I can't believe I'm doing this—in public, no less.* Keri's eyes widened as Alex's toes teased their way up. She felt the heat between Keri's legs and pressed the sole of her foot into her crotch. A bullet of raw sensation shot up Alex's thigh and into her already pounding clit. The blue of Keri's eyes grew hazy with need. *God, I want to see those eyes when you come for me again.*

"You haven't touched your food. Is something wrong?" Alex asked.

"I guess I'm too excited," Keri answered truthfully. Alex's foot against her already swollen clitoris was more than she could bear. Food was definitely the last thing on her mind. *How does she so completely unravel me with just one touch?*

"I know the feeling." Mischief played across Alex's face. She looked up as Beth tapped her shoulder.

"Get a room," came a soft suggestion meant for Alex's ears only, but Keri heard as well.

"That's an excellent idea." Alex glanced around, hoping no one was paying attention. To her relief, the other officers seemed oblivious to the conversation at her end of the table.

While the officers finished their dessert and talked among themselves, she went to each and thanked them for their work and dedication during the investigation. She vowed to send letters of commendation to their agencies, along with a summary of the operation. When she got to Keri, she knelt on one knee, as she'd done with the other officers, and leaned into her body space. Her arm slid along the back of Keri's chair and she could feel her lover's heat rising.

"You, my lead detective, were amazing. Have no doubt that you will receive the highest commendation I can substantiate. You have every reason to be proud of yourself."

Keri's generous mouth blossomed into a wide smile. "Thank you."

Her thoughts weren't on the case. Alex was too close, her fragrance too strong, her presence too compelling. The hard pain between her legs grew with every breath. She thought her insides would explode from want.

Alex leaned in closer and whispered, "Follow me home."

Keri's eyes sparkled as she struggled to swallow. When words would not come, she simply nodded.

Alex felt her body might betray her right there, on one knee in front of Keri. She wanted so desperately to claim her mouth, to announce her feelings. Instead she said, "Good. Give me a few minutes to wrap up and I'll meet you outside."

She talked with Beth a few more minutes, then addressed the group for the final time. "Folks, I hate to leave, but I've got lots of paperwork to finish if you're all to get your commendations. Please stay as long as you like. You have an open tab at the bar." With that, she headed toward the exit.

Keri watched Alex go and wanted to run after her. How long would she wait? Trying to appear nonchalant, she walked around the table talking and joking with the officers for what seemed an eternity. *I can't bear this any longer.* "Guys, I'm afraid I have to go."

It took every ounce of her patience not to bolt for the door as she accepted handshakes and pats on the back. The ache between her legs grew with each step toward the parking lot until a full-blown hunger gripped her.

Alex stood near their vehicles. She started toward Keri, then stopped just out of reach.

"I want you so much." Keri reached for her.

"Don't." Alex held up her hand. "If you touch me right now, I'll take you where you stand. Let's get out of here."

They practically ran to their respective vehicles and began what seemed an interminable drive to Alex's house, only two miles away.

CHAPTER TWENTY

Alex unlocked her front door, pushed it open with her foot, and pulled Keri into her arms, surrounding her in a full-body hug. "I thought we'd never get here."

"Is this really happening?" Keri pressed her tender pelvis against Alex's and felt her respond in kind. The contact created such excruciating pleasure it forced a long, gushing breath from Keri's body. "Please make love to me. I can't wait anymore."

Alex cupped Keri's chin and brought their lips together in a delicate kiss. As the softness turned demanding and grew like a fever between them, she led Keri into the bedroom and lowered her onto the down comforter.

Moonlight filtered through the trees outside and cast a flickering, candlelike glow across Keri's body. Alex stood over her and admired the devastating natural beauty of this woman, who lay ready to give herself over to desire. She prayed for the ability to give Keri what she needed. This time Alex wanted to show her how she felt, not just feast like a hungry animal.

Stretching her body along Keri's side, she stroked her face as she looked into her lust-hooded eyes. She understood that look, the consuming passion to move beyond the anticipation of love to its physical consummation. "You are so beautiful." Her lips met Keri's with the hunger of a woman starved. As her hands slid under the thin red top and teased a puckered nipple, her own breasts and pelvis throbbed.

Keri arched her body. "Please touch me. I ache for you."

Alex peeled Keri's top over her head and slowly unzipped the form-fitting silk pants, pushing them aside to allow her trembling fingers to enter. Her mouth captured a breast and tongued it as her hand slid down Keri's taut stomach into the slick moisture between her legs.

"Oh, my God," Keri breathed. Alex's fingers felt laced with fire as they separated the wet folds of flesh and massaged her engorged clit. "Oh, yes…that's it…" Her entire body shook with sensations beyond all she'd experienced before.

Her appreciative moans inflamed Alex even more. They were the sounds of uncensored vulnerability, totally raw and primal. Alex absorbed them like the elixir of life itself. *You are so perfect.* She draped her leg over Keri's and allowed her painful, soaked crotch only the lightest contact. Sparks released another flood and she tilted her pelvis backward. She was so hot. One easy stroke would send her over the edge and she didn't want to come that way, not this time.

Alex kissed her way down Keri's body to her navel, circling the rim with her tongue. At the same time, she dipped her middle finger into the warmth of Keri's body while milking her clit between thumb and forefinger.

"Ahh…" Keri's hips rose off the bed to deepen Alex's thrusts, her moans filling the air. "Yes, yes. Oh, it's so good. Don't stop."

She was getting close to the edge. Alex withdrew her fingers.

"Oh, no! Don't stop…please."

Disbelieving eyes met hers. Alex just smiled and licked her passion-covered fingers. "I want to feel you come against my lips. I have to see your eyes when it happens." She worked Keri's pants down her legs and off the side of the bed.

"Hurry," Keri pleaded. She'd never imagined wanting anything so much. Alex kissed her slowly, then more deeply before licking a fiery trail down her abdomen into the burning between her legs. When Alex's tongue flicked against her swollen flesh, every sensory nerve defaulted to that point. Each stroke magnified the current inside her body. It felt as if her insides were melting even as the pressure in her pelvis increased.

"Look at me," Alex commanded. "I want to watch you come."

"Now, baby. I'm coming now…" Keri entangled her fingers in Alex's hair and pulled her closer as the first tremor of orgasm gripped. Gazing into Alex's eyes, she let her body have its way and just released. "Oh…yes, that's it. Don't stop."

Pleasure consumed her as the series of spasms started low in her belly and continued over and over. She'd never felt like this and never wanted it to end. She felt herself being drained and simultaneously refilled as she watched Alex stroke her spent body.

Alex almost came watching Keri at the moment of release. Her brilliant blue eyes were hooded and cloudy with emotion. Her pleading moans pierced the hot air around them and settled in Alex's core. She'd been so beautiful in her surrender.

Alex kissed the insides of Keri's thighs and slid slowly up the length of her body. The fabric of her slacks rubbed painfully against her sensitive flesh, which begged for release. She squirmed to reposition her pulsing clit and minimize contact as she settled next to her lover. Their ragged breaths filled the silence of the room.

After several minutes, Keri tilted her face to Alex's and kissed her lightly on the lips. "Thank you for that." She stared, noticing for the first time that Alex wasn't naked. "You still have clothes on?"

"Guess I got a little carried away." Alex smiled.

"I'm sorry. I should've… It's just so hard to think when you're touching me."

Alex pushed slightly back to look into Keri's eyes. "God, I love it when you say exactly what's on your mind. It's probably one of the biggest turn-ons for me." She felt a surge of heat between them. "I'm sorry. I've embarrassed you."

"It's okay, but I need to tell you—"

"Must we talk now? I mean *just* now?" The pain in Alex's groin seemed to rise with each word.

"Oh, my God. You feel so good." Keri slid her hand up Alex's back and into her hair, almost embarrassed by the level of her need. "I never knew holding anyone could feel this way. My whole body's aching for you again. Does that sound crazy?"

Each honest declaration was like an aphrodisiac, each touch like liquid fire. Alex felt herself tumbling further under Keri's spell. She'd never had such an overwhelming desire to sexually devour another woman. Had Keri tapped some base instinct or were her desires too seldom satisfied and her emotions too closely guarded?

"It's not crazy at all. Now *please* stop talking." She brushed her lips over Keri's, broadcasting her passion. Her legs trembled and she hesitated. She needed to do one more thing before she allowed herself to let go completely. The words swelled in her throat, words she'd chained to her fear of intimacy and trust, words that she had to say and Keri had to hear.

"Keri, I—"

"Please, let me go first," Keri insisted. "If I don't say this now, I'm going to explode." At Alex's nod, Keri took a deep breath. "I'm in love with you and I want us to be together." There it was. Short, simple, and so true that her entire body felt lighter.

Alex tried to speak but her words had no sound. Emotion rushed at her like a blast of humid, summer heat. She burned with its intensity while simultaneous moisture seeped from her pores. Halting gasps racked her chest and tears slid down her face.

Keri took Alex's hands gently in hers. "Does this mean you love me, too?" She didn't really need a verbal reply. Alex's physical responses were enough.

"More than my next breath. I've never felt these things before. Without you, it's like going through the motions of life. I think about you all the time and want you to be safe and happy. And my body craves you."

Keri touched the silky smoothness of Alex's face and a surge of excitement charged through her. How deep were these newfound sexual and emotional hungers that suddenly consumed her? She trailed her thumb across Alex's invitingly full lips and felt a spasmodic jerk deep in her core.

"I love you so much, Keri, but…" A heavy sigh signaled that Alex was about to disturb the serenity of their perfect haven.

"Don't," Keri begged.

"Don't what?"

"Don't start with that damn list. It's professionally unethical. I live with my parents. You're a captain now. Have I left anything out?"

"Actually, you've covered it pretty well, but I prefer to call them legitimate reasons."

"Well, I've heard your reasons," Keri said tenderly. "And they just sound like excuses not to get close. We can work through anything, if we really love each other."

Her body burned with a painful, all-consuming need for this woman. Thunder and lightning clashed inside her, frightening with its rumbling announcement but illuminating with a piercing display of directed brilliance. What she'd craved in her life had been totally obscure but was now utterly specific and vital to her very existence. It was her love for Alex. Nothing had ever been so right, as perfect as this moment.

"I love you," Keri said again.

"Oh God, how I love you." Alex's breath came in excited gasps. "But we need to talk about this." She wanted Keri to understand what to expect, but the words tasted bitter in her mouth. She wanted Keri more than life itself.

"I've already decided what I want and how I feel about it. We fit. I know you feel it, too." Keri wedged her leg between Alex's thighs and lowered herself to bring them together. Alex grabbed her naked butt and forced her to match her own frantic humping. She'd never been this hot and out of control for any woman. Her crotch was soaked and she was only seconds from climax.

Keri pushed herself up on her hands to look at the woman beneath her. "I certainly hope you're not about to come, Alex Troy. I've waited too long for this."

Alex's disappointed groan brought a chuckle that was quickly smothered by a plea. "Can I touch you?" Keri blushed as she asked.

"Yes, please." Alex unbuttoned the confining shirt and discarded it with her bra. She brought Keri's hand to her breast.

Keri thought how beautiful Alex looked: her lips were deeply colored and swollen from their endless kisses, her nipples puckered and demanding Keri's touch. Skin so soft and yielding welcomed her. A bolt of excitement shot between her breasts and pelvis as she took a dimpled nipple into her mouth. She sucked the delicate tip and massaged the mound of flesh beneath it with her fingers. Each suck pulled her clitoris tighter as it became more engorged.

She reached for Alex's trousers. "Can I?"

"You can do anything you want." Alex edged closer to orgasm with each request. She'd never had a woman ask permission.

Keri slowly peeled the clothing away. Alex's exposed skin was flushed and glistening. Beads of moisture clung to the chocolate brown triangle between her legs.

Smiling, Keri repositioned herself for easy access. "I had no idea your body could tell me so much. I think you want me." She ran her index fingers along the juncture of thigh and torso.

"If you don't touch me," Alex groaned, "I'm going to die."

Something Keri had once heard echoed in her mind: *It's emotional, almost like instinct. Every touch feels like an extension of your own body. It's raw and tender and hot all at the same time.* She finally understood what Pat had said to her that day a long time ago. Her already engorged clitoris pounded with each stroke of Alex's tender flesh as though she herself were being teased. She moved as if from years of experience making love to Alex. She kissed her way across Alex's abdomen, down the insides of her thighs, and was rewarded with a pleading whimper. Instinctively she knew what Alex wanted and savored her ability to give such pleasure.

Alex clawed Keri's back. Her body screamed for the release she knew would only take seconds once this beautiful creature touched her. She panted and in a voice choked with desire said, "Please, Keri. I need you."

She trusts me—and she loves me. Eyes liquid with desire gazed into hers and Keri lowered her mouth to Alex and stroked her with a passion that promised her faith was justified. She'd never felt so vitally needed in her life.

"I know what you need, baby," Keri replied, infused with the passion and intimacy of the moment, jubilant at the level of trust it required, rejoicing in the arousal that threatened to render her helpless.

She tickled a tormented path between Alex's legs. Her fingertips dipped into the silky wetness and tentatively inched inside, stroking the velvet lining in time with Alex's increased upward thrusts.

"How beautiful you are." Alex's breathing increased. Her hand covered Keri's and held her firmly in place. "I need to feel you inside me, part of me, please don't stop."

"Trust me." Keri lowered her head and caressed with tiny tongue strokes. Gradually, teasing with each flick of her tongue, she reached Alex's center and was rewarded with the salty-sweetness of her desire. "Um…I do love the taste of you."

The instant Keri's hot tongue touched her clit Alex arched with raw current. A low whimper increased to a resonant growl deep in her chest and threatened to strip her throat with primordial screams. Knots of repressed energy coiled tighter in her abdomen as tremors signaled her imminent orgasm. "I'm not going to make it much longer."

"Trust me," Keri whispered again as she felt a quiver against her tongue.

The muscles in Alex's thighs tensed and Keri's own lust spiraled. Making love to Alex was bringing her more pleasure than she'd ever experienced, without even being touched. Her body vibrated as every nerve sparked with arousal. Soon, no matter how tightly she clamped her legs against her tender clit, she wouldn't be able to control the pending release. *How is this possible?*

Alex's panting increased as she tried to reach between Keri's legs. "I want you to come with me. Let me touch you." She was desperate for more contact. A sharp nibble on her aching flesh brought her closer to the edge.

"Don't worry. I'm with you." Keri felt Alex's legs tremble against the sides of her face. "Come for me, baby. Right now."

"Oh my God, Keri, please don't stop!" Alex pleaded. Her body stiffened. *I couldn't stop if I wanted to.*

Keri was unable to speak, concentrating now on the tingling release rising from her toes and burning a path between her legs. She plunged deep into Alex, alternately withdrawing and stroking her frenzied body. "Oh, yes, this is how it's supposed to feel," she gasped as she yielded to her own desire.

"Oh, yes…" Alex groaned helplessly with her.

Contractions racked Keri's body with each spasm of her pulsing flesh. Passion grabbed her by her throat and she wailed in continuous, contented waves. At that moment, Alex pulled her on top and entwined their legs. Their bodies arched and convulsed in orgasm until they collapsed, exhausted, side by side on the bed.

A sense of peace descended on Alex as she lay in Keri's arms. Her body continued to quiver with mini-spasms, then eventually relaxed. When she finally could, she brushed her fingers lightly across Keri's sweat-drenched forehead. "Are you all right?"

"I've never been better. I'm just amazed. I knew it would be different this time, but nothing like this." Disbelief echoed inside her flushed body. "How have I lived without you so long? I truly love you, Alex."

Alex pulled her closer and kissed the top of her head. "You have no idea how much you mean to me. When you were hurt during the arrest, I was crazed. And I put you in that position. I can't do that again. It would kill me."

"But I'm fine and we're here together—where we belong, by the way. Before you say anything else, I've got a gift for you."

"I thought you just gave me that. You're a natural, my dear," Alex replied with a mischievous grin.

"Actually, you're the one who gave me the gift. I never imagined I could feel this way about anyone. So my gift is small in comparison."

"You've given me back my life. What more could I ask?"

"Permission to enjoy it." Keri grinned. "Madame Lieutenant, soon to be Captain, you're looking at the newest member of the Drug Enforcement Administration, Granville Division."

A look of astonishment covered Alex's face. "What do you mean? You quit the department?"

"You bet. I applied with DEA after the first time we made love. I'm starting in three weeks. I told you I wanted to be a narc."

Trying to hide her joy, Alex asked. "But why? You love the job so much and you'd just proven yourself. You could've had anything in the department you wanted."

"Except you. I knew you'd never consider a relationship with me as long as we worked together. And I love you too much not to give it a try."

"You really are too smart for your own good. But there might be another way."

"What do you mean?" Keri asked.

"It seems I'm quite wealthy."

Keri rose on her elbow and looked into Alex's shining brown eyes. "Wealthy as in you don't have to work anymore?"

"Wealthy as in neither of us would ever have to work again if we didn't want to…ever." Alex smiled at the look of shock on Keri's face. "But I don't suppose a life of leisure would interest you, would it, Officer Morgan?"

"That's Special Agent Morgan, and I really want to catch bad guys a few more years. I'll reserve my leisure activities for the bedroom. With you." She kissed Alex, then teased her bottom lip between her teeth before letting go.

"By the way, I love you, Keri Morgan." Alex gathered her lover in her arms and pulled her closer to her sweat-drenched body.

"I know."

"But this won't always be so easy—the relationship or getting your way with me." Alex grinned and slid her hand down Keri's stomach to the heat between her thighs.

"Then we better practice. A lot." Keri gave Alex a languid kiss. "I have a feeling we'll need the entire three weeks before my new job to get out of the bedroom. But trust me. I can handle it."

Alex let herself float on a wave of true happiness. "I do trust you, with all my heart."

About the Author

VK Powell is a thirty-year veteran of a midsized police department. She was a police officer by necessity (it paid the bills) and a writer by desire (it didn't). Her career spanned numerous positions including beat officer, homicide detective, field sergeant, vice/narcotics lieutenant, district captain, and assistant chief of police. Now retired, she lives in central North Carolina and devotes her time to writing, rewriting, traveling, and volunteer work.

You can visit her online at www.powellvk.com.

Books Available From Bold Strokes Books

Heartland by Julie Cannon. When political strategist Rachel Stanton and dude ranch owner Shivley McCoy collide on an empty country road, fate intervenes. (978-1-60282-009-8)

Shadow of the Knife by Jane Fletcher. Militia Rookie Ellen Mittal has no idea just how complex and dangerous her life is about to become. A Celaeno series adventure romance. (978-1-60282-008-1)

To Protect and Serve by VK Powell. Lieutenant Alex Troy is caught in the paradox of her life—to hold steadfast to her professional oath or to protect the woman she loves. (978-1-60282-007-4)

Deeper by Ronica Black. Former homicide detective Erin McKenzie and her fiancée Elizabeth Adams couldn't be happier—until the not-so-distant past comes knocking at the door. (978-1-60282-006-7)

The Lonely Hearts Club by Radclyffe. Take three friends, add two ex-lovers and several new ones, and the result is a recipe for explosive rivalries and incendiary romance. (978-1-60282-005-0)

Venus Besieged by Andrews & Austin. Teague Richfield heads for Sedona and the sensual arms of psychic astrologer Callie Rivers for a much-needed romantic reunion. (978-1-60282-004-3)

Branded Ann by Merry Shannon. Pirate Branded Ann raids a merchant vessel to obtain a treasure map and gets more than she bargained for with the widow Violet. (978-1-60282-003-6)

American Goth by JD Glass. Trapped by an unsuspected inheritance and guided only by the guardian who holds the secret to her future, Samantha Cray fights to fulfill her destiny. (978-1-60282-002-9)

Learning Curve by Rachel Spangler. Ashton Clarke is perfectly content with her life until she meets the intriguing Professor Carrie Fletcher, who isn't looking for a relationship with anyone. (978-1-60282-001-2)

Place of Exile by Rose Beecham. Sheriff's detective Jude Devine struggles with ghosts of her past and an ex-lover who still haunts her dreams. (978-1-933110-98-1)

Fully Involved by Erin Dutton. A love that has smoldered for years ignites when two women and one little boy come together in the aftermath of tragedy. (978-1-933110-99-8)

Heart 2 Heart by Julie Cannon. Suffering from a devastating personal loss, Kyle Bain meets Lane Connor, and the chance for happiness suddenly seems possible. (978-1-60282-000-5)

Queens of Tristaine by Cate Culpepper. When a deadly plague stalks the Amazons of Tristaine, two warrior lovers must return to the place of their nightmares to find a cure. (978-1-933110-97-4)

The Crown of Valencia by Catherine Friend. Ex-lovers can really mess up your life…even, as Kate discovers, if they've traveled back to the eleventh century! (978-1-933110-96-7)

Mine by Georgia Beers. What happens when you've already given your heart and love finds you again? Courtney McAllister is about to find out. (978-1-933110-95-0)

House of Clouds by KI Thompson. A sweeping saga of an impassioned romance between a Northern spy and a Southern sympathizer, set amidst the upheaval of a nation under siege. (978-1-933110-94-3)

Winds of Fortune by Radclyffe. Provincetown local Deo Camara agrees to rehab Dr. Bonita Burgoyne's historic home, but she never said anything about mending her heart. (978-1-933110-93-6)

Focus of Desire by Kim Baldwin. Isabel Sterling is surprised when she wins a photography contest, but no more than photographer Natasha Kashnikova. Their promo tour becomes a ticket to romance. (978-1-933110-92-9)

Blind Leap by Diane and Jacob Anderson-Minshall. A Golden Gate Bridge suicide becomes suspect when a filmmaker's camera shows a different story. Yoshi Yakamota and the Blind Eye Detective Agency uncover evidence that could be worth killing for. (978-1-933110-91-2)

Wall of Silence, 2nd ed. by Gabrielle Goldsby. Life takes a dangerous turn when jaded police detective Foster Everett meets Riley Medeiros, a woman who isn't afraid to discover the truth no matter the cost. (978-1-933110-90-5)

Mistress of the Runes by Andrews & Austin. Passion ignites between two women with ties to ancient secrets, contemporary mysteries, and a shared quest for the meaning of life. (978-1-933110-89-9)

Vulture's Kiss by Justine Saracen. Archeologist Valerie Foret, heir to a terrifying task, returns in a powerful desert adventure set in Egypt and Jerusalem. (978-1-933110-87-5)

Sheridan's Fate by Gun Brooke. A dynamic, erotic romance between physiotherapist Lark Mitchell and businesswoman Sheridan Ward set in the scorching hot days and humid, steamy nights of San Antonio. (978-1-933110-88-2)

Rising Storm by JLee Meyer. The sequel to *First Instinct* takes our heroines on a dangerous journey instead of the honeymoon they'd planned. (978-1-933110-86-8)

Not Single Enough by Grace Lennox. A funny, sexy modern romance about two lonely women who bond over the unexpected and fall in love along the way. (978-1-933110-85-1)

Such a Pretty Face by Gabrielle Goldsby. A sexy, sometimes humorous, sometimes biting contemporary romance that gently exposes the damage to heart and soul when we fail to look beneath the surface for what truly matters. (978-1-933110-84-4)

Second Season by Ali Vali. A romance set in New Orleans amidst betrayal, Hurricane Katrina, and the new beginnings hardship and heartbreak sometimes make possible. (978-1-933110-83-7)

Hearts Aflame by Ronica Black. A poignant, erotic romance between a hard-driving businesswoman and a solitary vet. Packed with adventure and set in the harsh beauty of the Arizona countryside. (978-1-933110-82-0)

Red Light by JD Glass. Tori forges her path as an EMT in the New York City 911 system while discovering what matters most to herself and the woman she loves. (978-1-933110-81-3)

Honor Under Siege by Radclyffe. Secret Service agent Cameron Roberts struggles to protect her lover while searching for a traitor who just may be another woman with a claim on her heart. (978-1-933110-80-6)

Dark Valentine by Jennifer Fulton. Danger and desire fuel a high-stakes cat-and-mouse game when an attorney and an endangered witness team up to thwart a killer. (978-1-933110-79-0)

Sequestered Hearts by Erin Dutton. A popular artist suddenly goes into seclusion, a reluctant reporter wants to know why, and a heart locked away yearns to be set free. (978-1-933110-78-3)

Erotic Interludes 5: Road Games, ed. by Radclyffe and Stacia Seaman. Adventure, "sport," and sex on the road—hot stories of travel adventures and games of seduction. (978-1-933110-77-6)

The Spanish Pearl by Catherine Friend. On a trip to Spain, Kate Vincent is accidentally transported back in time—an epic saga spiced with humor, lust, and danger. (978-1-933110-76-9)

Lady Knight by L-J Baker. Loyalty and honor clash with love and ambition in a medieval world of magic when female knight Riannon meets Lady Eleanor. (978-1-933110-75-2)

Dark Dreamer by Jennifer Fulton. Best-selling horror author Rowe Devlin falls under the spell of psychic Phoebe Temple. A Dark Vista romance. (978-1-933110-74-5)

Come and Get Me by Julie Cannon. Elliott Foster isn't used to pursuing women, but alluring attorney Lauren Collier makes her change her mind. (978-1-933110-73-8)

Blind Curves by Diane and Jacob Anderson-Minshall. Private eye Yoshi Yakamota comes to the aid of her ex-lover Velvet Erickson in the first Blind Eye mystery. (978-1-933110-72-1)

Dynasty of Rogues by Jane Fletcher. It's hate at first sight for Ranger Riki Sadiq and her new patrol corporal, Tanya Coppelli—except for their undeniable attraction. (978-1-933110-71-4)

Running With the Wind by Nell Stark. Sailing instructor Corrie Marsten has signed off on love until she meets Quinn Davies—one woman she can't ignore. (978-1-933110-70-7)

More Than Paradise by Jennifer Fulton. Two women battle danger, risk all, and find in each other an unexpected ally and an unforgettable love. (978-1-933110-69-1)

Flight Risk by Kim Baldwin. For Blayne Keller, being in the wrong place at the wrong time just might turn out to be the best thing that ever happened to her. (978-1-933110-68-4)

Rebel's Quest: Supreme Constellations Book Two by Gun Brooke. On a world torn by war, two women discover a love that defies all boundaries. (978-1-933110-67-7)

Punk and Zen by JD Glass. Angst, sex, love, rock. Trace, Candace, Francesca…Samantha. Losing control—and finding the truth within. BSB Victory Editions. (1-933110-66-X)

When Dreams Tremble by Radclyffe. Two women whose lives turned out far differently than they'd once imagined discover that sometimes the shape of the future can only be found in the past. (1-933110-64-3)

Stellium in Scorpio by Andrews & Austin. The passionate reunion of two powerful women on the glitzy Las Vegas Strip, where everything is an illusion and love is a gamble. (1-933110-65-1)

Burning Dreams by Susan Smith. The chronicle of the challenges faced by a young drag king and an older woman who share a love "outside the bounds." (1-933110-62-7)

Fresh Tracks by Georgia Beers. Seven women, seven days. A lot can happen when old friends, lovers, and a new girl in town get together in the mountains. (1-933110-63-5)

Turn Back Time by Radclyffe. Pearce Rifkin and Wynter Thompson have nothing in common but a shared passion for surgery. They clash at every opportunity, especially when matters of the heart are suddenly at stake. (1-933110-34-1)

Promising Hearts by Radclyffe. Dr. Vance Phelps lost everything in the War Between the States and arrives in New Hope, Montana, with no hope of happiness and no desire for anything except forgetting—until she meets Mae, a frontier madam. (1-933110-44-9)

Innocent Hearts by Radclyffe. In a wild and unforgiving land, two women learn about love, passion, and the wonders of the heart. (1-933110-21-X)

Justice Served by Radclyffe. Lieutenant Rebecca Frye and her lover, Dr. Catherine Rawlings, embark on a deadly game of hide-and-seek with an underworld kingpin who traffics in human souls. (1-933110-15-5)

Justice in the Shadows by Radclyffe. In a shadow world of secrets and lies, Detective Sergeant Rebecca Frye and her lover, Dr. Catherine Rawlings, join forces in the elusive search for justice. (1-933110-03-1)

A Matter of Trust by Radclyffe. JT Sloan is a cybersleuth who doesn't like attachments. Michael Lassiter is leaving her husband, and she needs Sloan's expertise to safeguard her company. It should just be business—but it turns into much more. (1-933110-33-3)

Storms of Change by Radclyffe. In the continuing saga of the Provincetown Tales, duty and love are at odds as Reese and Tory face their greatest challenge. (1-933110-57-0)

Distant Shores, Silent Thunder by Radclyffe. Dr. Tory King—along with the women who love her—is forced to examine the boundaries of love, friendship, and the ties that transcend time. (1-933110-08-2)

Beyond the Breakwater by Radclyffe. One Provincetown summer, three women learn the true meaning of love, friendship, and family. (1-933110-06-6)

Safe Harbor by Radclyffe. A mysterious newcomer, a reclusive doctor, and a troubled gay teenager learn about love, friendship, and trust during one tumultuous summer in Provincetown. (1-933110-13-9)

shadowland by Radclyffe. In a world on the far edge of desire, two women are drawn together by power, passion, and dark pleasures. An erotic romance. (1-933110-11-2)

Love's Masquerade by Radclyffe. Plunged into the indistinguishable realms of fiction, fantasy, and hidden desires, Auden Frost is forced to question all she believes about the nature of love. (1-933110-14-7)

Honor Reclaimed by Radclyffe. In the aftermath of 9/11, Secret Service Agent Cameron Roberts and Blair Powell close ranks with a trusted few to find the would-be assassins who nearly claimed Blair's life. (1-933110-18-X)

Honor Guards by Radclyffe. In a wild flight for their lives, the president's daughter and those who are sworn to protect her wage a desperate struggle for survival. (1-933110-01-5)

Love & Honor by Radclyffe. The president's daughter and her lover are faced with difficult choices as they battle a tangled web of Washington intrigue for…love and honor. (1-933110-10-4)

Honor Bound by Radclyffe. Secret Service Agent Cameron Roberts and Blair Powell face political intrigue, a clandestine threat to Blair's safety, and the seemingly irreconcilable personal differences that force them ever farther apart. (1-933110-20-1)

Above All, Honor by Radclyffe. Secret Service Agent Cameron Roberts fights her desire for the one woman she can't have—Blair Powell, the daughter of the president of the United States. (1-933110-04-X)